Praise for *Double Dog Dare*

Double Dog Dare is a sweet and funny contemporary story. I enjoyed it very much and had many opportunities to smile and laugh. If you love a heartwarming story about falling in love, Then I dare you -- double dog dare you even, to get yourself a copy of this great book.

~Long and Short Reviews

Double Dog Dare is a charming read filled with memorable characters, lots of laughs, and tons of fun.

~Romancing the Book

This is one I would recommend to anyone who likes a clean contemporary romance with a heartfelt story. I am looking forward to Jennifer's next book!

~Beck's Book Picks

Double Dog Dare

Double Dog Dare

Jennifer Johnson

DOUBLE DOG DARE

"We're All Mad Here."
~The Cheshire Cat

When Cheris McDowell wakes up in a hotel room next to the husband she doesn't remember meeting, she decides the only practical solution is a quiet divorce.

Too bad the rest of the world disagrees.

As an Internet advice guru, Cheris ought to know how to fix the mess she woke up to, but when her own web master conspires to keep the marriage going, Cheris is at a loss.

Geoff Arrowood III, her new husband, isn't helping the situation. He's much too charming and looks a little too good in a Tuxedo.

Will Cheris choose a little storybook madness or the sensible advice of the wisdom she's followed all her life?

Chapter One

I wonder if I've been changed in the night? Let me
think. Was I the same when I got up this morning? I almost
think I can remember feeling a little different. But if I'm not
the same, the next question is 'Who in the world am I?' Ah,
that's the great puzzle!
—*Alice in Wonderland* by Lewis Carroll

The vice tightened around her skull waking Cheris with
its torment, and she gripped her head.

Was she dying? She had to be. Nobody in this much
pain could be *okay*.

Nausea gripped her stomach. Cautiously, she opened
her eyes, thankful, at least, that the room was dim. The
curtains drawn though the lightened edges attested to the
fact that the sun was up. With her hands pressed against her
scalp in an effort to stave off the deathly ache, Cheris
turned her head slowly.

Where was she anyway? This wasn't her bedroom. This
looked like a hotel room. She scanned the rest of the room.
Nice but...

There was a man in bed with her!

His back was to her, but it was definitely a guy, still
asleep.

What happened last night?

Trying not to jar the bed to wake him up, Cheris slipped from the mattress and gulped. Whose white button-down shirt was she wearing? Probably his. How low had she sunk? A one night stand.

Her? Not in a million years. No way.

But the evidence was so damning.

Cheris searched the carpeted floor for her clothes, and spotted her bra but not the ruffled blouse Janie, her best friend, insisted she wear to the art gala last night. Some of Janie's painted work had been featured and the private party had been lively even at five o'clock when Cheris had arrived.

She'd held a glass of champagne and pretended to drink it for the toast. The only other beverage she'd consumed had been some punch. It must have been alcohol.

Oh, no.

What an idiot she was. A stupid, stupid...

She grabbed her linen skirt with her panties tucked inside hanging from the shade of the lamp on the bedside table.

Cheris McDowell did *not* throw her clothes on the furniture. She placed them neatly in a pile in the dirty clothes hamper. The man in the bed sighed and turned onto his back, flinging his arm across the bed to where Cheris had been. In sleep, his face was relaxed, his dark hair tousled. She glanced at him noting his bare shoulders and chest as she tiptoed past the bed. *Ah, thank you,* she thought as she spotted her purse on the dresser. She grabbed it and entered the bathroom. She didn't dare turn on the light or even close the door afraid of waking him, whoever he was.

Who was he? How could she do this?

She stripped off the shirt without bothering with the buttons. The scent of male cologne wafting from the material triggered an image of tawny eyes behind trim glasses gazing at her from the face in the next room.

"You may kiss my hand, sir."

Her voice and her outstretched arm.

Her hands shook so badly, it took her several tries to get her bra fastened and her straps on her shoulders. Wrenching her arms into the big shirt, she tried not to think about its owner. Quickly, she tugged on her panties and skirt. Who knew where her blouse was, or her shoes? She wasn't going to look for them. She had to get out of here before he woke up.

Talk about awkward.

Hello. I'm Cheris. I know we slept together, but I didn't catch your name.

Cheris' throat closed up.

She hurried out of the bathroom and quietly opened the door leading to the hallway. Clicking the door shut behind her, she sprinted down the passage to the elevator.

She entered the lobby attempting to act nonchalant, as if she knew where she was, as if she didn't have a headache the size of the iceberg which sank the Titanic, as if she were wearing shoes.

A woman behind the desk smiled at her.

"Do you have today's paper?" Cheris asked her as she rifled through her purse.

Wallet?

Check.

Cell phone?

Check.

Keys?

Check.

"We have *The Herald Times, The Mountain Journal,* and *The Independence.* Which would you like?"

Since Cheris had only asked for the paper to find out where she was, she answered, "The local one."

The woman handed her *The Mountain Journal.*

The news of Serenity, Kentucky, the paper touted. Serenity was a tourist hideaway and about an hour and a half away from Cullsbaeir, her home.

Why had they come here, and how was she going to get back?

Cheris massaged her temple with one hand. She spotted the doorway next to the counter labeled 'Sundry' and went to find something for her head.

After purchasing a bottled water out of the machine, a travel pack of Aleve, and a pair of flip flops, Cheris asked the clerk about the closest car rental place.

"Is something wrong with your car?" the young woman asked.

Cheris debated on her answer.

"You're in room forty-three twenty, right? I checked you in last night. I had to pull a double." She stuck her tongue out in exhaustion. "The morning desk help didn't show up so I'm here until three." Typing on the keyboard in front of her, she peered at the screen. "I remember you giving your husband a hard time because he didn't know your license plate number."

"My husband." Cheris rubbed her closed eyelids attempting to relieve her agony. "Right."

"Blue Prius?"

Relief washed over her. Her car! Her car was here. Oh, thank the Lord, her car had made it to this side of the nightmare. Cheris raked the flip flops off the counter and shoved her feet into them. "Of course. I should take my car. Thanks."

She strode toward the front door hoping the parking lot wasn't too big. Asking the woman where they parked might make her suspicious. Cheris pressed the unlock button on her keyring and listened for the telltale beep.

And there it was in the second row. Cheris heaved a sigh of relief.

This could have been so much worse. So much. Guilt niggled at her for leaving the man in the hotel room without a shirt or a way home, but too bad.

That's what he gets for having a one night stand and lying to the hotel clerk about being married.

What a piece of scum. Revulsion crawled up her spine.

Cheris opened the door of her car and sat inside. Hmm. Her feet didn't reach the pedals which meant someone else had driven them here.

Him, probably.

Goodness knew she hadn't needed to drive if she didn't even remember how they got here. Cheris turned the key and cranked the engine. When she placed her hands on the steering wheel, she paused as she studied her left hand.

And the wedding band on her ring finger.

Putting the car in gear, the tires squealed as she tore out of the parking lot and got away from there as fast as she could.

Before she hit the main drag, she pulled the ring off and dropped it in the cup holder. It clattered as it settled.

What have I done?

****

When Cheris arrived at her apartment, she headed to the kitchen and retrieved another bottle of water from the refrigerator hoping to erase the not-quite-gone pain in her head. The pain reliever had taken most of the ache, but had done nothing for the regret of a night she couldn't remember.

Why had she been wearing a ring?

Cheris drank half of the contents of the bottle before sitting it on the counter. Her next task was to take a shower as if she could wash away what she had done.

If anybody found out....

On her way to the bathroom, the doorbell pealed. Against her better judgment, she pivoted and walked to the door peering through the keyhole.

Janie.

This was *her* fault.

She was the one who insisted Cheris come to the opening last night to support her best friend in the gala.

"You have to be here," Janie'd declared. "My mom and dad won't come because they have a bunch of my old fogey relatives in town who can't take the vagina imagery of my *Secret Garden Grown Up* piece. I need you to video me with all the big wigs admiring my art."

Where was Janie's Flip camcorder anyway?

Cheris grasped the knob and pulled.

"What in the heck are you wearing? Where did you disappear to last night?" Janie began without preamble as she walked in the apartment.

"Hard to say," Cheris hedged. She walked to her purse and rummaged through it. Where was the Flip?

"Are you okay?"

Definitely not here. "Umm. Why do you ask?" Cheris closed the bag, picked it up, and put it in its cubby hole under the counter separating the kitchen from the living room.

Janie collapsed on Cheris' couch and propped her feet on the coffee table. "Some people got into Gary Sheirer's Drink Me/Eat Me stuff in his Wonderland exhibit, and it's created mayhem throughout the tri-state area."

Cheris raised her other hand to her head cradling it. "The punch?" Yes. Cheris had been in the Wonderland room. She had eaten a petit four and drunk the sweet beverage from an oversized thimble.

"It was an interactive exhibit. That's why no underage people could be at the party."

"But it wasn't—"

"Labeled alcoholic? I know. Neither were the cakes. One or the other was fine, but combined?" Janie grinned and shook her head. "They had to pull a woman off a water tower she climbed after the gala. A man got arrested for streaking in downtown Central Park, and there is another man missing. Got any Diet Coke? I'd kill for one."

"Oh, Janie." Cheris retrieved a can for her friend and handed it to her.

"Most people got the message from the Drink Me and Eat Me signs, but I guess a few brave dummies thought it'd be cute to see if they'd shrink and grow."

A flash of the sleeping man rushed through Cheris' memory. Last night he had stood in the Wonderland room with her.

"I dare you," he said.

"I don't take dares," Cheris replied.

"What about a double dog dare?" He winked, and Cheris stomach fluttered. "Do you take those?"

Cheris gasped at the recollection.

"What's wrong?" Janie asked. "You didn't do the *eat me, drink me* stuff, did you?"

Cheris sighed. "Did I give you back your camcorder last night?"

Janie cocked her head at her friend ignoring her question. "You did, didn't you? Huh. Well, that's surprising. Ms. Let-me-fix-your-life Hip Granny ate and drank unknown substances."

Hip Granny, the web giant who organized homes and lives, who advised on health and relationships, who did *not* get drunk and wake up next to a strange man.

"I'm not Hip Granny."

Janie snorted. "You are soo the Hip Granny."

"Annie Hill is the Hip Granny."

"That woman hasn't done anything but interviews in over a year, *Granny.*"

Janie was one of the few people who knew Annie had retired leaving Cheris as the practical advice guru. It was easy to impersonate the older woman via the World Wide Web when all people saw were typed words.

"Look, Janie, I'm going to go take a shower."

"*Are* you okay? You didn't do anything crazy last night, did you?"

Knock. Knock. Knock.

Cheris formulated an answer as she stepped to the door and opened it. On her porch stood what she did crazy last night.

A squeak escaped her mouth as she stared at him.

How did he know where she lived? How did he get here?

With a white plastic bag in his hand and wearing a snug undershirt with Tuxedo pants, the man stared back at her. His disheveled hair and unshaven face testified to the fact he had come straight here from the hotel.

"Hi," he said.

"Who is it?" Janie asked.

Good question.

Janie appeared next to her and pulled the door open wider. "Oh, hey, Geoff. What are you doing here?"

Geoff? Cheris turned to her friend. "How do you...?"

Janie gawked. She pointed at Cheris' oversized Tuxedo shirt then Geoff's black pants. A huge grin split her face. "Are you kidding me? You two slept together last night? I love it!"

Janie grabbed the man's arm and pulled him inside. Cheris moved so as not to get hit by the door or...Geoff.

He studied her while Janie took the bag from his hand. "What's this?" She smacked her lips as she set the bag on the counter and opened it. "Oh. Evidence." She reached inside and pulled out Cheris' turquoise shirt, her matching high heeled pumps, and the Flip recorder.

"How did you know where I lived?" Cheris asked him. Geoff. *Who are you? Did you get into the Drink Me/Eat Me concoction too?*

Geoff's gaze moved from her to Janie and back again. He adjusted his glasses. "I found out."

Janie placed her hands on her hips surveying them both. "My brother and my best friend doing the dirty deed!"

"Your brother!"

He reached beneath his glasses and rubbed the bridge of his nose with thumb and forefinger. "Nothing dirty, Janie, so would you leave so I can talk to Cheris alone?"

"You're Janie's brother?" Cheris scowled at him before turning her attention to her friend. "How could you let me go off with him like that?"

"I didn't know he'd take you to Serenity to have illicit sex with you. Why Serenity, anyway? Aren't the beds here in Cullsbaier good enough? Seems like a long drive just to—"

Geoff held up his left hand with the gold band prominent on his ring finger. "To get married."

"We're not!"

"You're not!"

Both women spoke in unison.

"Real nice anniversary present, you jerk! Mom's going to throw a hissy when she finds out."

Geoff turned his back on his sister and faced Cheris, his caramel colored eyes appealed to her. "You don't remember?"

Cheris shook her head. "We're not."

"Not anything?"

"We talked at the Wonderland exhibit, but I wouldn't have...I wouldn't have....We're not m...m...m" She took a shuttering breath.

He broke eye contact, reached into his pocket, and pulled out a folded paper. "The courthouse closes at nine pm on Fridays in Serenity." He glanced over his shoulder. "Janie, please? I'd like to talk to my wife by myself."

"I'm not," Cheris whispered.

Without another word, Janie walked to the door, opened it, and left shutting the door softly behind her.

Cheris gripped the edge of the paper sliding it out of Geoff's hand. Walking to the counter, she opened the papers and spread them on the surface. A copy of a marriage license and a smaller perforated sheet of *the original to be given to the legally married couple.*

Groom: Geoffrey Watkins Arrowood, III.
Bride: Cheris Leigh McDowell.

She turned stricken eyes to the man standing next to her. "It isn't legal. We were both drunk from that...food and drink."

"I wasn't."

"It can't be binding because I was."

Geoff said nothing.

"Why would you marry me if you weren't high on that Wonderland elixir? Is this a joke to you? Marry some stupid drunk woman and sleep with her?"

"You—"

"Don't. Please. There's nothing you can say to make this all right."

"How about let's see if we can make this work?"

"You're insane."

Geoff shrugged. "You look good in my shirt."

Cheris dropped her head and studied the shirt. She raised her chin and marched into her bedroom slamming the door shut behind her. In less than a second she had whipped it off of her body, wadded it up in a ball, and threw it to the floor. Stepping on the material, she crossed her room and pulled a neatly folded shirt out of her bureau drawer and stuck her head and arms in it.

There now.

Picking up the offending object in her fist, she rejoined the crazy man in her living room.

"Here you go." She shoved the shirt at him and strode to the front door opening it in invitation. "Please leave now. I have a headache, and I cannot deal with lunatics at the present moment. I will contact you later, at which time we will discuss how to get unmarried."

Geoff didn't move. "You don't have my number."

"I know your sister. I know *her* number." The implications of the statement were cosmic.

Janie the artist. Janie the rebel. Janie the wild woman who would try anything and do anything a second time so everybody would know the first time hadn't been a fluke. Janie whose current boyfriend had served time in jail.

"Janie's my sister." Geoff entered Cheris' kitchen, and she ducked to watch him through the opening between the overhead cabinet and the bar. "Twin sister, actually. But we're not very much alike." He plucked a marker from its holder next to a small dry erase board displayed on her refrigerator. Next to her grocery list, he wrote his name and a telephone number. "I'm staying at the Days Inn on Vincent Avenue if you'd rather talk in person."

He replaced the marker and strolled toward Cheris.

He paused in front of her. "Okay?"

Cheris shook her head.

"It will be." His warm gaze caressed her before he exited the apartment.

Cheris stood at the open door and watched him shake out his shirt and slide his arms into it while he punched a number on his cell phone and spoke into it.

Suddenly he stopped and did an about face. He lowered the phone. "Hey Cheris?" he called.

Cheris waited in silence as they watched each other across the span of the walkway.

"You look good in your shirt, too."

She stepped behind the threshold as her heart thumped in her chest and closed herself away from the sight of Geoff Watkins Arrowood, the third, with his rumpled unbuttoned shirt and ebony dress pants in the early spring sunshine.

A memorable quote from the Queen of Hearts entered Cheris' mind, and she bit her lip in mirth.

Off with his head.

Chapter Two

"It's a poor sort of memory that only works backward"
—*Through the Looking Glass* by Lewis Carroll

Cheris surfed the web looking for a way out of her marriage. It seemed that even if she was under the influence the marriage was legal if it was signed by the appropriate parties. Cheris picked up the document which Geoff had left behind. County Clerk. Witness. Bride. Groom. She checked each name, each signature. The witness had been Gloria Kloes who had written her title as well. Administrative Assistant to the City Commissioners.

Administrative Assistant. What was she doing there at eight-thirty on a Friday night anyway? That's ridiculous. Darned dedicated public servants.

Cheris pulled out a blank file folder and picked up a pen. Poised over the manila tab, the pen stilled. What should she label this folder in which she would keep the marriage license until she and Geoff could go see a lawyer?

Marriage?

Mistake?

Finally, she decided on *License* and slipped the papers inside and placed it behind her *Life Insurance* folder in the filing cabinet.

How could this have happened? Why couldn't she remember anything? Had Janie introduced her to Geoff?

Cheris stood from her chair, pushing it under the desk and going to the bathroom pantry to retrieve a spray bottle of cleaner and a dust cloth. Beginning at the bureau in her bedroom, she wiped each surface.

No. Janie had not introduced them.

Cheris had filmed Janie with her *Secret Garden* exhibit before moving to the other rooms, admiring the other artistic renditions of classic children's stories, the theme of the gala. The Wonderland room had been exquisite with a vaporous water pipe in the shape of a club teetering on the edge of an oversized mushroom on a bed of real Fescue, a warped table with a black tea service arranged to resemble a spade, and a heart topped scepter lying across a gilded throne.

In the corner sat a stark white façade of a house. To one side toddler-sized furniture was arranged—an armoire, a marble topped sideboard, and an Elizabethan style chair. On the opposite end the furnishings were large and blocked. A skeleton key balanced at its side on the edge of the table above Cheris' head, and the wooden chairs big enough to sit three people. Arranged on a doily of one of the chairs were small punch filled milk glass cups etched to resemble thimbles and snowy petit fours on a china platter. A man stood next to the chair eating one of the delicacies.

Dressed in a Tuxedo in front of the completely white exhibit, he seemed to belong within the display. His nearly black hair, a little too long, curled at his neck, and he wore small gold rimmed glasses. Cheris glanced around the room to find they were alone. Was this why he thought it permissible to deface the art?

"You're not supposed to eat that, are you? That's part of the exhibit," Cheris advised.

"We're part of the exhibit." His eyes glittered in amusement from behind the clear lenses. He held out the cake to her. "Take a bite."

"I'm not eating after you. I don't even know you."

"Afraid you'll catch cooties? I've had all my shots."

"There is no vaccination against lice, and you don't catch them by sharing forks."

"How astute of you. Come here." He motioned for her to follow him to a row of mirrors. "That's why there are no characters because we are the characters. See?" He walked to a mirror next to the wall, and Cheris followed. Though their faces were theirs, their bodies had morphed. The man was now The Mad Hatter, and Cheris the Chesire Cat. She smiled in delight.

"Keep your smile, and watch what happens," he advised.

"What?"

"Show that gorgeous grin and look into the mirror."

Uncertain, Cheris glanced at her companion, so tall, next to her. He nodded toward the glass surface, and Cheris turned her attention back toward it watching in amazement as the fluffy stripped cat disappeared, then Cheris' own face until only her mouth remained in the darkened mirror.

"Oh." She breathed the word out.

"Indeed."

"How does it do that?"

"I think the appropriate response is *Curiouser and Curiouser.*"

Attraction for the stranger tugged at Cheris. He seemed familiar to her though she didn't know why. "Have we met?"

"No, we haven't." He met her gaze in the next set of mirrors. "It appears that I am now the Queen, and you are the Mock Turtle. Can we switch? It's so unbecoming to want to decapitate everybody."

Cheris stepped to the shiny frame centered among the rest. Instead of a whimsical character, there reflected were the petit fours on the doily and blood red punch in oversized white thimbles.

Cheris moved her hand in front of the reflection and pivoted her body to stand in between the mirror and the display nearby. How odd that it showed the display but not her. In a moment, she understood that it was not a mirror at all, but a receded crevice. Feeling a bit like Alice, she reached her hand inside the rectangle.

"You should take a cake to reflect the one I ate."

"I take the cake?"

"Most definitely."

Cheris paused. She glanced over her shoulder, judged

which one to pick up before doing so. Withdrawing her hand, she bit into the delicacy, its lightness surprising her. She wondered if she could get the recipe from the artist, maybe cover the exhibit on *Hip Granny* on art appreciation and the senses?

She swallowed and sighed in contentment eyeing the blood red punch.

Drink Me

"I dare you," her companion murmured.

"I don't take dares," Cheris replied shooting him a disdainful look.

"What about a double dog dare?" He winked, and Cheris' stomach fluttered. "Do you take those?"

It was silly, really, letting this stranger impel her to anything. Studying the thimbles on the tray and comparing them to the one behind her, she did notice one less cup. Squaring her shoulders she stepped forward into the looking glass and retrieved the drink. Bringing it to her lips, she sipped once and discovered it to be mild yet sweet— similar to cantaloupe in the peak of its season.

"Mmm. Very nice." She tilted the cup and drained it. "I've never tasted anything quite like it." She licked her lips and tilted her head. Picking up another glass, she set the empty one in its place. "Go over there and drink one."

The man raised his eyebrows, but walked to the chair. They faced each other as he determined the correct glass to pick up.

"Yes. That's the one." Cheris drank from the second glass enjoying the cool liquid. "I've got to find out what this stuff—oh!" She gasped as she tripped over the frame.

At once he was at her side steadying her. "Careful there, Alice. It's the rabbit hole you're supposed to fall into."

Oh. My. Goodness.

Cheris' hands were on his arms, her fingers sliding over the material, reveling in the solid flesh underneath. She raised her face and blinked up at him. "Whoever you may be," she drawled. "I have always depended on kindness in strangers."

***After dusting the apartment from top to bottom, Cheris turned on the television to the classic movie channel and lay back on the couch. She remembered very little after her Blanche DuBois quip last night. That was probably a good thing. She didn't really want to know the sordid details of a quickie ceremony in the Serenity courthouse or what had happened after that in the hotel room.

She shivered in disgust before reaching for the telephone and dialing Geoff's number. Dealing with it now was better than putting it off until later. They'd make an appointment with a lawyer first thing Monday morning and begin divorce proceedings.

When his voice mail picked up, Cheris ignored the goose bumps on her arms at the timbre of his words. She left a brief message asking him to call her.

Did he live in town? How come Cheris had never met him? Sure she knew Janie had a brother and that her parents lived in Cullsbaeir, but she'd never met any of them.

What kind of man would marry a woman he just met? He had to have known she wasn't in her right mind. What had she said last night? What had she done?

Cheris groaned and scrubbed her face with her hands. Rolling on her side she watched Doris Day jump on a horse to go rescue her love interest. Cheris had seen the movie a dozen times and knew the man Doris fancied herself in love with would not be the one she'd sing about in the moonlight by the end of the movie. With her lids heavy, Cheris settled against the cushions. Her eyes closed once, twice before sleep claimed her.

Bam! Bam! Bam!

In her deerskin outfit, Cheris aimed her gun firing in rapid succession from atop her galloping horse.

"Cheris, honey? Are you in there?"

Honey?

Cheris fell off the couch becoming fully awake when her butt hit the floor.

She jumped up, ran to the door, and threw it open. "Danny!"

Geoff dressed in suit and tie stared at her. He turned behind him as if searching for someone then back to Cheris. "I'm Geoff. We met last night and apparently again this morning. Who's Danny?"

"What?" Cheris shook her head, the vestiges of her movie-inspired dream dissipating.

"You called me Danny." Geoff wrinkled his nose at her. "You're not cheating on me, are you? What a shame since we're technically still on our honeymoon."

Cheris gawked. "There is no honeymoon! What were you thinking last night? At least I had an excuse for doing something so imbecilic."

Geoff grinned and nodded. "Imbecilic. I knew I'd arrived when Janie threatened me with the wrath of Mom."

"Don't act so proud of yourself. We're going to have to get a lawyer, you know."

"Really?"

Cheris stepped back and motioned for him to come inside. No use in the neighbors hearing of her divorce plans. When Cheris closed the door behind him, the room seemed to have shrunk to the size of her too-small closet. "What are you doing here anyway?"

In his tuxedo last night, he had looked like a movie star fitting in well on the set of the Wonderland exhibit. Today his grey suit with the red tie loosened, Geoff exuded confidence and comfort. His hazel eyes behind his eyeglasses had been what she had noticed first last night. Their unusual color was the same as Janie's. That's why he had seemed familiar to her. They twinkled at her now.

"I received your message. I thought I'd come by instead of calling you back. Is your headache any better?"

"My headache?" Cheris snorted. "It just came back."

Geoff closed the distance between them, reaching his hand up to touch her, but Cheris retreated.

He sighed. "Give me a break here. Don't you think if I wanted to maul you, I would have done it last night when you were more than a willing participant?"

"Don't you dare talk about last night. You make me sick!"

Geoff shook his head sorrowfully, walked to the door, opened it, and left shutting it softly behind him.

What?

Cheris stood there shaking. What just happened? He leaves without a word?

Knock. Knock. Knock.

Cheris reached forward, twisted the knob, and pulled.

"Hi." Geoff smiled congenially. "I'm Geoff Arrowood. We met last night at the gala." He offered her his hand. "I apologize for coming by unannounced. I got your voicemail, and your apartment was on my way back to the hotel."

Cheris hesitated before grasping his hand and wished she hadn't as a current of electricity shot up her arm through her body and all the way down to her toes.

Geoff continued, his hand still enveloping hers. "I know you know who I am, but I thought since we were never properly introduced—that you remember anyway—we could start over."

"Oh."

Geoff nodded and waited.

"I'm...umm...Cheris McDowell."

"You're friends with my sister, Janie." Geoff's handshake maneuvered into a handhold, his thumb stroking the flesh over her knuckles. Cherish glanced down at their hands.

Geoff closed his eyes briefly before directing a sheepish grin her way. "Sorry," he said as he dropped his hand. "Starting over," he muttered. "Want me to go out and knock again?"

Cherish giggled. "That's okay." She opened the door wider. "Come on in." She stood aside as he entered. The door closed again. She glanced back and saw the blanket she had covered up with during her nap lying askew on the floor. She strode over, snatched it up, and folded it. "Have a seat, and I'll fix us some iced tea." She placed the neatly folded blanket on the back of the couch.

"Please don't go to any trouble." He shifted from one foot to the other.

Why didn't he sit down? Why was he so tall?

Giving him a wide berth, she headed toward the kitchen. Once there, she clutched her chest and blew out a breath. For a moment she closed her eyes, willing the stampeding beat of her heart to slow. *He's Janie's brother. I can do this. I can act civil and not wonder what we did, how it felt...*

Stop! He is Janie's brother. Give him food and drink. Discuss a plan to fix the problem. Invite him to leave. Okay?

Yes.

Good.

Cheris shook her head and decided not to dwell on the fact that she was talking to herself, and answering back. What had the Cheshire cat said to Alice?

We're all mad here.

Yes. That about summed it up.

Cheris pulled out a serving tray and retrieved two glasses from her cabinet filling them with some tea she had brewed earlier in the day. Surveying the pantry, she grabbed a jar of mixed nuts to go with the beverage.

Mixed nuts.

Very appropriate.

In a few minutes Cheris entered her small living room with a tray carrying two glasses of iced tea, a plate of sliced lemons, and a candy dish containing the metaphor for her and the man sitting on her couch. The dish had been a gift from Annie Hill. What would she say if she knew Cheris had woken up next to Geoff without any memory of marrying him?

The tray banged against the coffee table, a result of Cheris' shaky hands. Tea spilled over the rims of the glasses, but if Geoff noticed he didn't comment. Perching on the edge of the couch a safe distance from him, Cheris picked up a Battenberg lace cloth, wrapped it around the glass and handed it to him.

The napkins were antique, another gift from Annie. On a whim, Cheris had placed them on the tray thinking that Geoff deserved Annie's Battenberg lace. Even if she never saw him again after the divorce, she'd never have another first husband.

"Lemon?"

"This is fine." Geoff drank deeply from the glass and rested it—half-full—on his knee. The bright gold band on his finger caught Cheris' gaze and held it.

Why was he still wearing the ring?

"Geoff." Even saying his name felt strange. "When I woke up this morning—"

"And stranded me in the hotel room in Serenity," he supplied.

The rational statement Cheris didn't finish flew out the window. "I'm sorry," she snapped. "I don't know the proper etiquette of one night stands."

"We're married. It's the exact opposite of a one night stand. It's a committed monogamous relationship."

"We are not having a relationship. Who meets and gets married in one night? It's the most ridiculous thing I've ever heard of."

"Yeah. That's what I thought, too."

"Then why'd you do it if you weren't under the influence of the cakes and punch?"

Geoff smirked. "You really don't remember?"

"If you knew me, you'd know I'd never do anything so irresponsible. Entering into a legal and binding covenant with a complete stranger and having…"

"Having?" Geoff prompted.

Cheris jumped off the couch and stalked the room. "Sex. Please tell me at least you…you know…used protection?"

"It's killing you, isn't it? Wondering what crazy things we did together last night?"

"There's a thing or two I'd do if I were no lady," she growled.

"Aha. I wondered."

"You wondered what?"

"If you quoted from old movies when you were sober. Who said that one? Audrey Hepburn? Deborah Kerr?"

It was Doris Day, but she wasn't telling *him* that. She stopped pacing and glared at him with her hands on her hips. "This isn't a joke," she snapped. "I don't know you. I don't even know if I like you. What I do know is that marriage is sacred to me, and because of that stupid stunt we pulled last night, I've cheapened it, made it into something disgusting and tawdry. Marriage is supposed to be for better and for worse, for richer and for poorer, in sickness and in health— "

"As long as we both shall live. Right. You want to do something tonight? Maybe go out to dinner?"

"Do I want to...? Have you heard a word I've said? Don't you care that you made some pretty serious promises to a complete stranger, that you got the state involved in taking advantage of me while I was drunk? I don't care if Janie's your sister. I don't know you, and I can't just pretend last night didn't happen. Me not remembering it makes it even worse."

"Cheris, I agree with every single thing you've said. I do. Marriage is sacred. It's a lifelong commitment. I get all of that. I also understand that you have some reservations about me because you don't know me and you feel I used poor judgment last night. Just go out with me tonight. We won't eat any cakes or drink any alcohol. You can ask me twenty questions. A hundred questions, and I'll answer every one. Give me the chance to show you I'm not as dumb as I acted last night."

"I don't trust you."

Geoff shrugged. "I suppose that's understandable. Give me a chance tonight to earn your trust."

Cheris sighed.

"Please?"

"Okay."

He picked up the china dish and tapped some nuts into his hand. "Very good. May I pick you up at seven?"

"All right."

"Good." He set the dish on the tray and popped the food in his mouth, winked at her and left.

Cheris let out a breath she didn't realize she had been holding. Why had she agreed to go out with that man? Why couldn't they just agree to meet at a lawyer's office first thing Monday morning and start the divorce proceedings? She didn't want to go out with him; she wanted to put this incident behind her and try to forget it ever happened. At least he had agreed about the big mistake they had made.

Hadn't he?

I do. Marriage is sacred. It's a lifelong commitment. I get all of that.

Cheris raised her hands to her cheeks in realization.

He hadn't agreed that last night was a mistake. He'd only agreed to *as long as we both shall live.*

Cheris lowered her arms and straightened her shoulders. Surely he wasn't seriously thinking of staying married. That was ridiculous.

Had the sex been that good?

Too bad she couldn't remember.

Chapter Three

"If a thing is right it can be done, and if it is wrong it can be done without; and a good man will find a way."
—*Black Beauty* by Ann Sewell

Cheris pushed the button of her computer screen, and the logo for *Hip Granny* appeared. She emailed Bill Conner, her supervisor about the exhibits at the gala the night before. With the unifying theme of children's classic literature, Cheris knew the art would be fun. She hadn't expected the breathtaking beauty and originality of it and proposed to Bill they dedicate a series on it for the web site. With the traffic Hip Granny received, it would be good publicity for the museum, and the potential for offshoot topics was rich as well: children's literature, reading to your kids, cultural icons, family outings, modern art, and artist bios. Cheris worked up the layout in her head. With the artists' permission, they could use a photograph from each exhibit as the focal point.

Peter Pan would have Dara Lassiter's mural of the Jolly Roger moored on Kidd Creek.

Cheris would use the green glass fortress from The Wonderful Wizard of Oz piece.

Black Beauty would focus on the magnificent onyx statue of a horse reared up on its hind legs.

For Janie's Secret Garden exhibit, they'd photograph the live plants cascading out from the six foot deep shadow box with its marble façade walls.

Topics Cheris did not suggest for the series: drunken black-outs, marrying in haste, quickie divorces, though avoiding the eat me/drink me display would be helpful information for anybody.

Cheris had been with Hip Granny for almost three years—ever since the original Hip Granny, Annie Hill, had handpicked her from among the lackeys at Net Enterprises, a franchised Web Media company which provided computer repair and service locally. On that fateful day, Cheris had been assigned to go to Annie's house to work on her computer.

When Cheris had knocked, a frizzy haired older woman in a leopard print dress opened the door of an enormous Tudor style house. She leaned heavily on a cane which matched her dress.

"What's the matter? Cat got your tongue? You've never seen anyone after knee replacement? It hurts like the dickens, I tell you."

Cheris shook her head. "I'm sorry, Ma'am. Please forgive me."

The woman cocked her head, her eyes narrowed. "Ma'am, eh? Did you drive the mile up my driveway to sell me something, or are you here to fix my computer?"

"The latter."

Rapid footsteps approached, and a woman wearing scrubs appeared at the door. "Mrs. Hill, why don't you wait and let me answer the door."

"Who knew where you were, Mary Frances? And I've got to get my computer fixed. Come on in, dear. I'm Annabelle Hill though most people call me Annie. What is your name?"

"Cheris McDowell, Ma'am. It is very nice to meet you."

"Mary Frances, go fix Cheris and me some tea. We'll be in the den."

"Oh, no thank you. I—" Cheris began.

"Now, young lady, you don't have to drink the tea, but I certainly do have to offer it."

Mary Frances hurried out of the foyer, and Annie ushered Cheris into a brick floored den with a lemon colored couch and a Victorian style Damask lounge chaise in a matching shade. In the corner sat an imposing desk with a computer monitor on its shiny surface.

Cheris laid her purse on the floor next to the desk and sat on the wooden office chair. She touched the power button and the blue screen of death appeared on the monitor.

Not good.

"Who are your people, Cheris?" Annie asked as she carefully lowered herself in a straight backed seat next to the wall.

Cheris knew this was the southern lady's way of asking who her parents were. Cheris dropped to her knees on the floor and disconnected the computer from the surge protector.

"I'm from West Virginia," she spoke as she worked, "A little town called Hermet. I'm sure you don't know my people." She glanced back and noted Annie studying her as if she were a specimen under a microscope.

"Oh, you might be surprised. I know lots of people."

"My mom works at a restaurant there called the Sugarbox Café. Her name is Sarah."

"I've been there. Excellent peanut butter pie, as I recall."

"The best in the state." Cheris connected the cord and powered it up again.

"And how in the world did a well-mannered woman from Hermet end up on her hands and knees in Cullsbaeir working on my computer?"

"Milton Stewart serves on the board of directors where I went to college. He was looking for a computer geek with knowledge in media and advertising so I went for the interview. He offered health insurance, and here I am."

"What would you tell someone who said they've got eighty-four thousand dollars in credit card debt?"

"I'd tell them to get on a budget, cut up their credit cards, pay the minimum on all of them except for the one with the smallest debt, pay as much as they could on it until it's paid off, then tackle the next one."

Annie chuckled. "Well, my dear, surely they should declare bankruptcy."

Cheris who had settled in the chair by this time had begun a viral check. She stopped and gazed at the older woman. "I don't mean to be disrespectful, Mrs. Hill—"

"Annie."

"Annie, but declaring bankruptcy is irresponsible. Now if it's medical bills, I would advise calling the medical providers and negotiating, but in my opinion bankruptcy needs to be the last option."

"In your opinion."

"Since you asked. I hope I didn't offend you. But Gerald, who owns the café, has been burnt a few times from suppliers who declared bankruptcy when they owed him equipment or food which had already been paid for."

"Very interesting. What would you say to someone who is so embarrassed at the state of their house that they won't allow their children to have friends over to play?"

Cheris, who had so far found fourteen different viruses on Annie's computer, shrugged. "Pick a room, have a family clean up day, and a yard sale to get rid of some of their junk. The next week, pick another room. Annie, I'm going to install some virus protection on your computer. You've got about a thousand cookies on here. It's not good for your computer."

"Cookies?"

"Yes Ma'am. They're spies that come into your computer from web sites you visit. *Hip Granny* even has them. That way we know how to market to people who visit."

The older woman sniffed. "It seems very unethical."

"Some of the cookies are. Ours are less invasive than most. But some of the web sites you've been visiting..." Cheris shook her head. "I'll install a program on here so that you'll have to give the cookie permission to be set if it's not a nice cookie."

"What do you think of wives chatting on the internet with men?"

"Are the men their husbands or dads?"

"I've heard enough." Annie clapped her hands together. "Just leave that old thing. I'm going to take you out to lunch."

Despite Cheris' protests that she wanted to get the older woman's computer working again, Annie had taken her out to lunch at a small posh restaurant in Cullsbaeir. From that day forward, Annie had taken a personal interest in Cheris, inviting her into the lives of the web visitors of Hip Granny to advise and inform. What Cheris did not realize at the time was that Annie was training her to be Hip Granny when Annie stepped down from the role.

With Bill's vision for selling anything even dirt, Hip Granny had become a lucrative internet enterprise selling everything from cleaning products, to how-to kits on organizing one's life and home, to debt and weight reduction plans, to relationship fixers.

Cheris had shown up in a few of Hip Granny's webcasts when they had demonstrated how to use Skype or some other techie topic. Though both Annie and Bill had approached Cheris about becoming a more visible presence on the site, Cheris had declined. She felt more comfortable operating the web cam than being in front of it.

****

His cell phone was ringing when Geoff stepped out of the shower of his hotel room. Grabbing a towel from the rack, he dried his skin as he summoned the call. He peered at the number on the small screen.

Janie.

"I hope you're planning on coming over here to Mom and Dad's pretty soon. I need a buffer between me and all of these elderly people."

Geoff expelled a breath. His parents' thirty-fifth anniversary party. He had completely forgotten. How was he supposed to go to the party and take Cheris out on a date at the same time? He rubbed the towel across his hair as he contemplated being in two places at once.

"Hey Dumb-dumb. Do not tell me you forgot the

party. That was your reason for coming home," Janie uttered in disbelief.

"I know. I know. Just calm down." Geoff picked up his watch from the dresser top. It wasn't even five o'clock. He had hoped to catch a nap this afternoon before his date. "What's the hurry? The party isn't until seven." The exact time he said he'd pick up Cheris. He slipped the band around his wrist and fastened it.

"The hurry is I'm losing my mind here. The house is filling up with all our crusty old relatives, half of whom I don't even know. I'm tired of their condescending remarks about me being an artist. I do very well for myself without any handouts from Mom and Dad. I had a spread in Southern Culture Today; I don't have to put up with this. Now be a brother and get over here and let them make over how brilliant you are, while I slink down to the basement and eat worms."

"I can be there in fifteen minutes."

"I'll give you twenty if you bring my new sister-in-law with you."

Geoff laughed as he shouldered the phone and rummaged through his suitcase for clean skivvies before throwing the phone on the bed so he could slip first one leg then the other in his shorts. "You haven't said anything to Mom and Dad, have you?"

"How crazy do I look?"

"Well, don't. Cheris is pretty shaken about all of this. I'm not planning on bringing her tonight. She isn't even sure she likes me yet. How crazy would I be to sic the Arrowood clan on her on our first date?" He picked the phone back up in time to hear his sister's reply.

"I thought last night was your first date."

"The first date she can remember." Pants next. He pulled the khakis off the hanger in the closet and stepped into them before selecting one of the pressed button-down shirts still in his hanging bag.

"You idiot. What were you thinking marrying her?"

"It's your fault, you know. You're always talking about

how wonderful she is, and you painted that picture of her—"

"What picture?"

"*Woman in Gold.*" He'd first seen the painting in Janie's studio last summer. A young woman reclined in a field, the soft curve of her hip contrasted with the lateral planes of the plants, and the fiery glint of her auburn hair complimented the hue of the golden wheat. Geoff was so struck by it that Janie had presented it to him as a Christmas gift last year. Then two weeks ago he'd been watching a tutorial on Net Enterprises about CMSs when he'd seen her again, talking about Drupal and caressing the computer keyboard instead of the blades of wheat which cradled her in the painting.

"Oh, Geoff," Janie gasped.

"What can I say, Sis? You know how much I loved that painting." He tucked the shirt in his pants and sat on the edge of the bed to retrieve his shoes.

"It's a painting," she said simply.

"Of Cheris."

"Well…I guess there was a likeness, but, Jesus, Geoff! You're supposed to be the smart one in the family."

"Tell me you don't think we're a good match."

"Couldn't you have waited?"

"Is this the rebel Janie Arrowood talking?"

"She's my best friend. She does not do spontaneous. Ever."

"Hope that goes for divorces, too."

"Just get over here. We can talk about it then."

Geoff disconnected and grabbed his keys. He'd make an appearance and shield Janie from well-meaning relatives before sneaking out for a couple of hours to spend with Cheris.

No such luck. Even with forty people milling through the house his mom had caught him sneaking out the door. She hadn't bought his excuse that he was going to the store for more ice, more milk, or more anything else. When he finally admitted he was going on a date, she commanded him to be back with his date in half an hour.

This was not how he had hoped to spend the evening gaining his new bride's trust.

The door to Cheris' apartment was open when Geoff walked up the paved path. Bluesy music played on the stereo, but she wasn't in the living room. Geoff paused at the doorway wondering if he should enter and how he was going to break the news to Cheris that she'd be meeting her in-laws tonight. Oh, he wasn't a total idiot. He knew she wanted out of the marriage ASAP, but somehow he had to stall her until she got to know him, until she realized he wasn't insane and until she was on board with his plan to love, honor, and cherish each other as long as they both shall live.

Cherish Cheris. It had a nice ring to it.

Movement from the corner of the sofa caught his attention. A large white cat with green eyes stretched and yawned.

So she liked cats.

"Here kitty," he called and knelt offering his hand in greeting.

The feline stood for a moment before cautiously moving toward Geoff who crooned to him. Finally within touching distance, Geoff scratched his big head. The cat had to weigh at least twenty pounds.

"Aren't you a big cat?" He crooned. "Where's your mistress, huh?"

The cat purred in reply, turning so Geoff could have better access to his back.

Muted footsteps approached, and Cheris entered. "Oh. Hello. I see you've met Timmy." She tilted her head, a quizzical expression on her face. "He's not usually so social with strangers."

For a moment, Geoff didn't speak his gaze traveling over Cheris who wore a black sleeveless dress and matching high heels. Her only jewelry was a pair of pink stones which dangled from her ears and an ornate silver toned necklace with pink highlights. But it was her hair he took notice of.

Last night she'd worn it up, secured loosely with a big barrette. Tonight it hung loose past her shoulders in big auburn curls. His fingers itched to reach out and touch her hair and find out if it felt as silky as it looked.

"If you'll give me one more minute, I'll be ready." Cheris pivoted on those spiked heels and walked from whence she came. In less than a minute she returned. Her hair had once more been pulled up and off of her shoulders. It was on the tip of Geoff's tongue to ask her to take it back down, but he concluded he hadn't earned the right to have a voice in her how she styled her hair. She looked pretty darn good with it up, too.

Beautiful, in fact.

She smiled at him, and his heart hammered in his chest. "So, where are we going?"

"Funny you should ask."

"Oh?"

"I'd like to take you out to dinner, but..." Geoff's voice trailed off. What could he say? *But my mom told me I had to take you to meet her.*

"But?"

"The reason I'm in town this weekend is because my parents are having an anniversary party. They've been married thirty-five years. In all of the excitement of...you, the party slipped my mind. I want to go out with you tonight, but I wonder if we could go to the party for a little while. Afterwards you and I can go get something to eat, you can grill me about my life, then I'll take you home."

"Do they know about our...mistake last night?"

Geoff's eyes narrowed. *So, eloping was a mistake, was it? Man, I sure have got my work cut out for me.* "No, they don't know about us getting married if that's what you're talking about."

"Do you promise that they won't find out tonight? It will just make it that much harder for them when we get divorced."

"You're my date. That's all they know."

Cheris picked up a black jacket of the same material as

her dress and turned to slip it around her shoulders. Geoff noted the graceful curve of her neck, and considered maybe the hair up had been the way to go after all.

"Come on then, Date," Cheris straightened her collar as she arched an eyebrow his way, "and make sure to take off your wedding ring before we get there."

Geoff couldn't help the smile which broke out on his face at her flirty tone. Last night had been a wild roller coaster ride. Tonight was turning out to be more like the Ferris wheel—a more sedate experience but what a breathtaking view.

Chapter Four

"What lies over *there?*" asked the Mole, waving a paw
towards a background
of woodland that darkly framed the water meadows on one
side of the river.
"That? O, that's just the Wild Wood," said the Rat shortly.
"We don't
go there very much, we river bankers."
"Aren't they-aren't they very *nice* people in there?" said the
Mole a trifle nervously.
—*The Wind in the Willows* by Kenneth Grahame

The drive over was quiet. Cheris detected a faint scent
of Geoff's cologne or aftershave. She inhaled the citrusy
scent.

Nice.

*What was it? Did he put it on all the time, or just on special
occasions?*

The SUV was different than what he had been driving
this morning. The other car must have been a rental,
probably one he'd had to get because she'd stranded him in
Serenity. Guilt nagged at her.

"I'm…sorry about leaving you without a ride this
morning."

"I accept your apology. Thank you for leaving me my
pants and wallet."

Right. She'd taken his shirt, too. "I only took your shirt
because I couldn't find mine."

"And you already had mine on," Geoff supplied. "It's
okay. If I'd known you were going to wake up with no
recollection of the night before, I would have…"

"What?"

"I don't know, set an alarm or something. I'm usually not such a heavy sleeper. I guess I was really tired. I don't blame you for panicking though—waking up in bed with me. I look pretty bad before a shower and shave."

Cheris decided not to think about her role in tiring the boy out, or how bad he hadn't looked all rumpled in bed. His slumbering form would be etched in her mind until she died.

Was it hot in here? She aimed the air vent toward her face.

Geoff pulled his car in front of a large antebellum structure which looked more like a museum than a family residence. Wide columns stretched from the floor of the stone front porch to the two-storied roof. Lights shown from nearly every window. Cheris gulped. Janie had grown up here? Cars lined the circular driveway and the perfectly manicured lawn. Geoff exited the car and walked over to the passenger side to open Cheris' door, holding his hand out to guide her. She took his hand and stepped out of the car still staring at the house.

"Hey." Geoff circled in front of her as he grasped her other hand. "This may be the last time we're alone tonight so I want to tell you that you look very beautiful."

Cheris felt warmth creep up her neck to her face. "At least one time in her life a woman should have a man tell her how beautiful she is. I give thanks that you are the one to tell me." Turning her face away from the house, she gazed at Geoff in the twilight of the evening.

He smiled. "Do I detect a movie quotation?"

"Ingrid Bergman said it in *The Inn of the Sixth Happiness.*" She pulled one of her hands out of his and strode up the paved walkway, pulling him with her.

He matched her gait. "That's a nifty talent, to be able to pull a quote from a movie to fit the situation."

"I do it when I'm nervous," Cheris admitted. What could go wrong? She was going to the anniversary party of the parents of her best friend as well as the man she'd slept with last night while drunk on cake and punch. *No potential for awkward conversation there.*

"Hmm. Interesting." Geoff murmured. "I didn't think nervous was in your repertoire. You sure didn't act nervous last night. In fact, your daring was a little scary at times."

"Please don't bring up last night. I'm already about to jump out of my shoes."

"I apologize." They were almost to the door. "Are you ready?"

"As I'll ever be." Cheris took a deep breath and pasted a smile on her face.

"Just think lovely wonderful thoughts," Geoff whispered as he pushed open the door and motioned for her to go ahead of him. Cheris glanced back to make sure he was coming in with her, and he winked as if he could read her mind.

Inside an airy foyer with granite floors and stairs leading to the second story greeted them. A distinguished man in a dark suit with a red tie approached them with a welcoming smile. "Geoffrey, glad you made it back. Hello, my dear."

"My dad," Geoff spoke in her ear, and Cheris shivered at the intimacy of the gesture. He drew back and made the introductions. "This is Chip Arrowood, my father who is celebrating thirty-five years of wedding bliss to my mom. Dad, this is Cheris McDowell."

"What a pleasure, Cheris."

She saw the family resemblance—same strong chin and captivating smile. Chip enveloped her hand in his, pulled her toward him, and kissed her cheek. The gesture surprised and pleased Cheris. Stepping back, he gestured toward a room through a wide doorway. A table overflowing with food dominated the space. "Go eat. Make yourself at home, Cheris."

Several people milled around the table filling glass vintage luncheon plates with food. Janie sat on the couch next to an older woman. When she spotted Cheris, she jumped up and hurried across the room to the couple. "Hi.

Oh, I'm so glad to see you. I just knew you were going to skip out on me."

"And miss the party? No son of mine would dare." A fiftyish woman joined their trio. Cheris recognized the tawny eyes of both children in her face. "You must be Cheris. I've heard so much about you."

Cheris shot a startled look at Geoff who shrugged.

"Don't panic. She pumped me for information the second Geoff left," Janie informed them.

"How romantic that Janie fixed you two up. I'm Margaret, but everyone calls me Monnie." She leaned forward and embraced Cheris. "Welcome. Welcome. Welcome. To our party. To our home. To our family."

Geoff and Cheris glared at Janie, but she waved her hand in defense. "I didn't tell her."

"Tell me what?" Monnie pinned each person with perceptive eyes. "Oh, never mind. We're glad you're here, Cheris. What a lovely name. We'll talk later about what Janie didn't tell me but obviously should have." Monnie aimed the latter part of the sentence toward her daughter and finished with, "Young lady." She looked past them toward the front door. "Oh, for heaven's sake. There is Larry Preston. I told Chip not to invite that man. Excuse me," she said hurrying into the foyer.

Cheris let out the breath she had been holding. Geoff cupped her shoulder. "See? That's as bad as it will get. You've met them. It's smooth sailing from here on out."

"Don't count on it, Romeo," Janie replied. "Mama knows something's up."

"She couldn't know unless you opened your big mouth." Geoff stepped closer to Janie so no one would overhear.

"I didn't say anything about the you-know-what, you big stupid oaf. What did you say?" Janie stuck her face next to his until they were huffing at each other nose to nose.

Cheris stood between them pushing them apart with her hands. "Stop it. Don't make a scene. Geoff, would you get us something to drink while Janie and I get a little snack from the buffet?"

Geoff immediately relaxed his stance. He adjusted his glasses. "Sorry, Sis. I should know you'd always keep my secrets, but you seemed a little too ecstatic over the...arrangement between Cheris and me."

"Well, yeah, I'm ecstatic. My bro hooking up with my best friend but putting Monnie Dearest into the mix so soon could put a damper on the honeymoon." When Geoff glared at her, she replied, "I was speaking metaphorically, *of course, a*bout the honeymoon and not saying that anyone in this room might have cause to take one."

"Well, no wonder she's suspicious if you've been making statements like that."

Cheris grasped Geoff's hand, caressing his fingers with her thumb. "I'm so thirsty. Please won't you get me something?"

He glanced down at their joined hands and nodded. Cheris broke the physical connection decidedly ignoring the warmth presently spreading from her arm to the rest of her body. Geoff pivoted and walked through a throng of people in search of drinks.

Janie raised an eyebrow. "He won't be gone long, you know."

"I know. I wish you had warned me about this." Cheris raised a hand indicating all of it—the house, the party, the family.

They walked over to the buffet table, and Janie handed Cheris a plate. "I think you would have been spared, but Mom caught Geoff trying to make a getaway. Big dope." They walked down the table side by side filling their plates. "Everybody knows when you're sneaking out, you use the back door."

Cheris studied her friend. "Janie, don't take this the wrong way, but are you sure you're not adopted?"

Janie chuckled. "You wouldn't know it to look at my dad, but my mom swears I'm Chip made over."

With brimming plates, they found a vacant corner of the room. Janie pinned Cheris with serious consideration.

"What are you going to do?"

She didn't have to be more specific. Cheris knew exactly what she was talking about.

"Go see a lawyer Monday morning and begin divorce proceedings though I can't seem to pin down Geoff about it." Cheris paused as she picked up a cucumber sandwich and examined it. "I can't believe that he would...that I would..." She dropped the food onto the plate and shook her head. All of the sudden the food didn't look so appealing. When Janie didn't reply, Cheris glanced at her, and the other woman held her gaze.

"You're perfect for each other. I don't know how in the world either one of you could have done something so impetuous, but I'm telling you, it's a match made in heaven."

Cheris lowered her gaze. "Please don't, Janie. I know he's your brother, but I don't know him. I didn't realize I would ever be capable of doing something like last night. I can't...I just can't..." What she wanted to say, she couldn't express. She set her plate on a nearby window sill, and sucked in some air from the stifling room. "I'm sorry." She touched her fingers to her aching temple and began to walk toward the door.

Air. She needed some fresh air, cool air.

"Oh, Cheris. Don't leave," Janie said following her.

Cheris spied Monnie and Chip near the front door and turned in the opposite direction.

She had to get out. She had to get out of here.

"Give me a minute. I just need a few minutes alone." Without waiting for a reply, she squeezed through several people and hurried through another door. Where was that back door Janie had talked about?

She entered a formal dining room which had a huge white cake sitting in the middle of the table. She stepped by several people, nodding politely as she did so.

Was there no secluded place?

Continuing on, she exited the room through a dark cherry doorway.

Another room with another table? How many tables did one house need?

This one had a plethora of beverages—both with and without alcohol. The bartender smiled at her expectantly. So, how come she hadn't passed Geoff on the way back?

Cheris shook her head and kept walking until she stood in front of another door, this one closed. She pushed it open and found a spacious kitchen with counters laden with food waiting to be taken to refill serving trays obviously. Only the light over the stove illuminated the room, and was void of any person, though Cheris knew that wouldn't last long. She spied another door—this one with a window lined with café curtains.

Ah, it must be an outside door.

Cheris strode across the room and opened it breathing deeply the night air through the screened partition. She pushed it open and stepped onto the bricked porch letting the screen door shut softly behind her. Crickets sang from bushes lining the porch. Cheris closed her eyes and breathed deeply for a few moments trying to empty her mind of all of the whirling emotions.

After a few minutes, the quiet calm of the evening soothed her soul, and she looked around with interest at the Arrowood backyard. A rectangular pool was just beyond the porch. Beside it sat a very small aged wooden structure. Cheris wondered if once upon a time it had been the servants' quarters. It looked so out of place next to the neat lines of the swimming pool. But then having seen the house, Cheris knew it was really the pool which was out of place. The rest of the surroundings had an old southern quality to it—a far cry from the cramped apartment she had grown up in over the restaurant.

Just another red flag as to why this marriage wouldn't work. Not that Cheris had any plans to try. The right thing to do was to shake hands and part ways. Marriages weren't built on one night in a hotel room but on mutual love and respect developed over time.

Settling on a wooden bench, Cheris inhaled and

recognized the strong scent of wisteria. She noticed the lavender-colored bush lit by the bright light of the moon.

Why hadn't they had the party outside?

It was so gorgeous out here.

The weather—though spring, still was warm enough for an outdoor party when as many people were in attendance as were here tonight. This backyard was made for people to enjoy it.

Cheris had always envisioned herself getting married in a church, but this backyard would be perfect for the reception afterwards. Never in any of her dreams had Cheris imagined her wedding in a courthouse in a tourist trap like Serenity. Never had she anticipated that she wouldn't even remember the event because of spiked punch and cake.

"Penny for your thoughts." Geoff's voice came to her from the other side of the screen door.

"They're not worth even that."

"Tell me. I can afford to be overcharged."

A flicker of interest lit within Cheris. She'd quoted from *Casablanca* and so had he. Did he like old movies too?

"I was just thinking how perfect this backyard would be for a wedding reception."

Geoff opened the door and walked outside, leaning against the frame after it closed. He handed her one of the drinks he held. She sniffed then tasted it and, thankfully, found it alcohol-free.

"I guess a quickie courthouse wedding isn't what most little girls dream of when they're growing up, is it?"

Cheris arched an eyebrow at him. He obviously didn't need a penny to read her thoughts. "No. It isn't."

"I did us a great disservice, didn't I? By not being level-headed enough to realize how crazy it was for us to get married without even knowing each other."

"I believe you did it because you are certifiably insane." She sighed and sipped her Coke. "I should have you committed. I can do that, you know, since I'm your wife. Just lock you up for thirty days. And while they do a mental evaluation on you, I could abscond with all your earthly goods."

"Ah, Cheris, everything I have is yours already. I believe it went something like *with this ring I thee wed, with this body I thee worship, with all my worldly goods I thee endow.*" Geoff pushed off the door and knelt down before her. He set his glass down on the bench beside her and reached up to tuck a strand of her hair behind her ear.

"Get up from your knees," she growled. "I hate your common jokes."

"You don't have to be nervous with me." Geoff rose, walked over to the poolside, grabbed the arm of a lounge chair and dragged it until it was a few feet from the bench.

"I don't know what you mean."

Geoff straddled the chair then reclined on it. He closed his eyes and sighed contentedly. "Yes, you do, you big fake. Mom made us watch *Gone with the Wind* every January on her birthday for years so don't you sit there and quote that movie to me, then deny it."

"I didn't deny it. Not exactly." If he knew the line, then he knew it's what Scarlet had said the Rhett when he proposed to her.

Oops.

"You told me you revert to movie quotations when you're nervous. After last night you don't have to—"

"I asked you not to bring up last night."

"So you did, Scarlet. I apologize."

They sat in silence for a few moments. Cheris watched him in the darkness, his relaxed pose, the curly dark hair a little too long on his collar, the strong chin, and handsome profile.

With this ring I thee wed, with this body I thee worship, with all my worldly goods I thee endow.

Had they really said that to each other last night?

Attraction pulled at her, motivated her to lessen the distance between them, to seek out the heat of his body in the cool of the evening. The intensity of the feeling surprised Cheris.

Was this her body remembering last night what her mind couldn't?

"I have a picture," Geoff spoke, opening his eyes and bracing his feet on either side of the lounger.

"What?"

"Come here." He gestured to the empty place on the chair in front of him.

Cheris shook her head. *He's crazy if he thinks I'm sharing a seat with him.*

"Don't be bashful." He held up his right hand for emphasis. "I swear I will give you a full thirty seconds before I ravish you. You can be halfway across the yard by then."

Cheris studied him indecisively.

"Don't I get any credit for behaving myself when you were naked from the waist down in bed this morning?"

"You were asleep."

"Not the whole time. As a matter of fact, when you slung your panties—"

"I don't want to hear what happened between us in that hotel room!"

"That is unfortunate as you would realize it wasn't as horrendous as you imagine."

Cheris snorted. "You're so conceited. I'm sure my enthusiasm was due to my inebriated state."

"I concur." He patted the space in front of him. "Now come over here. You're much more level-headed now. I'm sure you'll behave yourself even if you sit with me. I want to tell you about this vision I have for the backyard."

She perched on the edge of the lounger. "And you behave yourself."

"A thirty second warning is all I guarantee," he whispered from behind her. Cheris sat ramrod straight ready to bolt. She refused to turn her head to look at him. Clearing his throat, he spoke in a normal tone. "Now then. You've got me thinking about this as a setting for a wedding reception. I always thought a wedding would be better in church, but you're right. To have the reception here would be perfect."

Startled, Cheris glanced at him.

Did I tell him that?

No, I did not.

How did he know?

Stop it. You're conversing with yourself again.

I know. Disturbing, isn't it?

He placed his hands on her head, and she jumped. "Sorry. I just wanted you to look at the pool." He withdrew from her. "We could put a fountain there, and some lights that shine up through the water. Colored lights. Wouldn't that be lovely?"

Geoff's hands again, one on her shoulder, the other on her scalp.

What was he...?

The clasp of her barrette opened, and her hair spilled down over her shoulders. She turned to catch a glimpse of him, but his hands directed her face toward the bushes lining the porch and the yard beyond. "Little lights in the bushes, I think. The reception would begin at twilight, and as the sun sets their prominence would add much ambiance to the setting."

With his fingers he combed through the tresses of her hair. Her body relaxed with the strokes and the soothing tone of his voice.

"We could run wide ribbon through the porch rails of the pool house. Maybe some magnolia leaves and blossoms tied at the top of the rails. We could have a bar on the porch—soft drinks or tea. No alcohol, of course. We wouldn't want to be the indirect cause of some poor woman getting carried off to Serenity because she's had too much to drink, would we?"

"Certainly not," Cheris murmured. She moved her head as Geoff brushed her hair to one shoulder exposing the curve of her neck.

"Let's see here. Ah, yes. The refreshment tables over there under the big oak tree. You know how many times I climbed that tree growing up? Scared my poor mom to death."

With heavy eyelids, Cheris glanced at the tall tree as Geoff kneaded her skin. "Naughty boy."

"We'll have cake and punch—the regular kind, not any of that Wonderland brew—on a table next to the wisterias." His breath warmed her skin, his body closer now, thighs cradling her hips, chest against her back.

When had he moved forward?

"Have you ever had hummingbird cake? I don't know why they call it that. It isn't made of hummingbirds, but it has fruit and pecans in it. My Aunt Nancy makes a killer hummingbird cake. I'll have to introduce you to her later. She's staying in my room which is why I was demoted to the Days Inn. I don't mind though. She's a sweetheart."

He tugged her jacket from her shoulders, the sleeves sliding down to rest at her elbows. "Is this okay? You feel a little warm."

Oh, yes, she did.

Sizzling.

"We need some tables, of course, so people will have a place to sit and eat. Round ones with ivory cloths and a candle in the middle in a hurricane globe so the breeze won't blow out the flame. Maybe some flowers around the outside of the glass. Azaleas, I think. Mom has a ton of those in the front yard. My cousin Paul can arrange them. He's good at that sort of thing." His fingers rubbed and worked the muscles of her neck and shoulders turning her to Jell-O.

"What else? What kind of food should there be?" Geoff drummed his fingers briefly on her shoulders. "There's this mix called trash, and it's cereal and nuts with white chocolate dribbled on it. Ever had it?"

"No."

"It's tasty. I had it at something I went to...what was it? Oh. A stupid faculty party. Man, I hate those things. Everybody wants to fix me up."

"A stupid faculty party?" Cheris leaned away as she pivoted to face him. "What are you, a teacher?"

"A professor. I teach at the Newbie River Institute. Science and Astronomy."

She stood and glared down at Geoff. "Newbie River? Isn't that in Georgia?"

"Just across the Tennessee line, yes," he said as he, too, stood up.

"What were you thinking? You married me, and you don't even live in the same state?"

"Well, nobody knows this yet, but I've accepted a teaching position at Pitching High School with some didactic work at the science museum and observatory owned by Smithson College. It's a pretty sweet deal."

"But you'll be in Georgia until, what, at least the end of May?" Cheris grabbed her jacket and shrugged into it. "I knew it! I knew you married me just for the sex."

"I would hope not. That's a terrible reason to get married, although, I have to admit, a great fringe benefit."

"Stop making jokes about it."

"I'm sorry, Honey. The semester is over May twenty-sixth, and commencement is the twenty-ninth. But I can come up here every weekend if you don't think you can live without me until June."

"If I don't think I can live without you? Here's a news flash, Geoff. I'm not planning on living with you ever. In case I haven't made myself clear, I'm going to a lawyer first thing—"

The porch light came on.

Chip Arrowood stood inside the screened door. "Aha. I heard the two of you were out here. Come on inside now. Monnie is chomping at the bit."

Geoff didn't move immediately. Instead he studied Cheris, though she couldn't read his expression because of the porch light reflecting on his glasses. The door opened as the older man held it as an invitation to enter. Cheris walked into the kitchen and followed Chip as he led them into an adjoining room and down a hallway that led to the front foyer. From behind her, Geoff's footsteps followed her before the noise was swallowed up with the noise of people in conversation. Men and women crowded the room their faces tilted toward the stairs where Monnie Arrowood stood a third of the way up with a glass of champagne in her hand. She smiled radiantly at them, and a sense of unease overcame Cheris. Geoff must have felt it as well because he grasped her arm to detain her. When she glanced behind her, the troubled expression on his face caught and held her gaze.

"Listen," he whispered. "I think we're in trouble here."

"What?"

"You see that embarrassed looking woman over there?" He indicated a young woman in a cream linen suit. "That's the principal of Pitching, and I think she may have disclosed my newly employed status here in town. For whatever is about to happen, I apologize."

"Why would you need to—?"

"Oh, no, you don't," Monnie declared from her perch on the staircase. "Geoff, you and Cheris come up here with me. Chip, don't you let them escape. Come on, now. Everybody's waiting."

With uneasy steps Cheris moved toward the staircase and Monnie. When she stopped at the foot of the stairs, the older woman held her hand out for Cheris to take which she did so obediently. "Chip, you and Janie come up here as well. I want to make a toast. But first, what brought us to this moment."

Janie appeared out of the crowd with three glasses of champagne balanced precariously in her hands. She refused to make eye contact with Cheris, a worrisome indicator. She gave a flute to Geoff and Cheris as she took her place next to them. Monnie positioned each of them in an appropriate group pose.

The photo op.

And Cheris was in it.

Oh, this was bad. Very bad.

"You all know my son Geoff who teaches astrology..."

Cheris turned astonished eyes to Geoff who stared

stonily ahead. "Astrology?"

Janie shook her head at Cheris and whispered through her bright smile. "Don't even bother correcting the woman. She's in tsunami mode."

"...and I told Chip, can this night get any more perfect, but our son has demonstrated I was mistaken. It seems Dr. Geoff Arrowood will be teaching at the high school right here in town beginning in the next school year and in June he's going to be the dynamic professor at the Winfield Space Museum."

At the word *dynamic*, Geoff pinched the bridge of his nose under his glasses while a murmur of delight arose from the crowd.

"Our Geoff is coming home," Monnie announced. "Wait now. That's not the toast. You all just quit sipping from your glasses. I'm not nearly finished."

Monnie grasped Cheris' hand. "This is Cheris, a dear friend of Janie's."

Geoff leaned toward his sister. "I am going to kill you," he whispered.

"Oh, hush, Geoff, my son. Nobody's killing anybody tonight."

Some of the onlookers laughed in response to Monnie's public reproach. "Cheris accompanied Geoff over here tonight which in and of itself is a coup d'état as he's never brought a girl home. Well, you know how young people are. They disappeared almost as soon as they got here."

Snickers from the audience.

"We old fogies know it as pitching woo," Chip supplied. The snickers became outright chortles.

"We call it making whoopee," a voice called out.

"How about playing footsie?" another suggested.

Cheris smoothed her loose hair back with a shaky hand.

"That's enough." Monnie held her hand up to quiet the crowd. "My son would never do such a thing to embarrass us. But lawzy, that boy is stubborn. I'd say to him, 'Aren't there any girls down in Georgia worth dating? Are you going to be a bachelor all your life? Why can't you settle down, get married, and give us some grandchildren?'" She grinned up at her husband. "Didn't I say all of those things, Chip?"

"Every word."

"Well, finally! Geoff decided he had found the right woman."

Oh, no. Oh, no. Oh, no.

"And up and eloped with her last night. Can you believe it?"

Cheris stopped breathing. Her skin burned from her neck to her scalp. From the step behind her, Geoff lay a steadying hand on her waist.

"Geoff is coming back home to Culsbaier and bringing a new bride with him. Cheris." Monnie turned to her and hugged her fiercely. She whispered. "Thank you, my darling, for loving my son."

Shock bolted through Cheris.

When Monnie pulled back, Cheris was astonished to see tears in her eyes. She nodded and smiled. "You two have made me so happy."

Chip raised his glass. "Lots of reasons to celebrate tonight. Let us drink to thirty-five years of marriage, five of which weren't all that bad," he said jovially. "Ah, I'm kidding. Seriously." Gathering Monnie to him, he gazed into her face. "Monnie, I love you more today than I did the day we married. I'd like to raise a toast to you, my beautiful bride. May the next thirty-five years be as good as the last thirty-five years. And to Geoff and Cheris, may you know the love and joy in your marriage that we've had in ours."

Everyone raised their glasses at the family then sipped champagne.

Chip handed his glass to Janie then swooped down and kissed his wife soundly among cheers of the gathered people.

"Now the newlyweds!" Someone in the crowd yelled.

"Oh, no," Geoff responded. "You all have had enough fun at our expense."

"They way they're acting, you'd think they were the old fogies, and Chip and Monnie were the newlyweds." This from an elderly woman who bore a remarkable resemblance to Monnie.

"Whose side are you on, Grandma?" Geoff called to her.

"Yours. Now give that gal a big ol' sloppy wet kiss that'll put your mom and dad to shame."

"Sorry, Grandma. You'll have to be satisfied with Mom and Dad's sloppy wet kiss."

The crowd booed. They actually booed!

Cheris sighed and rolled her eyes. "'Youth is wasted on all the wrong people,'" she quipped. Stepping up one stair, she stood next to Geoff. Pecking him on the lips, she then glared at all of the jerks below her. Ignoring the tingling on her mouth, she said to them, "There. Happy?"

"No!" came several responses.

"You call that a kiss? You all should be ashamed of yourselves."

I do not know you people, but I hate you all.

She handed her champagne flute to her mother-in-law, the old bag. "Hurry up," she growled as she plucked his glasses from his face and tilted her head to him. "Let's get it over with before they lynch us."

"Are you sure?" He asked even as he cradled her jaw in his hands and moved closer to her.

Cheris closed her eyes. "Yes, I'm sure. Be quick about it."

The first touch of his lips on hers was tentative, light. But Cheris felt a zap of electricity shoot through her body. Geoff's hands moved from her head to wrap around her waist, nudging her closer, closer. His mouth moved, and oh boy, he deepened the kiss.

Oh, my gosh. He's French kissing me in front of his parents. In front of the elite of Cullsbaeir, Kentucky.

And, he's pretty darn good at it.

Cheris kissed him back and moved her arms to return his embrace. Earlier the heat she felt had been from embarrassment, but the flames licking her body now was nothing but pure bred lust from the pit of her stomach to her toes. Too soon, Geoff raised his head though he still held her. With effort Cheris opened her heavy eyelids and found him gazing at her.

He winked.

Cheris' foot went backwards nearly off the stair, and Geoff steadied her.

"Was that quick enough?" he whispered.

Was it...? What was he talking about? The kiss had lasted eons, not nearly long enough. Cheris became aware of catcalls and clapping.

Ugh! Public Display of Affection! So tacky. So unlike me.

Cheris covered her face with her hands and wished the wood beneath her would open up so she could escape the humiliation.

"That's what I'm talking about. Don't hide your face, honey. In fact, plant another one on my grandson," the elderly woman yelled.

Cheris lowered her hands but couldn't meet anyone's gaze. She shrugged out of Geoff's arms and held up his glasses in the vicinity of his face. Maybe he wasn't so blind that he couldn't see them. In a second, they were gone.

Chip squeezed her shoulder and patted his son on the back. "And may we be here one year from tonight drinking a toast to my grandson."

"Or granddaughter," Monnie added sipping champagne.

"Twins, then. Better get busy, Geoff, my boy." Chip laughed.

****

"This is a nightmare," Cheris said to her reflection. Her friend and sister-in-law met her eyes in the bathroom mirror. Soon after the spectacle on the stairs Cheris had grabbed Janie and retreated to the upstairs bathroom.

"Poor thing," Janie sympathized. "I don't know how

Mom found out. I promise when she came to me, she already knew about it. The only thing I told her was when, and that was under much duress."

"How are we supposed to get a quiet divorce when half the town just got that fairy tale out there?"

"I don't know. But you better pull yourself together. Mom's got it in her head to have some kind of after-the-fact wedding reception ASAP."

"Are you serious? We have to stop her!"

"Good luck." Janie snorted. "Tsunami Monnie is my nickname for her. When she makes up her mind about something, there's no hope."

"But you. She's not that way with you, is she?"

"No, but it has taken years of disappointment and shattered dreams to lower her expectations of me." Janie tapped her finger against her chin as she studied her friend's mirrored image. "Unfortunately, you're the epitome of the daughter she's always wanted. Little Miss Goody Goody. I'm afraid she's going to sink her teeth into you and not let go."

"Oh, great. Just great."

A brisk knock sounded on the bathroom door. Cheris didn't move or speak. She wasn't ready to go back out there and undergo the gauntlet of well wishes.

"Cheris, dear. It's Annie Hill," came the voice from the hallway.

"Oh, please don't tell me Annie witnessed what happened out there." Cheris sagged against the sink.

"Buck up," Janie counseled before turning the knob and pulling it open.

There stood the original Hip Granny smiling reproachfully. She rapped her cane on the floor twice. "Come out of there, please. I know you don't like being the center of attention but that's what happens when you get married. Everyone wants to make a fuss over you."

Cheris' feet refused to move. Annie rapped the cane against the hard wood floor again and arched an eyebrow.

Oh, help me. I'm being bullied by old women!

She lurched out of the bathroom feeling about as graceful as Igor. "Annie, it's not what you think."

"Did you get married to Geoff Arrowood the third at some time last night or this morning?"

"Yes, that's true, but—"

"Then it is what I think."

"But, Annie. I didn't...what I mean is..." Cheris looked around for some help from Janie and saw her walking down the stairs. "Janie!" she cried.

"See you later, Sister."

The jerk.

Annie chuckled. "If you didn't want this spectacle then why didn't you wait until after the party to tell everyone?"

"It was supposed to be a secret," Cheris mumbled.

Annie clucked her tongue. "You ought to know better than that. Secrets have a way of getting out."

"This one was best left untold."

Annie placed her arms around Cheris' shoulders and guided her toward a settee in the hall. She pushed her down gently and sat down next to her. "Sweetheart, after that kiss on the stairs..." She shook her head. "For goodness' sake, you took his glasses off. That simple gesture demonstrates a deliberate willingness to show your deep affection very publicly. My Gerald wore glasses, you know."

She nodded and sighed in contentment, a far off look in her eyes. "How I love that man. Even though he's been dead fourteen years, there's not a day that goes by that I don't think about him. And thank God for the time we had together." She turned to Cheris. "I am so happy for you and Geoff. You know, I worried so that you were here by yourself with no family. Well, anyway, there's no more worrying, is there? Because you've married into one of the most respected families in Cullsbaeir. Even with Janie, but we love her, too. Because she's..." Annie dropped her voice to a whisper. "...an artist. And she's talented enough that she can get by with it." Her voice returned to a normal tone. "Now then. Milton Stewart is downstairs."

The owner of Web Enterprises!

"He, his wife Ellie, and I want to have a dinner party when you get back from your honeymoon. You know, sort of a shower, but more formal with a sit-down meal."

"Honeymoon! Geoff and I aren't going on a honeymoon."

"Well, sure you are. Milton said to take two weeks off."

"I can't take two weeks off. I need to work."

"Honey, this isn't Bill who you can distract with pretty trinkets; this is Milton, the CEO of all of the Web Enterprises. No one says no to him. Not even me. Now I don't want to hear this *I need to work*. It's a paid vacation. But don't get any ideas about being a happy homemaker. I've invested too much time in you to lose you to the bliss of housework and babies."

The bliss of housework and babies?

Cheris' stomach rolled uneasily.

With some effort, Annie stood up leaning heavily on her cane. "Now then. I labored all the way up that staircase to have this little heart-to-heart. I hope you will help me get back down."

Chapter Five

The sun shone bright and the birds sang sweetly, and
Dorothy did not feel nearly so bad as you might think a
little girl would who had been suddenly whisked away from
her own country and set down in the midst of a strange
land.
—*The Wonderful Wizard of Oz* by L. Frank Baum

Cheris sat in Geoff's car as he went around to the
driver's side. When he sat down in the seat and closed the
door, he sighed heavily. Staring for a moment through the
darkened windshield, he finally turned the key in the
ignition and started the engine.

What was he thinking?

Cheris stole a glance at him. His morose expression
reflected her mood.

After she had accompanied Annie downstairs, Monnie
had put her and Geoff together then proceeded to
introduce them to every person at the party.

Every single person.

Cheris was pretty sure Monnie had dragged in a few
hobos off the street to introduce them to as well. Cheris'
face hurt from smiling so much, and her head hurt from
the stress of acting like a fraud. Without any verbal
communication between them, both she and Geoff had
played the happy newlyweds the entire night. Cheris
realized it was useless to attempt to explain the truth to
anyone. Not only had Hip Granny embraced the romantic
story, but Geoff's new boss had as well.

What could she say, really?

Thank you for your good wishes, but I was under the influence of

Wonderland potion last night and can't even remember getting married.

It had been horrible. The lie. The great, big, disgusting lie.

Geoff turned the car into the parking lot of her apartment. Pulling into a space, he cut the engine and released his seatbelt.

"I guess, there's only one thing to say," he announced.

"What?"

"Well, Stanley, here's yet another fine mess you've gotten us into."

A giggle bubbled up from Cheris' throat and escaped from her mouth. She opened the door and left the vehicle. The giggle grew until waves of laughter overcame her at the absurdity of every single moment since she had awoken this morning. She caught sight of Geoff who now stood with hands in pockets watching her, and she laughed some more. Holding her side to quell the stitches, Cheris staggered toward the walkway and her apartment. Her mirth echoed in the still night air, and though she didn't know exactly why, but it was funny.

Really funny.

Tears streamed down her face, and she wiped her cheek then dug into her purse for her keys. When she unlocked her door and threw it open Geoff followed her as far as the threshold. Cheris collapsed on her rocking chair and gulped in a couple of breaths.

Her gaze focused on the man who waited silently for her to do what, she didn't know. Though they had spent the last six hours together, she knew little more than she did this morning when he stood in roughly the same spot with undershirt and tuxedo pants. Tonight was supposed to be dinner and conversation. She was supposed to interrogate Geoff and gather evidence on his character.

Instead they had gone further into this upside down world inviting all of Geoff's family to join them not to mention Annie Hill and Milton Stewart.

And if Mr. Stewart knew that meant Bill Connor, her

boss, would find out, and within an hour he'd figure out a way to capitalize on it and make more money for Mr. Stewart. It would get on Hip Granny and her mom would find out.

Cheris buried her face in her hands and groaned.

"Are you ready?" Geoff asked.

For whatever it was, no she wasn't.

Her front door clicked shut. But he was still here. She didn't have to see him to know. Like the sound of air parting when someone enters a room though their footsteps are silent, she knew. The very molecules of the room shifted at his presence. And her own molecules, well, they didn't shift so much as they...err...vibrated.

Not too long ago, she had been talking to someone at the party. Geoff had been somewhere else, but Cheris had known the second he had entered the room.

How?

Some crazy feeling—awareness—those molecules...or something. She had turned her head, and there he had been, those beautiful eyes behind his glasses meeting and holding her gaze.

The recognition of it made her uneasy because it hinted at a history with him, and the only history she had was what she couldn't remember.

She lowered her hands, but didn't make eye contact. "For what?"

"To ask me questions. I told you earlier I'd answer as many as you wanted to ask."

Cheris leaned her head back against the wooden chair. "It's late."

"Really? Nothing you want to know?"

"Did you...know who I was last night at the exhibit?"

"Yes."

"Why didn't you tell me who you were?"

Geoff meandered into the room. He paused at a framed photograph of her and Janie. "It didn't come up. Not then."

Cheris' throat closed up. Again with the lost time. Had

she lived an eternity after the punch and cake?

"When did it? Before or after we got married?"

"Before. We talked about having Janie as a witness." He sat down on her couch and leaning forward, he clasped his hands between his knees.

Her troubled gaze met his. "Why didn't we?"

"You sure you want to know?"

"Yes."

"You said it would take too long."

"Why was I in such a hurry?"

"The courthouse closed at nine. We were pushing it."

"Yes. We were."

Geoff didn't reply, only leaned back against the couch cushion and stretched his arms across its length.

"What are we going to do?"

"We could go to bed. Everything looks better in the morning." He yawned as if to punctuate his statement.

"Go to bed? Go to bed?" Cheris exclaimed as she jumped out of the chair. "Don't you care that half the town knows we're married?"

Geoff followed suit. "Now, Cheris—"

"Don't you *Now, Cheris* me. We've got to figure out a way to get out of this marriage gracefully before my boss gets a hold of it and broadcasts it on the World Wide Web." What a nightmare it would be if her mom found out.

"It'll be all right, sweetheart."

Their postures felt familiar to her. Had he tried to placate her last night with a *Now, Cheris* and *It'll be all right, sweetheart?*

"Have we already had this conversation?" she snapped.

"No."

"Something similar though. What was it?"

Geoff blinked at her. He ran a hand through his hair. "What?"

"It was…it was about making love."

Cheris' jaw dropped in disbelief. What had he done to her last night?

He'd cajoled and talked her right out of her panties.

That's what he had done.

The ache in her head exploded, and she gripped her temples.

"I can't talk about this right now." She marched across the carpeted floor to the hallway and her bedroom. Behind the closed door she took a shuddering breath. No. She couldn't talk about it, didn't even want to think about it, wished she could wake up in the morning and find all of this was a very bad dream.

Geoff Arrowood could show himself out. She was done with him for tonight.

With jerky movements, Cheris stripped off her clothes, not even bothering to hang up her dress. She pulled on a nightshirt and collapsed on the bed staring at the ceiling lit only by the street lamp outside. She'd wait a little while for Geoff to leave then she'd go back out there to the bathroom, brush her teeth, take something for her head, and remove her make-up.

She'd give him twenty minutes.

He'd be gone by then.

Cheris turned on her side, and in the silence of the dark the events of the last twenty-four hours welled up from her heart and gathered in big tears which fell down her face.

At nearly eight the next morning, Cheris awoke with puffy eyes and mascara splotched all over her pillowcase. She yawned and stretched before sliding off the mattress and stripping it.

Monday was usually her day for washing sheets, but she'd rather erase the evidence of her tearful night. Today was a new day and the start of a new week. She'd do some laundry and go to church, maybe get some new insight on her situation.

She gathered the bedclothes in her arms and walked into the hallway to the shuttered doors which hid the cubby with the washer and dryer. Opening one side, she bumped it wider with her hip and dumped the sheets in the open machine. Then she pulled her gown over her head and shoved it in there as well. She started the load and stepped into the bathroom to take a shower.

Under the hot spray, she ruminated on Geoff's words.

Everything looks better in the morning.

Yeah, it did.

She'd make an appointment with an attorney in the morning. She'd talk to Annie and explain to her what happened. Annie was the original Hip Granny. She'd been giving practical advice for years. She'd be disappointed in Cheris' actions, but she'd probably have some ideas about how to handle a quiet divorce.

It'll be all right.

Cheris smiled and shook her head in irony.

Geoff's words again.

Well, Stanley, here's another fine mess you've gotten us into.

He was funny, and, yes, he was cute, too. He had a way of adjusting his glasses that was endearing. She'd only seen him without them when he'd been asleep yesterday morning. And, well, when she'd pulled them off his face on the stairs last night. The color of his irises without the eyewear had mesmerized her.

Turning off the faucet, she pulled a towel from the rack and dried herself before wrapping it around her body and tucking the corner in front. With her hair still wet, she picked up a brush from the basket on the corner of the counter and pulled it through the dripping locks. Humming the tune from Laurel and Hardy, she headed toward the kitchen to turn on the coffee maker.

And screamed bloody murder.

Because there standing there peering into her open refrigerator was Geoff. At her startled cry, he stood up straight and slammed the door shut, then tried to shield himself from the brush she threw at him.

"Geoff, what are you doing here?" She exclaimed. "You scared me half to death!"

"Sorry. " He reached down and rubbed his leg where the brush had hit him.

Geoff wore the same clothes he had been wearing last

night except they looked as if he had slept in them.

Slept in them?

"Do not tell me you spent the night here last night," she demanded.

When Geoff stared at her without answering, she stamped her foot.

The towel loosened though Cheris didn't notice.

"Answer me."

Eye glass adjustment. "Was that a question? It sounded like an order." Geoff turned away from her, leaned against the counter, and studied the wall across the kitchen from him.

Now what was he doing? He can't even look at me when I'm talking to him?

Cheris moved to stand in front of him and glared up at him. "Did you sleep here last night? *Uninvited?*"

"Yes." Geoff inched away from her, sliding along the counter toward the stove. "I'm sorry. I was waiting for you to come back so we could work something out, but I guess I fell asleep on the couch."

"You fell asleep on the couch." Cheris took the place he had abandoned, facing him. When she leaned against the counter, the towel slipped about half an inch. "What is wrong with you? Why couldn't you take the big, fat hint and leave?"

Geoff glanced at her from the corner of his eye and swallowed hard. "Sorry."

His jaw was rough from a night's growth of beard, his hair tousled from sleep. Sleep he had gotten on her couch. Her heart sped up a bit at the picture of him rumpled and...something else. What was it? Vulnerability maybe, or nervous tension. Her indignation softened, but she held onto it.

It was not okay for him to be here.

Definitely not.

He'd crossed way too many boundaries already.

"That's just great. You're sorry. Oh, well, that just fixes everything, doesn't it?" Cheris stood staring at his profile waiting for him to say something else, but he was silent. A pulse beat in his throat.

The doorbell rang, and she stalked out of the kitchen.

"I don't think you should answer that," Geoff called.

"This is my home, and you don't have a say in what I do in it, *Geoff Arrowood.*" Cheris wrenched open the door on the last word.

Her friend Janie waited on the front porch with a bag from the Jolly Pirate Doughnut Shop in her hand. Her mouth hung open in shock then she doubled over with laughter. Cheris narrowed her eyes at the greeting.

"What's your problem?" she snarled.

"And good morning to you, too," Janie said recovering from her chuckles. "May I come in?"

Oh, no. *Not with your brother inside.*

Janie would jump to the wrong conclusion.

As in leap the tallest building of wrong conclusions.

"No."

Janie's eyebrow rose at the answer. Cheris grabbed the first excuse which jumped in her head.

"I'm sick. I think I've got the stomach flu."

Janie grinned. "Cheris, my friend, if I hadn't noticed his truck in the parking lot, I would have figured it out when you were yelling at him as you opened the door."

Cheris adopted an innocent expression. "Who?"

Janie rolled her eyes. "Please. How stupid do I look?" Janie pushed her way inside. "Don't worry. I have enough for Geoff, too."

Janie marched into the dining room and laid the bag on the table. She nodded to Geoff. "How about getting me a cup of coffee, Brother?"

Without a word, Geoff looked through the cabinets for coffee.

"This isn't what it looks like," Cheris said as she followed her. After Geoff had perused the third cabinet, Cheris entered the kitchen, reached up and took a canister from the top of the refrigerator and handed it to him. Her movement had caused the towel to slip dangerously low, and Cheris retucked it. She opened the dishwasher and set three coffee cups on the counter.

Janie grinned like the Cheshire cat as she watched her. She chuckled. "Well, that's good because from here it looks pretty damaging. Would you say so, Geoff?"

"Nothing happened," Cheris responded before Geoff could. "He just fell asleep on the couch. Right, Geoff? Tell her."

"Nothing happened, Janie." Geoff winked at his sister and filled the coffee pot with water from the sink faucet.

Cheris punched his arm. She gripped her towel when it slipped. "Stop encouraging her."

"Well, really, Cheris. If you want me to believe this is all so innocent," Janie said as she studied her friend critically. "Then you better get your butt back there to your room and put on some clothes."

Cheris glanced down at herself and gasped. Clutching the towel which hung precariously around her, she ran into the bedroom and shut the door.

Twenty minutes later, she emerged from her bedroom fully dressed. Janie sat at the table sipping a cup of coffee. When Cheris scanned the apartment for him, Janie spoke.

"He's not here. He went back to the hotel."

"Good." Cheris walked into the kitchen and poured coffee in one of the two cups sitting on the counter.

"He said he'd call you later."

"Whatever." Cheris sat across from her friend and reached into the bag. Her fingers closed around a cruller. Mmmm. Yes.

"You don't have to pretend with me."

Cheris' attention moved from the cruller to her friend who stared at her with a kind gaze. Cheris bit into the doughnut and chewed. "There is no pretending." She swallowed. "I told you what happened. It's all a mistake, and I'm going to see a lawyer tomorrow."

"If you keep sleeping with him, then I don't see how anyone is going to believe you."

Cheris glared at her friend as she chewed. It was

obvious she was happy to have Cheris as her sister-in-law.
Janie stayed until it was time for Cheris to go to
church. They walked to their respective cars.

"You could go with me, you know." Cheris unlocked
her car.

"And spoil my reputation? Not on your life." Janie
smiled unrepentantly at her friend as she climbed into her
own her own car and shut the door. She rolled down the
window as she backed the car out of the parking space.
"Besides, I imagine you've got some confessing to do to the
priestess."

"She's a reverend not a priestess." Cheris raised her
voice to be heard as Janie drove off.

Janie was referring to the pastor at Trinity Church
where Cheris was a member. Reverend Kelly Thomas was
the same age as Cheris and had caused quite a stir when she
first came to Cullsbaeir as she was the first female pastor
the church had ever called. But in her two years at Trinity,
she had proven herself to be a compassionate pastor and a
gifted preacher. Everyone in the church loved her. Cheris
stared thoughtfully at Janie's departing car then entered her
own vehicle. Maybe Janie was onto something after all.
Maybe Kelly could offer Cheris some good advice about
this mess in which she found herself.

After the worship service, Cheris shook Kelly's hand
and asked if she had a few minutes to talk. The minister
affirmed that she did and to wait for her in the courtyard,
an airy rectangular space carpeted in the middle with real
grass, framed by blond bricks, and bookended with two
dogwood trees. Cheris settled on one of the wooden
benches and waited.

About fifteen minutes later Kelly, minus her black
robe, heaved a big sigh of relief as she sat down next to
Cheris. The woman leaned her head back and smiled as the
sun shone on her face. For a few minutes they sat in
silence. Kelly sighed again contentedly and turned to
Cheris.

"Okay, I'm ready."

"Ready for what?" Cheris asked.

"I'm ready to listen to you, to hear what's on your heart."

"Thank you because I'm in a big mess here."

Kelly nodded but said nothing. Cheris began her story with videotaping Janie at the gala opening Friday night and ended with the fiasco in her towel this morning. Kelly made sympathetic noises during the telling.

"So you can see, I'm in way over my head."

"Yes, it is a very difficult situation," Kelly agreed.

"What do you think I should do?"

"What do you want to do?"

"I want to go back to Friday and relive my life over again."

"Ah." Kelly nodded. "How different all our lives would be if we could go back and undo the past."

"The thing is, if I had not had the cake and punch that night, I would have never done anything so irresponsible."

"Sometimes alcohol gives us permission to do the things we don't think we're capable of. Then if something goes wrong, we can blame the drink." Kelly softened her remark by patting Cheris' hand.

"Do you think that maybe somewhere inside I really wanted to marry Geoff? How could I? I didn't even know him. A complete unknown to me."

"He's not a complete unknown now. From what you've learned about him so far, is he someone you can imagine yourself with?"

"Well, I don't know. He seems really nice and considerate, but what kind of man would…well, you know, with someone who was too drunk to say no?"

When Kelly didn't say anything, Cheris turned to her. "You don't think I really wanted to…and I'm just using the Wonderland elixir as an excuse, do you?"

Kelly shrugged. "I don't know that, but what I do know is you shouldn't beat yourself up over what has already happened. You can't change it anyway. The challenge before you is how you will make the right choices from where you are now."

"What are the right choices? Don't you think I should divorce him and put it all behind me?"

"Cheris." Kelly shook her head. "I can't tell you what to do. What I can tell you is that sometimes things happen in our lives which we don't choose and we don't like, but God often uses those things for the good. Remember Joseph? His brothers sold him into slavery. His own brothers. But because they did that, he ended up in Egypt and saved an entire nation from famine."

"So, you're saying God's hand was in this?"

"I'm saying God will work with us in any situation if we just give a little leeway."

"Give a little leeway, huh? Like you were preaching today—erring on the side of grace?"

"Yes. However God leads you to do that."

Cheris stared at the bricked border wishing it was yellow and led to a place where she could find the answers. "Guess I've got some things to think about."

"I hope you will let me know what happens, and how I can help you."

"I will. Thanks, Kelly."

Cheris walked back to her car slowly as Kelly's words ran through her mind.

Is he someone you can imagine yourself with?

Is he?

You again. Get out of my head.

I was here first.

"Shut up, both of you," Cheris muttered as she settled herself in her car, put the key in the ignition, and turned it.

Nothing happened.

Cheris stared in disbelief at the dashboard.

What was wrong with her car? She hadn't had problems with it in months. She turned the key again.

Nothing happened again.

Expelling a breath, she opened the car door planning to find Kelly and asking her if she knew any Sunday mechanics when Janie's little Toyota pulled into the parking lot.

Janie's car stopped next to where Cheris stood, and Janie rolled down the window. Cheris saw her own reflection in Janie's mirrored sunglasses.

"What's taking so long? I thought we'd go grab some lunch. I've been waiting at your apartment for, like, almost half an hour."

"My car won't start."

"Yeah?" Janie parked her car and got out. She walked over to Cheris' car and slipped into the driver's seat. With the same results as Cheris, she pulled the latch for the hood and walked around to the front and raised its lid.

"What do you know about cars?" Cheris asked as she watched Janie stare critically at the engine.

"I know gas makes them run." Janie pursed her lips and shrugged. "Let's take my car to lunch. I'll call Bobby and ask him to come by and take a look-see. Leave your keys under the floormat."

Uh-oh. Not the felon.

Bobby was Janie's bad boy boyfriend. "My car's not going to turn up missing, is it?"

"Don't be a smart ass. Bobby hasn't done anything like that since way before."

Since way before what?

Cheris slid her key off of her key ring and put it where Janie had directed.

It was probably better not knowing.

Janie closed the hood and wiped her hands down the side of her blue jeans. Cheris didn't trust Bobby, but he did know cars. Cheris suspected that he had worked in a chop shop at some time in his past and that was why he had to check in with his parole officer ever so often.

Cheris grabbed her purse and sat down in the passenger side of Janie's car. When Janie started up the engine, she gunned the accelerator, and they were on their way.

"Don't worry about the car. I'm sure it's a little something. I bet Bobby will have it up and running before we get back from lunch." Janie merged with traffic and headed toward town.

"I just hope he doesn't commit any felonies while driving it."

Janie didn't reply. She bypassed the main thoroughfare in town where all the restaurants were located and continued north.

"Hey, where are we eating anyway?"

"Oh, just this place I know about. Great food." Janie turned left into a little sub-division and drove down a tree-lined avenue.

"What's the name of it?" Cheris asked. When Janie didn't answer, Cheris repeated her question.

"Huh? Oh. Didn't I tell you?"

"No, you didn't." The neighborhood seemed familiar. Large turn of the century homes dominated immaculately manicured front lawns. Unease prickled her skin. "Janie...Oh, no. Janie. If you're my friend, you'll turn this car around and take me home."

"Of course, I'm your friend, Cheris. How could you think anything else?"

The evidence mounted. Cheris recognized the house as Janie pulled into the circular driveway, parked it, and jumped out with keys in her hand.

"No, no, no!"

Janie crouched down and looked at her friend through the open door. "I am also your sister-in-law, at the moment anyway, and we are going to have a nice lunch in the nice backyard with our nice family. Not the extended family, mind you. They've all gone home, which is a relief. Just Monnie, Chip, you, me, and Geoff."

"Give me your keys," Cheris demanded.

"No way. Mom has promised this will be only lunch and chit-chat. No talk of weddings, receptions, or anything like that. She promised me, and I'm going to hold her to it."

"You're a dirty, scheming jerk. You did something to my car, didn't you?"

Janie shook her head and spit in on the pavement.

"Did you even see the priestess this morning?"

"Did you just spit on your parents' driveway? Are you sure you're related to them?"

Janie grinned. "I thought for sure she'd put you in a better mood."

"Was she in on this, too?"

"Of course not. I was hoping you would talk to her though."

Cheris stared stonily through the windshield at the perfect house.

"Well, did you?"

"Oh, all right," Cheris snapped as she threw open the door and stomped out of the car. "But you better be careful. I'm beginning to think you have confidence in Kelly's ability to provide counsel."

"I'm not a complete heathen," Janie commented as they walked around the side of the house and to a wooden gate. "My parents did take me to church every Sunday when I was growing up."

"Too bad none of it stuck."

"Yeah, yeah, *Granny*." She opened the gate revealing the backyard Cheris remembered from the night before.

On the other side of the pool sat Chip, Monnie, and Geoff at a round glass-topped table under the shade of an umbrella. Slumped in a wrought iron chair Geoff was neatly dressed in khaki pants and a forest green golf shirt. Monnie was the first to spot them, and her face broke into a wide smile as she waved them over.

"Hello, girls. Come on over and have a seat."

From the startled expression on Geoff's face, Cheris knew he hadn't been expecting her for lunch. Cheris' steps faltered when he half way stood up, then took his seat again. Cheris' stomach fluttered. She forced her feet forward toward the table. Chip and Monnie beamed at her. Geoff's expression was unreadable.

"So glad you could join us for lunch, Cheris," Chip said standing up as they approached.

Geoff stood as well.

"Okay, here now. Janie, you sit here between me and your dad," Monnie directed as she moved over one chair. "Cheris, you can have the seat next to Geoff."

Dutifully, Cheris sat down without looking at him, her skin burned from...what? Was she embarrassed? Nervous?

Why should she be nervous? She was having lunch with her in-laws.

She had in-laws.

"Here, dear, how about some ice tea?" Monnie poured the drink from a crystal pitcher into a glass. "Come on, Chip. Help me with the food."

They stood up and walked the short distance to the back door. When it closed behind them, Janie sat forward and grinned. "A hundred bucks says I get called in to the house to help prepare lunch and give the lovebirds time alone."

"I don't think either one of us is dumb enough to take that bet," Geoff replied.

The door opened and Monnie stuck her head through the crack. "Janie, come in here a minute, would you?"

"Do I know Monnie Dearest, or what?" Janie grinned at them before bouncing into the house.

Cheris stared at the frosted glass table top. The silence at the table deafened the chirps of the birds in the trees.

"Will they come back?" She glanced at Geoff, and the corner of his mouth upturned in a smile.

"Eventually. After all this *is* supposed to be lunch, and I see no food on the table."

"Do you think they know something's up with us?"

"Most definitely. Before you and Janie arrived, I was getting lectured about how to treat women, how to be a good husband, what makes a good marriage." He shook his head in derision. "They think the quickie Serenity wedding was not a good start to happily-ever-after. As if I hadn't figured that one out already."

"You should humor them. I know they mean well."

"I know, but I've been running my own life pretty well for the last ten or twelve years. All of the sudden they have all the answers." Geoff crossed his arms on the table and rested his chin on them.

"They're married. It seems to me they probably do have a lot of the answers…about marriage anyway."

He seemed so morose. Cheris reached forward and smoothed a hand over his hair to offer comfort.

"This is my problem."

"So, you made your bed, now you're going to lie in it, is that right?"

Geoff tilted his head and studied her face. "All by myself. All by my married self. In bed." His eyes sparkled at her, the image of him not by himself in bed becoming clear in her head.

Cheris' heart raced.

No. She didn't want to think about that! "Marriage is more than what happens in a bedroom," she snapped.

Geoff straighted. "Exactly what I was trying to tell Mom and Dad. But they insist sex is the glue that holds a marriage together. Can you imagine how traumatic it is to hear that kind of stuff from one's own parents?"

Cheris gazed at Geoff's deadpan face and chuckled. "I suppose until they enlightened you today it was your belief that they found you under a cabbage leaf."

"That's absurd. It was the stork that brought me."

"The stork, huh? How very difficult it must be to find out your parents have had sex at least twice in their thirty-five year marriage."

"Once. We're twins, remember?" He shuddered. "I hope they haven't said anything to Janie about it. Her uncorrupted ears couldn't take it."

"Now I know you're being ridiculous."

"What? You know something about my sister you're not telling me?"

"I know she's got a crazy brother."

"He is crazy, insane. About you." Geoff grasped her hand and stroked it, his finger turned her palm up and caressed the soft flesh at her wrist.

Cheris watched their hands. "How could you be? You

don't even know me."
  "I know you more and more each moment."

Chapter Six

> "I've just been imagining that it was really me you wanted
> after all and that I was to stay here for ever and ever. It was
> a great comfort while it lasted. But the worst of imagining
> things is that the time comes when you have to stop and it
> hurts."
> —*Anne of Green Gables* by L.M. Montgomery

Monnie stood at the window watching the young couple. "Oh, Chip. He's holding her hand. Isn't that sweet? Maybe they're patching things up."

"What's to patch up? They've only been married two days." Chip took plates out of the cabinet and set them on the table.

"Don't act like you don't know they've been having problems. You told me yourself last night she said she'd never live with him. What kind of marriage is that?" Monnie held the curtain still peering through the glass.

"I shouldn't have told you what I heard." Chip opened the refrigerator door and pulled out several covered bowls. "That was their private conversation. Besides don't underestimate your son's power of persuasion. You know once he sets his mind on something, he gets it. I saw that drive when he wrote his dissertation in seventeen months. He's set his mind on that young lady out there, and I'm afraid she doesn't stand a chance."

"Doesn't she have a choice?" Janie walked into the kitchen with freshly laundered cloth napkins in her hand.

"She certainly does, and as I live and breathe, she'll choose Geoff Arrowood."

"How can you be so sure?" This from Monnie.

"Because he has my irresistible charm. Any woman is powerless against it." Chip placed the plates on the service caddy along with the leftovers from the night before.

"Oh, Dad, your modesty is inspiring."

"You watch him. No one else exists when she's within fifty feet of him. He's in love, and he's going to make sure she's in love before it's all said and done. Would you agree, Monnie?"

"I sure haven't seen him so focused since he finished up his doctorate," Monnie commented from her lookout.

"After all those years you harassed him about not settling down." Chip shook his head. "And all along he was just waiting to find Cheris. Monnie, I think that's everything. Let's go get to know our daughter-in-law."

****

The door opened, and Monnie and Janie walked out with smiles on their faces. Chip followed pushing the caddy laden with food and dishes. Cheris extricated her hand from Geoff's and clasped her hands in her lap. Chip and Janie sat down as Monnie set dishes on the table.

"I hope you don't mind leftovers, Cheris. We have so much food from last night." She took the lids off several bowls, and unwrapped finger sandwiches. Setting them on the table, she nodded and sat down. "I tell you what. I love parties, but it's work putting one on. That's why we're eating out here—not a clean surface in the whole house."

They passed the dishes around the table, and each person filled their plates. Soon everyone was eating. No one asked Cheris specifically about herself allowing her to volunteer whatever information she felt comfortable. Geoff was quiet, and Cheris stole glances at him wondering what was on his mind. Wasn't he comfortable with his family? One time he caught her staring at him, and he winked.

Just like he had the night before at the party on the stairs.

"Cheris." Monnie's voice captured her attention. "I saw you and Annie Hill talking at the party last night. Isn't she just a darling?"

"Yes, she is," Cheris agreed. "She's been like a

grandmother to me since I've lived here."

"Is that right? You know I love Hip Granny's website. I've gotten several good tips from there."

Janie laughed. As *Hip Granny* Annie Hill was the local celebrity in town. Very few people knew Cheris had taken the reins from Annie in every responsibility but promotion. Annie still did webcasts and TV talk shows. Her picture was the one on all the publicity. But it was Cheris who researched topics, wrote the columns, and organized lives on the web.

"You've done a few podcasts," Geoff commented.

"You've seen them?"

He nodded, his gaze warming her and making her heart skip a beat or two.

"I've never heard of such a thing. What is it? A podcast?" Monnie asked.

"It's an audio or video clip on the internet. I...I have two of them on *Hip Granny*. I'm IT there. At Annie's insistence, I demonstrated some helpful computer technology for users to take advantage of."

"Well, isn't that interesting? Geoff, how did you know about the podcasts?" Monnie smiled at her son and waited for an answer.

Geoff quirked an eyebrow at Janie who squirmed. Cheris watched the silent exchange with interest. "Come to think of it, Janie," he said at last, "I believe you told me *Hip Granny* had some computer tutorials on their site."

"So that's how you fixed them up?" Monnie asked Janie.

"Well..." Janie shook her head as she watched her brother. "Yes. That was the beginning of it, Geoff. Other than I must have mentioned Cheris a time or two as my friend. But that was *it.*"

Geoff smirked. Cheris' eyes narrowed.

He had something on Janie.

What could it be?

"We'll have to look at those podcasts, Cheris. Won't we, Monnie?" Chip commented. "What do you think Hip

Granny will do when Annie retires? She has to be at least seventy."

"Yes, Cheris, *is* there someone who will take Annie's place?" Janie jumped on the topic with all fours.

Oh, boy.

"There has been some conversation about it. As far as I'm concerned, there will be no publicly disclosed changes in the person who is Hip Granny."

A chorus of understanding sounded around the table.

"Sounds like you're not allowed to tell us."

Cheris picked up her glass and drank deeply from it. Oh, she was allowed to tell, but she didn't want to, and she hadn't allowed anyone else to either. The only reason Janie knew was she had found Cheris' contract one day when she had been at the apartment. Cheris had threatened her life if she ever breathed a word about it.

Every once in a while Bill approached her about coming out as the organizing guru, but she'd convinced him that Annie was the essence of Hip Granny. She was a success as the seventy plus hip grandma. If the public found out she was a twenty-something single woman, the implications would be similar to the New Coke disaster of the mid-eighties.

It didn't matter that blind taste tests had shown it was preferred.

Coke was more than a taste. It was familiar, and people didn't like change.

Whenever Bill began to harass Cheris about being the new *Hip Granny*, she sang the jingle from the old commercial.

Well, she didn't know if it was the jingle or not. She'd made it up. Bill didn't know. No one did, because New Coke has been a failure.

And Hip Granny wasn't a big enough icon to overcome a marketing disaster like that.

Bill was all about the money, so singing the jingle always worked on him.

"So, Mom and Dad, when are you leaving on your

trip?" Geoff, obviously aware of Cheris' discomfort, changed the subject.

"I don't see how we could possibly go anywhere now." Monnie smiled at Cheris' curious expression. "Chip and I had been planning on taking a little trip to Savannah. That's where we went on our honeymoon. But we've been thinking about postponing it for a while. I mean, we can go there any time."

"Why wouldn't you go?" Geoff asked.

Chip and Monnie exchanged glances. "With the party and all, who can even think about leaving on a trip?"

Cheris suspected their son's newly married status was the reason.

Oh, please go on to Savannah. Maybe by the time you get back, we can have this straightened out, and you can stay on your side of the railroad tracks.

"You thought it was a good idea before the party. What's changed?" Geoff persisted.

Monnie shot him an *I'm the mother and I said so* look. When Geoff did not back down from the glare, Chip cleared his throat.

"Son, you've got to admit, you gave us quite a shock last night."

"Therefore you're not capable of taking a trip you've been planning for months?" Geoff murmured.

Cheris' eyes widened at his serious tone. She glanced at Janie who watched Geoff just as intently. Tension thickened until Cheris could hardly stand it.

No.

No way was she going to be culpable in this family starting a feud.

"Geoff, sweetie, could you show me to the powder room?" Cheris touched his shoulder as she stood up.

With his jaw still clinched, he finally broke eye contact with his parents to look at her.

"Please?" She trailed her hand down his arm to clasp his fingers.

Geoff allowed her to pull him to his feet and toward

the back door. He held it open for her and followed her inside. Through the kitchen and down the hall they walked until he gestured her toward a door.

Cheris turned to face him. "I don't really have to go."

"Then why—"

"Because I wanted to diffuse that situation before someone said something they would regret."

Geoff sighed angrily, pivoted, and began to walk away. Cheris hurried around him and blocked his path. "How can you blame them for wanting to stay to be with us?"

He ran a hand through his hair and glared at the wall.

"They just found out their only son ran off and married someone they've never met. Of course, they want to stay here and get to know me. They're excited and anxious. Did you see your mother's face last night on the stairs? She had tears in her eyes. Please don't be angry at them because they don't want to miss a very important part of their son's life."

"And which part is that, Cheris? The one in which their only son has divorce papers served to him, or the one in which they find out that the only reason they have a daughter-in-law was because their son coerced her into getting married while under the influence?"

Cheris faked a calm pose. She'd counseled Webbers to 'fake it to make it' and followed that advice now. Breathing deeply, she adopted a cool expression, and loosened her already-tensed muscles.

"The point is, if they want to stay here, it's their choice. Not yours. Not mine." Cheris ran her hands up and down his arms wanting him to relax. "Right?"

Geoff sighed again and shut his eyes. "Right."

"So, we're going to go back out there and be pleasant. If you don't want to see them this week, don't come over here. It's that simple."

"It's never simple when it's your own family."

No kidding. If her mom ever found out, there'd be teeth gnashing of Biblical proportions.

"Agreed."

Geoff leaned back against the wall pulling her with him. When had they begun to hold hands? She stumbled against him, and Geoff dropped her fingers to wrap his arms around her.

"If you're really moving back here, you need to get used to them having a more active role in your life." Cheris tried to sound matter of fact when she said it, but instead her voice had taken on the characteristics of a twenty year smoker on a hike up the Alps. He surrounded her, his body and the clean scent of Dial soap.

She'd never thought of Dial as sexy, but *on him*. . .

"Will I have to get used to you having a more active role in my life?" His voice reverberated against her.

Her stomach flipped, and tingles which had begun there rippled outward. A sure sign of desire.

Geoff was turning her on.

Geoff Arrowood, her husband.

"I. . .I don't know."

"That's not an outright rejection. Perhaps we're making progress."

Progress?

Lust was progress?

Geoff bent his head, and touched her lips with his briefly. "I want to kiss you. Really kiss you."

"You'll behave yourself with your parents?"

"If you'll kiss me for two minutes I promise to behave myself with them."

"Two minutes?" That sounded way too long to Cheris.

Geoff tapped a finger on her back. "A two minute kiss, and a two week reprieve on the divorce. Will you accept those terms?"

"You think you can change my mind in two weeks?"

"Is it a deal?"

"No sex," Cheris countered.

"No sex unless you, fully sober, consent," Geoff amended.

"I still don't trust you."

"You should. I'm trustworthy."

"The marriage license says otherwise."

"What a sad culture we live in that marrying a gal before you bed her mars one's character."

"The honorable man would have dropped me off at home instead of spending the night with me in Serenity."

"I've got an idea." Geoff looked at his watch and pushed a button on it until it beeped. "I'll set my watch for two minutes. We'll kiss until the alarm sounds, and when I stop, that will prove you can trust me."

Cheris had her doubts.

"Shall I get you a stick so you can beat me off if you need to?" Geoff glanced around the hallway. Finding nothing suitable, he walked into a small sitting room under the stairs.

Cheris followed him.

"Aha." He turned to her and picked up an umbrella which must have been propped inside the doorway. "You can do some serious damage to me with this."

"We better just go back out there. You killed the mood with all of this negotiating and umbrella-waving."

Geoff grinned as he placed the umbrella in her hand. "I dare you."

"I don't take dares." Recognizing their words from the art gala, she gasped and popped her hand over her mouth. The umbrella clattered to the floor.

"Aha. Not all of Friday night has been forgotten then."

With a constricted throat, she managed to ask, "How many dares did I take?"

"You took two, and gave one."

"The first was the punch."

"Yes," he confirmed.

"I don't remember much after that. Do I want to know the other two?"

Geoff stepped closer to her. "The second was you double dog daring us to get married."

"Are these in chronological order?"

"Yes."

"Then I know I don't want to know the other one."

Smoothing a strand of hair which had escaped from her clip, he gazed down at her. "You have absolutely nothing to be ashamed of about Friday night."

"I found my underwear on the lampshade."

"Even at your most uninhibited, your elegance took my breath away."

"What's elegant about a double dog dare?"

"You." He raised his arm to look at the watch on his wrist. Pressing a small button on its side, he then linked his fingers through hers and stepped in front of her now, closer.

Cheris' heart pumped hard against her ribs. Lowering his head, Geoff's lips touched her cheek, a light brush on the skin, to her ear.

"I'd love to kiss you, but I've just washed my hair." Even as she whispered the words, she couldn't place what actress had said them in which movie. She'd bet it was black and white though. Some brassy actress for sure.

Geoff's mouth was at her neck now. He trailed soft kisses down to her shoulder moving aside her collar to expose the skin. His leisure path back up her neck soothed her nerves, comforted her. Both of her hands were free now, and with one she grasped the back of his shirt, feeling his flesh underneath, learning the texture of this man, her husband, enjoying touching him, reveling in his tasting her. His lips were nearly to hers now, and she tilted her face enough so that her mouth met his, and—

Wow.

Twenty minutes later they joined the trio outside. Cheris was too embarrassed to make eye contact. She was sure they all knew what she and Geoff had been doing.

And it wasn't visiting the powder room.

It had also lasted much longer than the allotted two minutes though when the alarm had sounded Geoff had instantly ended the kiss. When she pulled him back to her, he resisted spouting some tripe about his trustworthiness being at stake.

"No, it's not," Cheris insisted. "I trust you now. You

stopped when the alarm sounded."

"Just so we're clear about that." Geoff leaned forward pressing his mouth to hers.

Now he held her chair for her as she sat down. Ever the gentleman, at least in front of his parents, she thought darkly. Thankfully no one mentioned the span of time they'd been in the house though when Cheris found the courage to look at their faces, she saw what she suspected.

They knew she'd been making out with Geoff, and they all looked pleased as punch about it.

Janie grinned like an idiot. Cheris thought about kicking her but was afraid somebody might see through the glass-topped table.

Geoff sat down and looked squarely at his parents. "I apologize, Mom, Dad. Certainly if you want to postpone your trip, it's fine with me."

Jaws dropped all around the table. Cheris bit her lip to keep from snickering. From his family's reaction, Cheris could tell his words had been unexpected. Three sets of eyes then settled on her.

What?

This wasn't her doing. She didn't make him come out here and announce his apology. She just wanted him to be a little more understanding about his parents' reason for wanting to stick around.

Somehow, Cheris made it through the rest of the lunch without incident. When she began making her excuses to leave, it was Geoff who stood to take her home. Of course, it was expected that he would go home with his wife, she determined, so she didn't complain.

Geoff drove her to the church to retrieve her car which started without any problem—more proof that it had been sabotaged in the first place. To her surprise, Geoff didn't ask to follow her home, but said he had some things to take care of.

"Can I come by later?" He leaned against the hood of a silver SUV she assumed was his since it had a Georgia plate. The sun reflected off the lenses of his glasses making it hard to read his thoughts.

Cheris, already seated in her Prius, shrugged assuming a nonchalant expression. What the heck did she care what his unnamed business was about?

She was only his wife. Not voluntarily, that she remembered anyway, but

Whatever.

He made no move toward her open window.

I guess no goodbye kiss for the wife.

Or was he waiting for an invitation? Him and his unnamed business.

Cheris shifted into reverse. "See you later then," she replied shortly as she pulled out of the space.

Not that I really care if he wanted to kiss me or not.

Yeah, right.

You again.

That's right. Me again. You wanted him to kiss you and you know it.

Not if he doesn't even want to tell me what he's doing this afternoon.

Cheris glared at her reflection in the rearview mirror at the red light on Oak Street.

I have got to stop having conversations with myself. It's a sign of insanity.

When she arrived at her apartment, she kicked off her shoes and stripped her clothes on the way to the bedroom. Finding an ancient pair of jeans which actually had holes in them she had put there through wear and tear, she slid them on, along with a Hip Granny T-shirt sporting the cartoon logo of Annie on it. She curled up on the couch and punched the remote of the television.

Oh, goody. An Audrey Hepburn double feature.

Who cares if she had seen both movies multiple times?

She could get lost in the world of happily ever after resolved in an hour and a half.

At the end of *Roman Holiday*, Cheris donned shorts, laced up her tennis shoes and headed to the exercise room in the apartment clubhouse to work out. She'd found at this time of day it was empty so she could exercise without obnoxious music blaring over the speakers or men in too-small Speedos running on the treadmill beside her.

She timed the treadmill for the forty minute course, and as she ran she thought of Geoff, the cute way he adjusted his glasses on his nose, his sweet and unhurried way of kissing her, and the fact that he didn't seem to like her hair up as he had unclipped her barrette last night out on the porch and again this afternoon in his parents' sitting room. She hadn't realized she didn't have it until the breeze had blown her hair in her face out on the patio, and Janie had smirked at her.

When the treadmill beeped signaling she'd completed the work out, she pressed the power button, stepped off of the machine, and headed back home to shower.

Soon she was washed and stood at her dresser wondering what to wear. It was nearly six, and she hadn't heard from Geoff.

When he had asked to come by, she'd given him a noncommittal answer. Who knew whether he would or not?

Should she call him?

Did she want to see him again today?

Shrugging, she picked up her jeans from the floor, slipped them on and grabbed a cotton camisole from her drawer. After she cooled off a bit more she'd put on something else.

The doorbell rang.

Hmm.

When Cheris opened the door, Geoff stood on her front porch, hands in his pockets smiling at her.

"Hi. I was just thinking about calling you." She stepped back and motioned him inside.

He didn't move from his spot. "Calling me what?"

"On the telephone, Smarty. Aren't you coming in?"

"I was hoping you'd go out with me."

Cheris looked down at the camisole and ragged blue jeans. "Let me change."

"No." Geoff reached forward and caught her hand. "You're perfect. Grab your shoes and keys. That's all you need."

She gestured to her top. "This is underwear. I can't go out in underwear."

"We'll be in a dark theater. No one will see you."

"We're going to the movies? Ugh. All I've done this afternoon is watch movies. I need a break from the silver screen. And I am not wearing a camisole to go out with you."

Geoff craned his neck and his gaze roved over her. "It's covering all the important parts. Mostly. I have no problem with you wearing it."

Cheris shook off his grip and crossed her arms to cover herself. "It doesn't matter because I don't want to see a movie."

"No movies then. Have you eaten dinner?"

Her stomach growled in response. Geoff's eyebrows shot up, and he chuckled.

"That sounded like a *no*."

Huffing, Cheris marched back to her bedroom and grabbed a polo shirt out of her dresser drawer. On the way back toward the living room, she pulled it over her head. If he didn't care what she looked like with wet hair and no make-up, then neither did she. But she *was* going to wear a shirt, by God.

In moments they settled in the SUV.

Cheris noted the floorboard void of even a gas receipt. "I suppose this is yours."

Geoff cranked the engine and shifted gears. "Yes."

"It looks brand new." She glanced in the back seat. It was as immaculate as the front.

"I've had it about a year." He maneuvered the vehicle out of the parking lot and onto the main thoroughfare. Within minutes they were parked in front of El Toro, a popular Mexican restaurant in town.

She studied the building before turning to him. Did he know this was her favorite place to eat?

"We can go inside, or I can get it to go. Your choice."

"To go where?"

"A surprise."

"I don't like surprises."

"You'll like this one. So, want to get take out?"

"No. Let's just eat here. Maybe I can worm the surprise out of you before we get there."

＊＊＊＊

Cheris stood at the doorway of the planetarium, her eyes following the curves of the high circular ceiling.

"What are we doing?"

"Having fun. Are you having fun yet?"

"Are we allowed to be here?" No one else was around. In fact, Cheris hadn't seen anyone else in the math and science building on the college campus.

They stood inside the carpeted room. Five rows of theater seats lined its perimeter.

"Of course, we're allowed. I'm faculty now at Smithson. Adjunct, but it still counts."

"I thought you were the *dynamic* professor at the museum." Cheris purposely chose the adjective his mother had used last night on the stairs.

Geoff arched an eyebrow at her. "She meant didactic, and the college owns the museum and planetarium. This," he held his arms wide. "was one of the deal makers."

He walked toward a large metal cylinder on a recessed stage in the middle of the room. "Have a seat. The best ones are there." He pointed to the east side of the room. "Second or third row in the center."

"Where are you sitting?"

"I'm sitting in the captain's chair." He disappeared behind a partition surrounding the cylinder.

"You're a nerd."

"Takes one to know one, Commander Gensa." His voice echoed off the blank walls.

Shoot. She must have told him she'd donned the female starship commander's costume from a popular SciFi movie for the Hip Granny franchise party in February.

"Is there anything I didn't tell you Friday night?" Cheris chose a seat in the second row and sat down. The back reclined slightly with her weight. Hmm. Comfy.

"You didn't tell me, but there's a framed photograph of you and a Sleechberg warrior in your apartment."

Oh.

The stark white walls began to soften to pearl gray and darker to mauve. A city skyline appeared near the bottom of the dome. The ceiling transformed into the twilight sky as a ghost of the moon rose from the seam of the wall.

Oh, cool.

Stars dotted the ever darkening sky, and Cheris sighed at the beauty of the sight.

Yeah, having a toy like this would definitely be a deal maker for a job.

"This is the sky for the coordinates of Culsbaeir."

"When?"

"One fifteen tomorrow morning."

Cheris shook her head. "I don't think so. I've never seen this many stars here even in the middle of the night."

"This is what you would see if we didn't have light pollution."

"Light pollution?"

"Artificial lights which prohibit stargazing. Street and building lights. Lit billboards. Headlights on cars." The ceiling lightened and many of the stars disappeared. "This is with Culsbaeir's lights. See the difference?"

"Wow."

The expanse lightened further becoming hazy. "Here's the view in New York City. In metropolitan areas air pollution inhibits viewing as well. If you can even see the sky with all of the buildings in the way."

"So the best place to star gaze would be a rural area," Cheris surmised.

"Even better a rural state with a sparse population."

"Or a country with no electricity."

"Not too many of those anymore." The night became dark once again, and the twinkling lights moved across the ceiling for a moment before coming to a rest. "Here's what the sky looked like on the night of your birth."

"I'm sure that wasn't framed in my apartment."

"No. But you had to show your driver's license at the courthouse, and I have a photographic memory."

Cheris shifted on the soft cushion. She wondered if anyone ever fell asleep in here. "Yeah? What's my license plate number?" She smiled when she said it remembering the hotel clerk's comments about it.

Geoff was silent for a moment before he rattled it off to her. Hmm. He must have memorized it since Friday night.

"What's on the front of my refrigerator?"

"A small dry erase board with my hotel phone number on it, a pen, a recipe for spinach salad with strawberry dressing, four magnets, and a drawing done by my sister."

Impressive.

"What's the recipe?"

"Frozen strawberries, which you crossed out, and wrote 'fresh', Red wine vinegar, Splenda, Salt, chopped pecans. Drizzle over spinach, chopped red onion, apple cut into pieces, English cucumber. Do you want measurements too?"

"No. What's on the end table next to my Commander Gensa picture?"

"A jar filled with buttons, a box of tissue, and a biography on the Fitzgeralds."

A bolt of light streaked across the artificial sky. "What was that?"

"What?"

"It looked like a shooting star."

"Oh. Yeah. A meteor. They show up every once in a while to keep things interesting. Here and in the nighttime sky, too."

The origin of his voice had changed. He must have moved. Cheris glanced toward the center of the room but didn't see him.

"See that?"

A red dot appeared on the ceiling and moved slowly in a circle. "That's the constellation Lyra." The dot stopped next to a star, and Cheris decided he had a laser pointer. "This is Vega, one of the brighter stars in the sky. About the third week of April you can see a pretty impressive shower when Earth plows through the tail of the Comet Thatcher."

"What's that really bright one there? A planet?"

He moved the pointer. "Here?"

"Yeah."

"Not a planet. That's Sirius. The dog star, and our nearest star neighbor. It's actually a binary star system. It's so bright because of its proximity to us and its luminosity."

"Hmm."

"Ugh. I'm sorry. I didn't mean to start lecturing."

"How close is it?"

"Two point six parsecs. About...oh...six point seven light years. I'm going to stop now before you run out of here screaming."

Cheris stood up, her eyes searching for him in the dark room. "Where are you?"

She saw him, then, on the floor in front of the section of chairs where she sat. He lay on his back with his knees bent. He sat up and aimed the pointer at himself before turning it off. "Ready to go?"

Actually, no, she wasn't. "What about those stars up there close to Sirius?"

The dot appeared again on the domed ceiling. "Here?"

"No." She pointed upward, and walked to where he sat on the floor. Geoff reclined and looked to where she indicated. "There. The three of them in a row."

The red dot moved to the three stars on the ceiling.

"Aha. Orion's belt. Mintaka. Alnilam. Alnitak." He indicated each star with the laser. "Orion's the hunter. Betelgeuse is his shoulder. Head is there. Body, and feet. That's his sword hanging from his belt marked by M42, the Orion Nebula."

Cheris craned her neck for only a moment before

walking a few feet away and lying down herself putting enough distance between them so he wouldn't get any ideas.

Wow. It was a better view from down here.

"I thought Orion was in the sky in autumn."

"It is. The star projector is giving us a summary of the major constellations. How'd you know when Orion was in the sky?"

"There's a poem about it called *Fair Use.* 'In the black expanse Orion, that great hunter, waits with arm raised, Arrow poised and twinkling belt—silent, searching. While below I pull my sweater to me thinking soon I'll see my breath. The hunter pays me no mind, so focused is he on his aim.'"

Geoff didn't reply, and Cheris turned her head from the glittering ceiling and sought his gaze. Darnit. She'd gone and quoted poetry. He, science teacher that he was, probably thought she was silly. The darkness didn't hide his burning gaze from across the carpet.

"Trembling," he continued the verse as he watched her. "The crisp leaves beside me hang on for dear life. They know the eminent fall and crunch underfoot. And I'll strike a match to them, breezy cinders, and bitter smoke. Will rise, rise, rise to that great one who may, at last, stop and look on me. And have his turn to gaze and wonder.'"

As Geoff recited the remainder of the verse, Cheris' heart beat hard in her chest. How could he possibly know that poem?

"How do you know that poem, and well enough to recite it? It's so obscure, I didn't think anyone else had even heard of it."

"It's about stargazing and burning things. Two of my boyhood interests." His head turned upward again, and the thin beam shot to the dome.

Cheris watched as the laser danced on the ceiling. "You were a pyromaniac as a child?"

"Every boy is a pyromaniac. I liked the poem because it was about stargazing in the autumn with the turning leaves and cool air."

Cheris sighed as she pictured Geoff as a little boy, fanciful and intelligent. "I thought you were the practical one."

Geoff chuckled. "Yes. I've been getting that a lot lately. Janie's the reckless one, and I'm the practical one, at least I was until Friday night."

Cheris sighed as she watched the stars march along the artificial sky. "This would be a neat place to watch a movie."

"You've had your break from the silver screen then?"

"Do they show movies in here?"

"It's possible. Got any requests?"

Cheris pursed her lips as she pondered his question. In a planetarium it ought to be Science Fiction. But which movie? *2001 or Star Wars.* They were no brainers, but her favorite was *Gensa's Genesis,* hence her own costume from the movie. It was too cheesy to admit it though.

"I don't know."

"Yes, you do."

Cheris swiveled her head and found Geoff had sat up and was watching her. She leaned on her hip and rested her head on her elbow. Tracing her finger along the pattern of the carpet, she studied him before choosing her words.

"'Don't test me. I didn't get here by playing games.'" At this point General Gensa had aimed her laser at Randeau Kilgan's crotch. Nonplused, he'd smirked at her and said—

"'No one's questioning your authority, General. But even you need time away from the bridge,'" Geoff quoted and peered at the remote in his hand. "*Gensa's Genesis,* it is. Let's see if I can get it for you."

The room lightened faintly, and Geoff jumped to his feet. Cheris strained her neck as she watched him walk toward the projector and disappear behind the wall surrounding it. The white noise of the projector ceased, and she heard a few bumps and rapid typing on a keyboard.

The whirring began again, and Geoff entered the

auditorium and settled himself on the floor. Aiming the remote skyward, he pushed a button, and the darkness resumed as the opening credits for *Gensa's Genesis* began.

Chapter Seven

I had considered how the things that never happen, are
often as much realities to us, in their effects, as those that
are accomplished.
—*David Copperfield* by Charles Dickens

"What are you doing here?" Bill Connors bellowed as
he glared at her over the partition which separated her work
space from the rest of the office.

Cheris looked up from her computer monitor and
blinked uncomprehendingly at him. "I'm working."

"Oh, no you're not." Bill shook his head. "Milt is
going to kill me if he thinks I've got you working on your
honeymoon."

"My what?" Cheris stared at Bill as heads popped up
from surrounding cubicles.

Bill strode to her desk, pushed a couple of buttons on
her computer, then turned it off. He picked up her purse
and handed it to her. "Your honeymoon. Milt said to give
you two weeks off."

"No, Bill. I'm staying." Cheris turned back to her
screen.

Pushing her chair back, he shoved her shoes she had
shed toward her with his big loafer. "Out. Out. Out." He
motioned for her to leave.

Cheris picked up her shoes and shouldered her purse.
"But I need to work."

"Not here you don't. Not when Milton Stewart says
you're on your honeymoon." He escorted her to the door.

"We're not taking a honeymoon."

"Not my problem."

He nudged her out the door and shut it as Cheris, in bared feet, stood on the front sidewalk in disbelief.

You've got to be kidding me.

The head of Net Enterprises gave her a mandatory vacation for her honeymoon? Some honeymoon. After they had watched the movie last night, Geoff had taken her home and promptly left. He hadn't come inside for coffee at her invitation. He hadn't kissed her. Not even a hug.

Cheris slipped on her shoes and decided to walk the few blocks to Janie's downtown studio, a converted store front on Main Street. As she walked in front of the building, she saw Janie through the large plate glass window. She knocked on the glass, and Janie waved her inside. The front room stretched the length of the space, its walls a soft marbled gray with art for sale hanging upon it. Paintings in various unfinished states rested on several easels throughout the room. The back had an office, a smaller studio for when Janie used models, a small kitchen, and a bathroom.

Cheris opened the door and walked across the spotless wood floor to where Janie stood in front of a framed canvas.

Janie smiled a greeting at her friend. "Hey, Sister. What's up?"

"I've been barred from work," Cheris groused.

"Why?"

"Because I'm on my honeymoon, apparently." Cheris stood next to her and studied the painting with its pastel colors and gentle rolling waves. Cheris knew better than to ask what it was, as Janie's standard answer was always, *not finished yet.*

"Hmm. Does Geoff know? Where is he anyway?"

"Am I your brother's keeper? How should I know?"

Janie arched an eyebrow, her smile widening.

"What am I supposed to do for two weeks?"

"How about what you did on your wedding night without the cake and punch? That way you'd remember it at least."

"Nothing's changed, Janie."

"The big ol' hickey on your neck from your little bathroom excursion yesterday tells me differently."

Cheris slapped her hand to her neck. She'd covered the mark with make-up this morning, but it must have worn off.

"Hey, guess who called me this morning?" Janie said, changing the subject. Cheris shrugged her shoulders, careful to keep her hand on her neck. "Your priestess. She asked me to come to the church and give an estimate on painting a mural for the nursery."

"Really?"

"Yeah. Something Biblical."

"Like Noah's ark?"

Janie snorted. "I'll only paint Noah's ark if I can put a few unrepentant souls drowning in the deluge of water."

"Ick, Janie. How morbid."

"What do you think that story's about? God said, 'I will wipe humanity from the face of the earth for I'm sorry I ever made them'. It's a terrible thing to put on a nursery wall."

"Oh, I'm going to faint. Janie Arrowood is quoting Scripture."

"Smart ass. Hand me that towel over there," Janie said indicating a paint-stained towel draped over a wooden backed chair. When Cheris handed it to her, she wiped her hands and stood up. "I would invite you to lunch, but it's barely ten o'clock. Guess we could get some coffee and a doughnut from the Jolly Pirate."

Janie's cell phone rang from the back office, and she strode across the room to retrieve it. When she returned, she had the phone pressed to her ear but her gaze was on Cheris.

"Hi, Mom....Not since lunch yesterday. Why?...Geoff spent the night at the house last night?....What time?...Maybe he just came over there to get some sleep because she won't leave him alone." Janie laughed as she winked at Cheris who had blanched. "No. Don't wake him up....Don't, Mom....No, I'm not giving you Cheris' phone number....When are you and Dad going to Savannah?....Well, in the mean time leave them alone....Try." An expression of irritation crossed her face. "I'm hanging up now....'Bye, Mom." Janie pressed the screen on her phone and shook her head. "My idiot brother crashed in his old bedroom some time after Mom and Dad went to bed last night."

"I thought maybe he'd have to go back down to work in Georgia."

"This is his Spring Break. He's got the whole week off."

"Oh."

"You and Geoff better come up with a plan to get that woman off your back. Otherwise, she's going to bug the hell out of you until they leave on Wednesday." Janie left the room and came back in a moment later with her canvas bag over her shoulder. "Come on. Let's get over to the Jolly Pirate before the PoPos take up all the stools at the counter.

****

Cheris lay among the golden wheat in a field gazing at Geoff where he stood at its edge. She wore the same clothes she had on the night of the gala, the white skirt and turquoise shirt, her legs and feet bare, her hair loose and spilling out on the ground around her face.

"Geoff," she whispered. "Geoffrey." She raised a hand, crooking her finger for him to come to her.

The aroma of fried bacon and biscuits wafted in the air. Geoff cast an irritated glance behind him. He didn't want to smell breakfast; he wanted to smell earth, wheat, outdoors, and Cheris.

"Geoff?" Cheris' voice didn't sound like Cheris. It sounded more like...

"Geoff, honey. Wake up. It's ten-thirty. How late are you going to sleep?"

His mother.

Geoff opened bleary eyes to find the gauzy image of

Monnie Arrowood standing inside his bedroom door holding something—a tray perhaps?

He shut his lids willing the dream back, wanting to recall the image of Cheris supine before him.

"Geoff."

Dishes rattled and weight settled next to him.

He sighed and gave up on getting back the vision. With resignation, his eyelids lifted, and he groped the nightstand for his glasses. When he placed them on his nose, his mother's determined face met his gaze.

"What are you doing here?"

He sat up careful not to knock over the tray she had set next to him on the bed.

"Aunt Nancy left Sunday morning. I thought I could have my room back." He picked up the coffee cup and sipped.

"Why aren't you at Cheris'?"

Geoff didn't answer. He placed the tray on his lap. If he was going to get the third degree, he might as well enjoy his mom's excuse for coming in here.

"Geoffrey Watkins Arrowood."

Oh, man. When she spouted the middle name, she meant business.

"Shouldn't you be at your wife's house, sleeping late in her bed?"

"I'm not welcome here?" He broke the biscuit in two and shoved three pieces of bacon in the halves before stuffing it in his mouth.

"What is going on with you two?" Monnie's expression moved from concern to anger back to concern.

"Nothing," he said as he chewed.

"Don't you give me 'nothing.'"

"Do you really expect me to disclose the private details of the relationship with my wife to you?"

"You're not too old for me to put you over my knee, young man."

"Yes, I am." He shoved the tray aside and bounded out of the bed. He grabbed his pants from the floor he'd shed last night and put them on. Coming here had been a mistake. He'd have to go back to the hotel. Or sleep in his car. Anything was better than this.

"Geoff, if you tell me what the problem is, maybe I can help."

His shirt lay on the top of the bureau. "No problems, Mom. We're fine."

"Then what are you doing here?"

He stuck his arms in the sleeves and pulled the material across his chest. "Sleeping."

"Won't she let you get any sleep at her house?"

Geoff risked a glance at the woman and saw her embarrassment. He suppressed a chuckle. His mom thought Cheris was insatiable.

Would he ever find out?

"We're cool, Mom. Stop worrying." He grabbed the second biscuit from the plate with one hand and his shoes with the other before striding across the room to the door. Where he went from here he wasn't sure. Maybe the college. Barbara Adkins, the department head, had shown him a vacant office. Usually adjuncts didn't get offices, but since he was going to be in charge of the planetarium, they'd found him one.

Mom followed him to the landing and down the stairs.

"Son, your father and I..."

Geoff tuned her out. From past experience he knew anything after *your father and I* was going to be a lecture, and he wasn't in the mood to hear it.

Last night he'd been as good as gold, the perfect gentleman. He'd taken Cheris out, fed her, listened and talked to her, taken her to the planetarium, and brought her home before eleven. He'd walked her to the porch, watched her unlock her door, and wished her a good night. Then he'd gone up to Coleman Hill with his telescope for some stargazing until nearly four. After he'd driven to Mom and Dad's and settled in his childhood bed, he'd watched the sun rise through the window until sleep had finally claimed him.

He was in love with Cheris.

Forgetting his socks, he paused at the bottom of the stairs and shoved his feet in his shoes.

"...and this is supposed to be your honeymoon anyway, isn't it? Even if you're not taking an official one. How can you bear to be away from her when you could be...well...making love?"

Yep. Definitely time to leave.

"See you, Mom." He made a sharp turn around the banister and headed to the door leading to the back carport.

"Don't leave now," Monnie protested.

Geoff didn't look back at her. "You just told me I should be with Cheris. Now you want me to stay?"

"Well, Geoff, really. I shouldn't have to tell you to go make love to her. Should I?"

The door loomed in front of him. Geoff grabbed the handle and pulled. He opened it wide enough to slip through then closed it quickly behind him. Jumping the three stairs to the concrete pad housing his mom's car, he sprinted past it to his vehicle.

The door swung open. "Can you all come for dinner?" she called.

Geoff didn't answer. His suitcase was still up in his room. No way in hell he was going back for it now. He'd have to see if Janie would retrieve it for him. He wasn't stepping back in the house to get more marital advice from Tsunami Monnie.

In his SUV, he jammed the key in the ignition and shifted gears reversing until the drive met the large paved circle in front of the house. He shifted gears again, turned the wheel, and headed to Janie's studio.

He'd determined Cheris needed space to process being married, and he was willing to give her some. But he also wanted to be with her, watch her eyes light up with humor or irritation, quote another movie to him, learn her ways—the bad and the good.

He couldn't very well make her fall in love with him if he wasn't with her. And he only had this week. Next week he'd be back in Georgia teaching.

With her working, that didn't give him much time.

Was this connection he felt to her about Janie's painting? Had he admired it so many times on his wall that when he had realized she was a flesh and blood person he'd somehow transferred his love of the picture to a woman who resembled it?

It was stupid.

It wasn't like him to be stupid.

Or reckless. Or irrational. Spontaneous.

And the biggest surprise of all of this is he knew how crazy it was, and he didn't care. He knew every single reason why marrying Cheris was the dumbest stunt he'd ever pull in his lifetime, and he jumped in with both feet anyway loving it every minute. Loving her every minute.

He grinned.

Stupid-in-love idiot.

****

Janie looked at the screen of her phone. "Hmm."

"What?"

"Geoff just texted me and asked if I'd go by the house and pick up his suitcase." Her fingers flew over the keys. It chimed, and she waited for the answering tone.

"What'd you say?"

"I asked whether he was kicked out, or did he leave voluntarily." She laughed when she read his next message. "Escaped and now homeless, he says."

"Can he stay with you?"

"He won't. Not if he thinks Bobby is there." She pressed a few keys on her phone and stuck it back in her purse.

"He and Bobby don't get along?"

Janie lowered her face and didn't answer immediately. "The night of the gala I asked Geoff if he'd go pick up Aunt Nancy and bring her. She'd called me and asked to come, and she wasn't sure where it was. When he came back, he and Bobby got into it."

"About what?"

"I don't know. They didn't fight or anything, but I got the feeling if I hadn't walked in, they would have. You were there. You don't remember any of it?"

Cheris sighed and shook her head. "If I didn't have so many blank spaces of that night, I think I'd feel better about the whole thing. You haven't asked either of them about it?"

"Bobby says Geoff was being overprotective, and Geoff said Bobby is a jerk, and I'm better off without him. As if I hadn't heard that before."

"You could do better, don't you think?"

Janie fiddled with her straw. "You know, Cheris, Bobby's never asked me to be anybody but who I am. I like that about him."

Cheris shook her head. "You think he's the only guy who could love you for you? He's not."

"I've played the field. The Arrowood name comes with a lot of expectations especially from boys on this side of the train tracks."

Cheris looked at her friend appealingly. "But, Janie. Bobby is..." she shivered involuntarily. "He's not just on the other side of the train tracks. He's the hobo who jumps the train and steals your mom's silver."

Janie sighed. "Look. I've got to go over to the church and give your priestess an estimate for that nursery mural. Want to go with me?"

****

Janie and Cheris stood in the nursery talking to Kelly about her vision for a new wall in the room when a thirtyish man in a suit walked in the door.

"David." Kelly smiled as she hugged him. "How are you?" Stepping back, she introduced him as a friend of hers from seminary who had recently taken the pastorate in Clarksdale, a town about half an hour from Cullsbaeir.

"We've asked Janie to give us an estimate for creating a mural on this wall, but the actual picture is up for debate."

"I suggested Noah's ark, but Janie says she'll only paint it if she can put some drowning people in the water,"

Cheris informed the newcomer.

"People do tend to overlook the judgment part of that story. They want to treat it like a children's fairy tale with the animals entering a quaint little ark two by two," David commented.

Janie shot Cheris a triumphant look. "So there."

"Can't you at least paint a rainbow? Rainbows are brightly colored. The babies will like that."

"What about a creation scene with all the animals and plants and water?" Kelly suggested.

"Could I paint a serpent waiting on the sidelines looking for its chance to pull some shit?"

"Janie!" Cheris exclaimed.

David rubbed his hand over his chin in thought as he studied Janie. "You know, some people say the serpent had legs until God cursed it. Wonder what your serpent would look like before the Fall?"

Janie returned his stare but said nothing, one of the few times Cheris had known the woman not to have a witty comeback.

From down the hall the telephone rang and Kelly excused herself. Janie followed her out and brought a metal folding chair back in the room.

"What are you doing with that?" Cheris asked.

"I need to measure the height of the wall." She unfolded the chair and set it against the wall.

"I don't think that's such a good idea," David commented.

"It's a better idea than standing on the rocking chair." Janie climbed onto it and unhooked a metal tape measure from the waistband of her jeans. She extended the tape and stretched as she attempted to lay it upward to the ceiling.

David stepped next to the chair. "Why don't you let me do that? I'm taller."

Janie paused in her work long enough to size up the man below her. Cheris waited for Janie to tell him to go to hell.

Instead she returned to her task. "I'm capable." But

the tape wouldn't cooperate. Janie stood on tiptoe trying to coax the measuring device to straighten. With too much of her weight near the back of the chair, it began to fold up. Janie lost her balance and started to jump off, but the seat caught her foot and she fell instead. David caught her and lowered her to the floor.

"Janie, are you okay?" Cheris gasped.

"Yeah, sure." Janie stepped away from David. "Fine." She glanced at him. "Thanks."

"Never had a woman fall for me before." He grinned. "How about I find a stepladder?" He said as he walked out of the room.

"Wow. That was a close call. Good thing he was there to catch you."

"Uh-huh." Janie folded up the chair and set it out of the way then stood and stared at the wall with her arms crossed in front of her.

Cheris waited for a quip from Janie, some clever remark and a chuckle, but none came.

"You sure you're okay? You're acting as if something's wrong."

"Please drop it, Cheris," Janie's voice quivered.

"You're hurt. Where?" Cheris walked to her friend, but Janie shook her head.

"Don't. Let's just do this and get it over with."

"Okay."

David came in with a ladder and set it next to the wall. "This where you want it?"

"Yes."

He straightened the prongs and gestured to the ladder. "May I?"

Janie shrugged. "Knock yourself out."

He took off his suit jacket and carefully laid it on one of the baby beds. Cheris noted the breadth of shoulders and trim waist under the crisp white shirt.

Nice.

David held his hand out for the measure, and Janie dropped it on his palm. Climbing the ladder he touched the tape to the ceiling with little effort. Grinning down at Janie, he passed the metal holder to her as the tape stretched to the floor.

"I used to do this kind of thing a while back, weekends helping my dad who is a carpenter."

"Was that before or after you married?" Cheris asked.

Janie's head whipped toward her.

David shook his head. "I've never been married." He descended the ladder. Then to Janie, "What else? This wall to that one?"

She nodded, handed him the end of the tape, and they walked to opposite ends of the room.

"It's like a dance," Cheris declared as she watched both of them crouch to the floor in sync.

"I wish you'd keep your trap shut," Janie snapped. She uncapped a pen with her mouth and wrote numbers on the back of her hand. "I can live without the commentary." They both stood and the tape rapidly disappeared back in its holder.

"I think you missed a measurement," David said. He plucked the pen from her hand, opened her palm and held it as he wrote on her skin before returning the pen to her. "If you will excuse me. I've got an appointment in Clarksdale." He picked up his jacket and left without a backward glance.

Voices in the hall signaled Kelly's return as David said goodbye to her.

"Sorry that took so long," Kelly said once she was back in the nursery. "What do you think, Janie?"

"I'll come up with some renderings, figure out an estimate, and get back to you."

"Great."

Janie didn't speak as they left the building. Still silent, she drove Cheris to her car behind Web Enterprises.

"I'm sorry for whatever I did," Cheris said.

"It wasn't you, okay? I'm in a mood, and I need to work it off." Janie glared through the windshield and drummed her fingers on the steering wheel impatiently.

"Probably the stress of being in a church after all these years. Too righteous, huh?"

Janie opened her hand and narrowed her eyes at the script David had written on her palm.

"What did he write?"

"My penance."

"What?"

"Out of my car. Now."

Cheris stepped out of the car a second before Janie gunned the engine and shot out of the parking lot, the door still open on the passenger side. When she squealed onto the street, the door shut with the momentum of the car as it turned.

What was wrong with her?

Chapter Eight

"Build a house?" exclaimed John.
"For the wendy," said Curly.
"For Wendy?" John said, aghast. "Why, she is only a girl!"
"That," explained Curly, "is why we are her servants."
—*Peter Pan* by J.M. Barrie

Cheris' steps slowed as she approached her apartment and saw Monnie Arrowood on the front porch.

"Hello, Cheris dear." She waved.

"Hi." Cheris walked by her and unlocked the door. "Please come in."

"I'm so sorry for dropping by like this." The older woman turned in Cheris' living room to face her. "I went by your work, and Annie told me you have two weeks off for your honeymoon."

Cheris grabbed her cell phone before placing her purse in its cubby near the door and walked toward the kitchen. "Have a seat, and I'll fix us something to drink."

"Oh, I couldn't possibly impose since you and Geoff are.... Is Geoff here?"

"No. No, he's not." She ducked into the kitchen, her eyes scanning Geoff's number on the front of her refrigerator while she texted him.

Ur mom at my apt. Lookn 4 u

She sent it then set the phone on the counter while she pulled glasses out of the cabinet. She remembered from Sunday lunch that Monnie drank tea so she put some water on to boil and pulled bags out of her tea canister. Her phone dinged.

Still there?

Yes

U need me?

Now there was an interesting question. Did she need Geoff? Was this just a friendly get to know you visit from Monnie? She texted back.

DK

His text came back within a minute.

Keep me posted. On my way.

Cheris sighed in relief. Yes. She did need him here. Janie had said their mother was overbearing, and Cheris had seen a hint of that on the stairs the night of the party. She had arranged them in the family pose and made the announcements while Chip had stood beside her and interjected a comment every now and then.

Cheris poured water in a pot and placed it on the stove. Monnie appeared at the door.

"Can I help you, dear?" As she spoke Monnie's gaze traveled around the kitchen. Was she looking to see how clean it was? Deciding if Cheris kept a neat enough house to be married to her son?

"I thought I'd make some iced tea."

"Oh?"

"Yours was delicious the other day."

Monnie smiled. "I use mint leaves."

"Would you like something to eat?"

"It is nearly lunch, isn't it? Have you talked to Geoff today? Were you two planning to eat lunch together?"

"Umm. We hadn't made definite plans." She filled the glasses with ice and placed them on a tray thankful to have something to do.

"How long have you two been dating? We had no idea whatsoever Geoff was even seeing anyone."

"It was definitely what you call a whirlwind courtship."

"I suppose he came to Culsbaeir to see you without letting his father or me know."

"No. He didn't." Cheris turned to the stove. Boil, dammit! She commanded the water.

"So, you would go and see him then?"

Crouching down, she opened a cabinet door, hid behind it and sent a quick text to Geoff.

HELP

"We met at one of Janie's exhibits. He swept me off my feet." Cheris opened the refrigerator and pulled out a block of cheese. The woman was getting cheese and crackers, and that was it. No way was Cheris going to sit down with her for a full meal.

"Chip and I were so worried he'd never meet anyone and fall in love." Taking the box which Cheris had set on the counter top, Monnie opened it and began arranging the crackers on a plate. "I'm so pleased he's found you right here in Culsbaeir."

"Thank you."

"I'm sorry about the comment at the party about you and Geoff having a baby. I hope it wasn't too awkward for you."

Cheris busied herself with the cheese. "It's okay."

"Have you two talked about children?"

"No."

"But you do want children, don't you?"

"Eventually. Yes, I think so."

"You have plenty of time. Are you two getting along?"

Her phone dinged, and she glanced at the screen.

Ten minutes.

"It's Geoff. He's on his way over." Cheris' fingers hit the tiny keys on her phone.

Hurry.

"So, is he staying here with you tonight? It seems odd that he wouldn't. Don't you think?"

"We're still…you know…trying to figure some things out."

"I was heartbroken when I saw that he'd spent the night with us last night. I can't imagine spending the night apart after only two nights of marriage."

"I wondered where he went." That much was true. After he walked her to her apartment, he'd said 'Goodnight' and left.

"Was it a fight?"

"Not exactly."

"What then?"

"I'm not really sure how to answer that, Monnie."

"If you two are having problems, you can talk to me. Maybe I can help."

Cheris didn't answer. She set the slices of cheese aside, and grabbed tea bags. Boiling or not, the bags were going in the water.

"I think I do know what this is about."

"Really?"

"Yes. You know Geoff went off to college at fifteen. He never dated girls in high school. He was too busy studying. As far as I know, he didn't date at college either. I mean, how could he being three years younger than everyone else? Then he went on to get his Masters and Doctorate. And in all that time, he never talked about a girl."

"Are you telling me you think Geoff's—"

"Not had much experience with women so if he seems

to…fumble a bit, I'm sure if you are patient with him and show him what to do, he'll learn. He's always been a very eager student."

Cheris bumped the glass with the pot nearly knocking it over. Oh, dear Lord, when was Geoff getting here? If he didn't hurry, she was going to lock herself in the bathroom.

Truth or dare?

"Geoff again. I think he misses me."
"You go ahead and text him back. I'll finish the tea."

Ur mom's giving me the truth. Thinks ur a virgin

Dare then

We got in trouble w/ that already

Double dog

Quit txting n get here b4 she suggests positions I teach u

Cheris smiled as she lay the phone on the counter.
"Did you all work things out then?" Monnie said as she handed Cheris her glass of tea.
"We'll see."
"Chip said he heard you say you two will never live together. Why is that?"
Sweat trickled down Cheris' face. Why was it so hot in here? She glanced at the stove to make sure she had turned off the eye. *Think. Think.* Cheris raised her glass and sipped. Her stomach roiled in protest. She chose her words carefully. "Geoff and I didn't really plan on getting married so quickly."
"But of course, you'll want to set up house now. I'd like to have a party for you two. Sort of an after-the-fact wedding shower. We're leaving on our trip tomorrow, but I

think I can pull something together rather quickly. Say in two weeks?"

Cheris stared at the woman who waited for her answer. Nausea slammed Cheris, and she clutched her stomach.

"I have to go to the bathroom." She skirted past the woman. "Will you excuse me?"

"Of course, dear."

****

Someone knocked on the door. Cheris, who sat on the side of the tub with a cloth pressed to her forehead, debated answering. She hadn't thrown up, but she sure had felt like she was going to.

What was wrong with her?

"Cheris?" Geoff spoke through the door. "Sweetheart, it's me."

She jumped up, disengaged the lock, and pulled the door open. Geoff stood there, an amused expression on his face. He leaned into her.

"Is this avoiding Monnie, or are you sick?"

Cheris shrugged.

"Would you like for us to tell her the truth?"

Cheris shook her head. "I don't think it would help. She'd be more determined to fix it. Maybe we should go for the dare."

"Got anything in mind?"

"You could kiss me and act like you know what you're doing."

Geoff grinned. "I like it."

"Where is she?"

"Hovering." He glanced over his shoulder. "Back there somewhere."

Cheris inhaled a steadying breath.

Bold. Be bold. She adopted a Bette Davis swagger. "Fasten your seatbelts. It is going to be a bumpy ride." Pulling back the door, Cheris launched herself in Geoff's arms aiming for his mouth.

Bull's Eye.

Geoff stumbled back against the wall with the force of

her embrace, his hands steadying her hard against his body, his lips meeting hers with confidence.

He hummed appreciatively, and Cheris decided he must be really enjoying *this* dare. He'd probably enjoyed the others, too. Not that Cheris could *remember*. But *this* was nice.

She clutched his head to her and arched her neck as he nibbled on her skin there causing tremors to shoot all the way down to her toes. When she couldn't stand it anymore, she dipped her face and knocked his glasses askew.

"Sorry," she whispered as he whipped them off his face, then his arms were around her again. Cheris melded her mouth to his, savoring his taste, learning the raspy texture of his unshaven face as it scraped across hers, the feel of his hair beneath her fingertips.

He pressed another kiss on her lips then drew back as if waiting.

"What are you..." doing not kissing me? Cheris finished the sentence in her mind when he shook his head at her, his eyes blinked. Once. Twice.

"She's gone."

"Who?"

"Monnie. Your front door just opened and shut."

"Oh." Right. The reason they were kissing in the first place. To get rid of her and her plans to have an after-the-fact wedding shower, her helpful advice.

Clearing his throat, Geoff stepped away from her.

Cheris wrapped her arms around herself. She missed the heat of his body. "I'm sorry if I took your virginity."

He grinned and stooped to pick up his glasses. Placing them on his nose and adjusting them, he replied, "You didn't."

"Yeah. I didn't think you kissed like a virgin. Not like I'm an expert or anything, but it seems if you've never done it before—kissing, I mean—you wouldn't be that good at it."

Turning, he walked into her living room. "Was that a compliment?"

Cheris followed as she considered his question and how she wanted to answer it.

He was only the best kisser she'd ever locked lips with. "Yes."

Standing in the middle of the room, Geoff's expression warmed at her answer. "Want to go get something to eat? You haven't had lunch yet, have you?"

Cheris snapped her fingers as she remembered the cheese and crackers she had set out for her and Monnie. "I'm not that hungry. I just came from eating doughnuts with Janie, and I fixed a snack tray for your mom." Cheris walked into the kitchen and picked it up. "Do you want some?"

"No. Come out with me. We'll go to Lilly Belle's, and you can sip on raspberry tea while I eat. Then I'll take you back to work."

Cheris poured the crackers back in the box and wrapped up the cheese. "I can't go to work. They've given me a mandatory vacation for two weeks."

"Work furlough?"

"Honeymoon."

Geoff didn't reply, and Cheris finished her task before joining him in the living room where he stood. When he saw her enter, he headed to the door.

"Ready?"

"I can fix you something to eat."

Geoff shook his head. "No, let's go out."

"We're supposed to be honeymooning. If people see us out, they'll know we're not."

Geoff sighed. "Why do you care what they think?"

Cheris shrugged.

"I'm positive people on their honeymoon eat, so let's go out to a restaurant. If we see anyone we know, you can jump me again, okay?" Geoff pulled the door open and walked out without another word.

Cheris grinned as she grabbed her purse and followed him. Putting on a show for the Cullsbaeir public would be a great excuse to kiss him again.

****

Sitting across from Geoff at Lilly Belle's tea room, Cheris sipped from a tall crystal glass while he waited on the blue plate special.

When the waitress set it before him, Geoff took his fork and meticulously separated the carrots, beans, macaroni and cheese, and chicken from each other. "Are most of your neighbors college students?"

Cheris wrinkled her nose at his actions. "Some, I guess. What are you doing?"

"I don't like my food touching on the plate. Aren't they bothersome to you?"

"I don't care if my food gets mixed up. It's going to the same place anyhow."

"Not your food. Your neighbors. Every time I've been to your apartment I can hear their music. Grunge. Typical college sounds." Geoff dipped into the macaroni and ate it.

"How come you don't mind cheese and macaroni together?"

Geoff smiled. "Cheese is okay on most everything."

"What about vegetable soup?"

"No. I don't eat cheese on vegetable soup."

"I mean do you like vegetable soup? Everything's touching in soup."

"Not a big fan. What about your neighbors?"

Cheris crooked her head and purposely misunderstood him. "I don't know if they like soup or not."

Geoff smiled. Finishing up the macaroni, he began on the green beans. "They are likely unable to hear you if you asked them. Does the noise keep you up at night?"

"I guess I'm used to it."

"Have you ever thought of getting a house?"

"I have a dream house in town, but it's not in my budget. Do you always eat your meal one food at a time?"

"Generally." Geoff ate another bite of the beans. "It's not in your budget. Does that mean it's for sale?"

"Last time I drove by it still had a sign out front. I doubt it's sold with the price tag they have on it and the market being what it is."

"What part of town?"

"The east side not too far from Janie."

"What makes it your dream house?"

Dropping her gaze, Cheris picked up her glass and drank. Why had she told him she had a dream house? "Do you dislike all soup, or just vegetable?"

"I like tomato, potato, French onion, and chowder."

"What about chili?"

Geoff shook his head. "It's not technically a soup."

"Neither is chowder."

"Is it the color?"

"Color isn't what makes it chowder. It's the thickness of it."

"I'm not talking about chowder. I'm wondering if the color is what made the house your dream?"

Oh.

"The architecture of the house? What is it? Ranch style? Tudor?" Geoff persisted.

"Brick. What kind of house do you live in?" Cheris asked hoping to get the topic away from her.

Geoff speared a carrot and brought it to his mouth and chewed before answering her. "It's a one story cookie cutter house with a double garage. Why don't you want to tell me?"

"It's stupid."

"No, it isn't."

She shot him a disdainful look. "How do you know? I haven't told you yet."

"I'll tell you why I'm a food freak if you'll tell me what makes this house your dream."

"Okay."

"When I was twelve years old, I started high school. My first day there, four sophomores cornered me in the cafeteria, held me down, and made me eat cole slaw mixed with tapioca pudding, chicken and dumplings, mustard, and blue cheese dressing."

Cheris shuddered. "That must have been awful."

Geoff shrugged nonchalantly. "Nah. I vomited all over them so they got it lots worse than I did. I was good at projectile spewing apparently. But after that, I didn't like any type of food mixed together."

"I...I grew up in a little apartment over a restaurant. The only yard there was a parking lot." Cheris felt her face heat up at the admission. She'd never told anyone this before, not even her best friend Janie. "I always wished I had a yard to play in with a tree and a swing hanging from one of its branches."

When Geoff didn't reply, Cheris looked up to see him watching her.

"I told you it was stupid."

Geoff placed his napkin next to his plate. He stood without breaking eye contact. "Let's go see it."

"What?" Cheris stood as well.

"The yard. The tree. The house. Does it already have the swing, or do you just imagine it there?"

"'Do you know what imagination is?'" She quipped.

He pulled a twenty out of his wallet and laid it on the table then motioned for her to precede him. When they exited the building, he spoke.

"'Oh, sure. It's when you see things, and they're not really there.'"

Chill bumps rose on Cheris' skin. In her anxiety, she'd reverted to an old movie dialogue, and he was following right along. "'That seeing can be the cause of other things, too.'"

At his SUV, he escorted her into her seat before walking around the vehicle and settling on the driver's side. He started up the car and he continued the conversation from the classic movie. "'To me imagination all by itself is a place. A separate country. Perhaps you've heard of the nation of the French. Even the British nation. But I like the Imagine Nation—'"

"Stop it."

"But I'm coming to the best line."

"You're not Santa Claus, and I am too old to play

pretend," Cheris snapped.

Geoff turned onto the road and headed toward Janie's. "If you don't want me to play the movie quote game, then you need to pick more obscure movies. Everybody's seen *Miracle on 34ᵗʰ Street.* Now, where's the house with the yard?"

Cheris shook her head. "Don't humor me. I hate that."

"I'm not humoring you. I'd just like to know if the tree has a swing."

"Yes, it has a swing, and, no, I don't want to go by and see it. I'm sorry I told you. It's just a silly notion I had one day when I was feeling sorry for myself."

"Because of where you grew up?"

Cheris didn't answer.

"Tell me about your parents."

Cheris snorted. "I don't like to talk about...that. Believe me. If you knew what I came from, you'd be more than happy to divorce me in case my bad genes might infect the decency of your family."

"Cheris." Geoff shook his head. "You bring a refinement to my family which compliments all of us."

"I'm just really good at faking it. You remember that. You're married to a fake and a phony."

"I think my sister is a pretty good judge of character."

"You've met Bobby, right?"

Geoff's mouth tightened, and he glared out the windshield.

Cheris watched him closely. "You don't like Bobby, do you?"

A pulse beat at his jaw. "Do you?"

"No." Cheris shuddered. "He creeps me out even more so since the Gala."

"Why is that?"

"I...I'm not sure. I think I remember him being there."

"What do you remember?"

"An image, really. He..." Cheris shivered. "I don't know."

Geoff turned into the entrance of Central Park, one of the jewels of Culsbaier. He pulled into a parking space and cut the engine.

Cheris peered out the window. "What are we doing here?"

"Going for a walk." Geoff pulled the keys from the ignition and leaned back in the seat. "If you want to, or we could neck in the car giving credence to our newly married status."

His expression gave nothing away, as if either choice seemed perfectly reasonable. Her stomach fluttered in anticipation. Oh, yes. That kiss back at her apartment had been... Cheris pulled the door handle and stepped onto the graveled ground.

Dangerous. That's what it had been.

Walking in the park was much safer.

****

"Geoff? It's Janie."

Geoff yawned as he held his phone to his ear. "What do you want?"

"I just got a call from Mom at the airport. What the hell is your problem? You know how she is. Why would you go over there to sleep again knowing how she reacted yesterday?"

Grabbing his glasses he put them on then looked at the clock on the bedstead.

8:20

He'd kept the same routine as the previous night—Cheris' apartment until eleven, observatory until four a.m., then falling asleep at Mom and Dad's around five, and awoken by well meaning female member of the family too soon afterward. He liked the routine until the last part.

"I thought Cheris and I had solved that problem."

"What? By making out in front of her? You just confuse the poor woman. She can't understand why you won't stay with Cheris."

"It's none of Mom's business anyway."

"She thinks you make it her business by sleeping in

125

your old room. Why don't you come over here and stay with me?"

Geoff sat up and planted his feet on the floor. He'd hoped when Mom and Dad left for the airport this morning, he'd be able to sleep in. "I think you know the answer to that."

Bobby. Geoff had had enough of the maggot.

"What happened at the gala between you and him that's got you so pissed?"

The image of Bobby pinning Cheris against the *Black Beauty* exhibit flashed in his mind. It had taken everything Geoff had not to charge over there and beat Bobby to a pulp for breaking his sister's heart and going after the woman who Geoff wanted for himself.

"He made a pass at my wife, thereby insulting my sister at the same time." Cheris hadn't been his wife in that moment, but that didn't make him feel any less territorial. By then she belonged to him as much as Janie did.

Janie didn't reply.

"Do you believe me?"

"Yes."

"Want me to come over and help you throw his stuff on the street?"

"Nope."

"You're dumping him though, right?"

Janie growled. "This is supposed to be about you keeping Cheris, not me dumping Bobby."

"I'm working on it, Sister, but there is some truth to absence making the heart grow fonder."

"Dude, you're such a geek. You're back in Georgia next week. Her heart isn't going to grow anything if you don't spend any time with her."

"I was with her nearly twelve hours yesterday."

"Were any of those hours in bed?" Janie asked.

"Not your concern," he answered.

"Geoffrey, lust is a powerful persuader. Jeez, I can't believe you're a guy sometimes."

"Lust may motivate the man, but romance woos the

woman."

"Not this woman. I'll take lust over romance any day," she declared.

"You're not Cheris. Changing the subject here, do you know the route Cheris takes when she comes to visit you?"

"Why?"

"She told me about a house she likes, but I can't find it. She said it's on the way to your apartment."

"Huh. She's never told me about a house." Janie clucked her tongue in thought. "I bet it's on Mary Jane Road. She always takes that street when she's driving me home. Bugs the crap out of me because it's out of the way."

Geoff grinned. "I'll check it out. Thanks, Sis."

Chapter Nine

He had not yet learned that the only safe male rebuke to a
scornful female is to stay away from her—especially if that
is what she desires. However, he did not wish to rebuke
her; simply and ardently he wished to dance the cotillion
with her. Resentment was swallowed up in hope.
                            —*Penrod* by Booth Tarkington

"You're not peeking, are you?"

From behind her hands, Cheris rolled her eyes. "No,
I'm not peeking, but I feel really stupid. Why can't I see
where we're going?"

"Because I want it to be a surprise."

The smooth motion of the car made it impossible for
Cheris to guess where he was taking her for their one week
anniversary. Not that Geoff had said anything about an
anniversary, but when he'd picked her up this afternoon,
the air around him had nearly crackled with excitement. He
hadn't told her where they were going for the second time
in their short courtship. Then in the car, he'd suggested she
put her hands over her eyes.

"I told you before. I don't really like surprises," said
Cheris referring to their trip to the planetarium.

"But you enjoyed the star show, or am I mistaken?"
The car stopped, and Geoff shut off the engine.

"Yes, I did like it. Can I look now?"

"Yes."

Cheris lowered her hands and saw it through the
windshield.

Her dream house sat so pretty in her dream yard with
her dream tree and hanging from it, of course, the dream

swing.

All there. All real.

Cheris blinked at the brick structure with its recessed porch and low wrought iron gate. Long windows with real white painted shutters bookended the front.

Cheris opened the door and slid out of the SUV and regarded the house as if it might vanish. She crossed her arms as she stood there for a moment before stepping onto the freshly mown grass.

"Is it okay for us to be here?"

"Yes."

Cheris walked toward the tree and sat on the swing. She held the chains and swayed with her toes against the packed dirt.

"How did you figure out which one it was?"

"A little investigating. Unfortunately, it's no longer listed."

Cheris moved a shoulder in dismissal. "Still a nice dream house. Wonder who bought it?"

"No one. The contract with the realtor ran out, and the owner didn't relist it."

"It's a shame for it to be empty."

"Real shame especially when you see the inside."

Cheris' eyes widened at his statement. "Have you seen the inside?"

Geoff held up a key between thumb and forefinger. "I have. Would you like to?"

She shook her head in disbelief. "How did you get a key?"

"My dad has a friend who's a realtor so I called him. He pulled some strings."

"Wow." Cheris stood, and side by side they approached the house. "It's nice to have connections."

"Sure is."

Cheris opened the gate running her fingers along the smooth metal as she did so. The empty porch testified to the house's vacancy.

Sad.

Geoff slid the key into the lock and turned it. With his hand on the knob, he looked at Cheris. "Ready?"

Cheris bounced on her heals in anticipation. She nodded, resisting the urge to open the door herself.

Geoff waited another second, then two, and pushed it open. She crossed the threshold and stopped in amazement.

Oh. My. Gosh.

There was a pool. An indoor pool.

Cheris' studied the lines of the large room lit mainly from the late afternoon sunlight through its glassed back wall. Spiral wrought iron stairs led to a walkway which connected the second story rooms to each other from opposite sides of the house. With their open space, both ends of the house reminded of Cheris of a miniature house without a back wall allowing some lucky girl to put her dolls in all the rooms.

Her shoes clicked as she crossed the tiled floor to a patio table set for two, a picnic basket on the floor next to one of the chairs.

"I can't get over this." Cheris glanced back at Geoff, but his warm gaze held hers. "Can you believe this?"

"You begin to understand why the cost is so exorbitant." He indicated the front wall, reminiscent of the front porch outside. "These are two houses connected by the pool room. Here's one house." He pointed to the open walls near the front door they had entered. "And that's the other house."

"What about that end of the pool over there?" Downstairs was a bedroom and above it another bedroom visible through sliding glass doors.

"That used to be the garage. It jutted out to the side. The one on the east side still has its garage on the front."

"Why in the world would someone leave this? It's gorgeous."

"One house belonged to a woman, the other to her adult daughter. The woman died, and her daughter is divorced with children and grandchildren who live in

Nevada and Florida respectively. I think she's living close to the one with the most grandchildren."

Cheris stepped to the rail on the porch leading into the east house. "How many bedrooms total?"

"Seven. Much too large for one person." He followed her as they entered the door and walked through the unfurnished rooms until they passed through a door which must have been an exit before the addition. It led to the western side of the pool room with three bedrooms each with their own bathroom. From the back bedroom they walked on the catwalk over the pool and leaned on the railing overlooking the cavernous room.

"Are you sure it's okay for us to be here?" Cheris watched Geoff as he rested his elbows on the metal banister.

"You don't think I'd break in to your dream house just to impress you, do you?" His mouth crooked in a smile making Cheris wonder.

She shrugged.

"I wouldn't. Larry Preston, my dad's friend, he *knows people*." Geoff made brackets in the air with his fingers. "He'd do anything for a friend, and if it eventually leads to a commission on a sold house, all the better."

Cheris' mouth dropped open. "You aren't thinking of buying this house, are you?"

Geoff laughed and shook his head. "I don't think so. My dream house has more bookshelves in it. Maybe a moat with an alligator or two to keep out the unsavory characters."

"Alligators in a moat?"

"What? You like a tree swing, I like a reptile-fortified security system. We're talking about ideal here."

The room was darker now as the sun dipped below the tree line in the back yard, and the lit sconces on the walls inside became more prominent.

They strolled further along the walkway to the eastern side of the house. The bedroom they walked into was nearly as large as Cheris' apartment. She could fit her car in the walk-in closet with room to spare. She cast one last longing glance at the sunken tub in the bathroom which could easily accommodate an alligator before they ventured down the stairs to the living room.

Cheris sighed. "This really is a dream house."

"Would you want to live here?"

"I don't know. The size is overwhelming. It certainly doesn't look this big from the outside."

Geoff nodded sitting on the oversized leather chair and propping his feet on the matching footrest.

"Are you sure it's okay for us to sit on the furniture?"

"Sure. The furniture comes with it. Larry said she took what she wanted with her, but still left enough to furnish this side of the house."

Cheris sat on the matching couch and sank into the butter soft comfort of the cushions.

Oh my. I need this couch.

"Nice, huh?"

Cheris ran her hand along the armrest. "Very nice."

Geoff didn't reply, but the silence was comfortable. In their time together this week, there had been several quiet moments. If conversation happened, it wasn't forced then, but another facet of the budding relationship.

And it was feeling like a budding relationship.

Geoff had tempered his time with her. If they spent a marathon of hours together one day, the next day he'd wait until the evening to see her. Each night he'd ask her plans for the next day, and if she had none, he'd suggest a place to visit, an idea to hang out at her apartment, or a plan for spending time together. Yesterday morning she'd been surfing web when she'd received an invitation to play an online game with him. They'd played nearly two hours before he'd called it quits via an IM and asked her out for dinner at the Riverfront Inn.

"I'm going back to Georgia in the morning."

Disappointment ballooned at his words.

"I'd rather not go, but classes start up again Monday, and I've got some things to do to get ready."

"I understand."

"Certainly you're welcome to go with me, or come visit if you get bored during your…vacation."

Honeymoon, actually. Not that they'd done much honeymooning. They hadn't kissed since she'd jumped him at her apartment for his mother's sake.

Hadn't even touched.

Well, except for when they had gone to see a SciFi flick. They'd both reached for the popcorn, and her leg had brushed his a few times as they sat next to each other.

Her cat Timmy had gotten more action even, settling on Geoff's lap like they were best friends while Geoff scratched his neck and smoothed his thick white fur.

Cheris would have shut the cat in the bathroom, but Geoff insisted he didn't mind. Cheris had minded. She hated to admit she'd been jealous of Timmy as she watched Geoff's fingers caress the animal.

"Thanks. I'll think about it."

"Are you hungry? I brought food." Geoff tented his hands and waited for her answer.

****

Lovely. She was so lovely.

Cheris sat across the table from Geoff and twirled a lock of hair around her finger. She couldn't have known how enticing the gesture was, how the copper of her hair reflected the flame from the tabletop candles, how the smell of chlorine from the pool elicited images of them swimming in it—bathing suits optional. In this moment, he'd mortgage his soul to give her this house if he could live with her here and share the gigantic bedroom upstairs for the next fifty or sixty years.

The king sized bed had looked inviting though when Geoff had pulled the comforter back earlier today, it revealed a bare mattress.

Not that he had plans for that bed.

Well, not exactly.

With so many sleepless nights this week, he'd about decided the bed—sheets or not—was looking good for actual sleep.

He suppressed a yawn and took his glasses off to wipe his eyes.

"Ready to go?" Cheris asked. "You look tired."

Geoff shook his head.

She held out her hand. "Let me see your glasses."

He handed them to her, and her gauzy figure moved. "Oh, my. Your eyesight is not very good, is it?"

"No."

"How well can you see me?"

Uneasiness niggled at him. What was she doing? "Not very."

"How many fingers am I holding up?" She teased.

"Give me my glasses, and I'll tell you." He held out his hand, but the glasses didn't materialize. "Cheris." He crooked his fingers.

"Interesting," she murmured. "Geoff Arrowood seems to be at a disadvantage."

"Come on."

"So, if I do this, you can't even see me, can you?"

He couldn't be sure, but it looked as if she had put his glasses down the front of her shirt.

So, should he go after them, or play dumb? "Are you teasing me?"

"Perhaps." Her suggestive tone left little doubt. He weighed his options. He could sit here on this side of the table conversing to her Monet image, or he could risk breaking his nose with a surprise attack.

Geoff skirted the table, but by the time he had jumped to her chair, she had vacated it scrambling around the table giggling all the while. With a quick retrieval, she now held her arm up and over the pool.

"Oh, dear. I hope I don't drop them in the water."

"Now, this is the Cheris I remember from Friday night."

"Oh, really? Did I nearly lose your glasses then too?"

"No, but you flirted…a lot. Can I have my glasses please?"

"Not…" Cheris began when Geoff lunged. "Ah!" He caught her and pulled her toward him so that they wouldn't end up in the water.

His glasses weren't as fortunate.

He heard the simultaneous gasp of Cheris and the plop as they broke the surface of the water.

Still.

He now was shoulder to knee with Cheris, his hands spanning her back and waist. Was temporary blindness worth the price of having her in his arms?

Oh, yeah.

"Geoff, I'm sorry." This close he could tell she was, too. Gone was the vixen who had shoved his glasses in her blouse. Had they gone into her bra, too? He hated to lose the scent of her skin to the chlorine.

"Are you now?"

"Oh, no. What are we going to do?" She attempted to pull away, but he held her for a few more seconds before releasing her.

"I suppose I'll retrieve them."

"No. I'll go."

"You'll go?"

"Yeah. In the water."

Geoff shook his head wishing he could read her expression. As appealing as the offer was, he thought it ought to be a last resort. "I'm sure there's a skimmer here somewhere. Let's look for it." Not as if he'd be much good at looking for anything right now.

They began their search. After he stumbled twice, Cheris had grabbed Geoff's hand and guided him throughout the house. They found nothing, but a closet in the enclosed greenhouse off the kitchen and a storage house in the backyard—both locked.

Back in the pool room, Geoff squinted at the water.

It was a lost cause.

Of course he couldn't see where his glasses were even with the underwater lights illuminating the bottom of the pool.

"Can you see them?"

"Well, sure. They're at the deep end."

Of course, they were.

Fishing his keys out of his pocket, he held them out to Cheris. "Would you go out to my car? There's a blanket in the very back. If you'll bring it in, I'd appreciate it."

If she wondered why he needed a blanket, she didn't ask, only took the keys and left. As soon as she walked to the front door, he shed his clothes. No use in humiliating himself further by stripping in front of her. With any hope he'd be in the water by the time she got back—maybe even with glasses in hand. He'd grab the blanket and cover up before she decided he had any plans for molesting her. He'd excuse himself and get dressed in one of the seven bathrooms.

Problem solved.

When he'd taken everything off but his skivvies, he dove straight to the bottom of the ten foot pool and felt around with his hands. When his lungs burned, he surfaced and took a deep breath.

"What are you doing?" Cheris astonished voice greeted him.

"Getting my glasses."

"Well, you're nowhere close. They're in the middle right there."

Geoff wiped the water off his face and peered up at her. "In the middle?"

"Yeah. How are you going to find them? You're blind as a bat."

He kicked to the side of the pool and held to its edge. "I can probably see almost as well as you underwater."

Big lie.

He couldn't see jack. The pattern on the lining made it impossible for him to make out anything down there. However, as close as Cheris stood to him, he could make out her legs pretty well, and the fuzzy short length of her skirt.

"You shouldn't be in there. I was the one who threw

them in like a stupid idiot."

"I believe I knocked them out of your hand when I grabbed you. Okay. I'm going down again." Without waiting for her reply, he submerged.

No luck. He came up for a quick breath and dove again.

Where were they?

Dammit. This was frustrating.

During the fourth time down, Cheris joined him. She swam to a spot about three feet away, then pulled on his arm tugging him upward. They both surfaced sucking in air before swimming to the side of the pool.

Crooking her arm on its edge, she held his glasses in her hand.

"I'm sorry. I'm so sorry, Geoff."

Sky blue.

The same bra she'd had on the night of the gala. The lace edging wasn't visible to him now, but the straps on her shoulders were. Obviously, she'd followed his lead—shed her clothes, but kept on the underwear.

He reached for his glasses and plucked them from her fingers.

"Please," Cheris appealed.

"What?"

"Please don't put them on. I'm...I don't have my clothes on, and it's embarrassing."

"I'm only wearing my skivvies here, and your eyesight doesn't handicap you."

She didn't respond.

"Will you trust me enough to let me see?" He waited for her answer, and the only sound was the lapping of the water.

"Okay."

He shook them, wiped his face and slipped them on. Cheris came into focus, her expression unsure.

"Thanks. Let's swim for a while." He pushed off and sliced through the warm water across the width. She hadn't moved when he reached the other side. "You like to swim?"

"Love it. I swim laps at the Y twice a week."

"Really?"

"Uh-huh."

"Think you can beat me from one end to the other?"

"Don't know. How good are you?"

He was terrible. He hadn't been swimming in years. "Oh, I think I could beat you easily. Me being a guy and all."

She laughed and swam to the end. He met her there.

"One length. Winner gets to dry off with the blanket first," Cheris proposed.

Oh, yes. He liked those stakes. If he won, he got the blanket first. If he lost, he got to watch her exit the pool to get the blanket.

"Ready? On my mark. Get set. Go."

They shoved off, and mid length Geoff realized even if he wanted to win, it was hopeless. Her strokes were clean and confident. By the time he reached the steps, she was crouched in the shallow water waiting for him, a smug look on her face.

"Two out of three," he said.

Cheris shook her head. "How humiliated do you want to be? Have you ever been swimming in your life?"

"I'll have you know I swam every summer at computer camp until I graduated high school."

"They have a pool at computer camp?"

"It was mandatory. We had to swim before they'd let us play on the computers."

"I'll bet it was mandatory." She snickered. "So you haven't swum since you were fifteen."

Geoff thought about it. "Yeah. That sounds about right. The water feels good, doesn't it?"

"Yes. Seems if the house is empty, they'd not want to pay to heat the pool."

"Larry came by earlier with me and switched on the pool lights. Maybe he turned the heater on as well."

"It'd take longer than a few hours to heat it."

Geoff nodded in agreement. "Who knows why? Maybe Larry likes to swim."

"I think I'll swim a few more laps."

Geoff watched her slice through the water, flip against the wall, and return. Before she reached him, she went under and swam away, resurfacing in the deep end. Resting his arms against the tiled rim, he leaned his head back and studied the reflection of the rippled light on the ceiling.

How he hated to go back to Georgia tomorrow.

Hated it.

But he had to. He'd done nothing to get ready for his Monday classes. Nothing.

A glimmer from the back window caught his eye, but in an instant the glass was dark again. What had it been? Headlights from a car? No. There was no street or driveway back there, only a large backyard with a bricked patio.

Cheris now crisscrossed the width of the pool with graceful strokes moving closer to him with each lap.

Man, she really liked the water.

No matter what happened between them, he'd make sure she knew she'd be welcome to swim at Mom and Dad's any time she wanted.

Movement from the front of the room captured his attention.

Two policemen strode toward the pool, their hands on their holstered guns.

Oh, boy.

"Hello," he called. "Is there a problem?"

"Is this your house?" One of the officers asked.

Geoff straightened and faced them. Uneasy because of having nothing on but his underwear, he nevertheless spoke matter-of-factly. "No, but we have permission to be here."

"According to the neighbor, no one is supposed to be here. Why don't you two come out of the pool so we can sort this out?"

Geoff glanced at his wife. Crouched a few feet from him, she held the tiled lip with her fingers as she peeked over its edge at the men uniform.

"We're not exactly dressed for an interrogation."

One man shrugged unconcerned for their predicament. The other motioned for them to move. Sighing, Geoff ascended the stairs, and stalking over to the blanket he picked it up before walking back to the end of the pool.

He unfolded it and held it in invitation. "Come on, Sweetheart."

Cheris shook her head, her eyes wide in fear.

"It's okay. Just a misunderstanding."

Geoff crooked his head studying her.

That wasn't pool water running down her cheeks. Those were tears.

"I need to help my wife out of the water."

Laying the blanket aside, he waded toward her as, out of the corner of his eye, he noted one officer moved closer.

What was going on here? Sure it was awkward, but nothing a call to Larry wouldn't fix.

He hoped.

Cheris trembled beside him.

"It's okay," he murmured as he attempted to pull her to a standing position. "Cheris, it's okay. I promise."

She resisted. "You said we could be here," she whimpered.

He bent his knees to meet her eye to eye. "We can."

"Then why are they here?"

"The neighbor didn't know we'd be here and did what a good neighbor should do. I'll call Larry, and he'll vouch for us." Placing his hand around her waist, he moved them through the water toward the edge of the pool.

She refused to go further, the water to her shoulders. "I can't get out. I'm practically naked."

Geoff met the watchful gazes of the policemen as he stood at the top step and grasped the blanket. "Gentlemen? Do you mind standing aside for a moment? My wife is reluctant to exit the pool while you watch."

They exchanged glances before pivoting and facing each other.

"Thanks." Geoff stretched out the blanket in front of his body. "All right, Sweetheart. Come on out."

For a few seconds she didn't move. Geoff nodded to her in encouragement. She squared her shoulders.

Shutting her eyes tightly, she stood, Venus rising from the sea. "All right, Mr. De Mille," she whispered as her lids lifted and she pierced him with her intense gaze, "I'm ready for the close up now."

Oh, man.

The bra and panties plastered to her flesh providing no barrier from his gaze.

Not a good thing since there'd be no way of hiding getting turned on in his own wet briefs.

He sucked in a breath, focused on the far wall, and thought of his freshman physics teacher whose nickname was *Killer.*

When that didn't work, he began reciting the elements of the periodic table by group. She stepped into the blanket at Strantium, a metal that is highly reactive chemically.

Very appropriate.

Adjusting the cloth around her, he pressed it on her shoulders covering her. He walked them over to their clothes in two piles next to each other. He handed her garments to her and pushed her to the door of the closest bathroom.

She glanced back at him uncertainly before stumbling across the tiled expanse to the threshold. Picking up his undershirt, he wiped his chest and arms before shrugging into his button down shirt.

"You guys have a problem with me getting dressed before I make the call?"

"I'll go with him," one officer spoke to the other.

He followed Geoff to the front part of the house and took his stance at the door while Geoff stripped off his shorts, dried off with his damp T-shirt, and slid on his slacks. Feeling in his pocket, he retrieved his cell phone and called Larry.

Larry—God love him—showed up in less than twenty

minutes with his cell phone to his ear.

"Very good. Yeah. I'd love that. Fantastic, my friend. Gotta go. Goodbye." He waved a hand in greeting. "So sorry about the confusion here," he called to them. He held the phone in front of him and aimed. "Gorgeous place, isn't it?"

He approached the policemen and introduced himself, calling them by their names.

Their radios crackled.

"That'll be your dispatch saying we're all legitimate." He smiled confidently.

Sure enough, the owner of the house as well as the neighbor had called the police department saying Larry's friends had permission to be in the house.

The older man shook the hands of the uniformed officers and thanked them for their prompt response.

"You all do a fine job. A fine job!" He reached in his pocket and pulled out his wallet. "I'm having an open block party next weekend in Vestavia Hills. Come out if you get a chance." Handing each of them a business card, he continued. "We'll have inflatables for the kids and a sixty inch flat screen television as a door prize. It's going to be big. Big."

After the police left, Larry shook his head. "Oh, Geoff. I'm sorry, buddy. What a terrible thing to happen."

Geoff had his arm around Cheris, her body flush against his side. When she'd come back from getting dressed, she hadn't spoken at all, hadn't reacted to anything.

He'd tried to reassure her, but she only stared at the floor and nodded.

"Of course, you're welcome to stay as long as you want. Days even. Lauren Cooper, the owner, is a sweetheart. She'd love for you guys to enjoy the house. She's just as torn up about this as I am." He held his camera in front of them. "Smile for prosperity. Your first bust, ha ha!"

Cheris stiffened.

Geoff patted her. "I appreciate it, Larry. Really."

"Sure thing. Sure thing. I better go. Left Natalie at the restaurant. She'll order lobster just to spite me for leaving her alone. If you all want to come to the block party next weekend, you're welcome, of course. Some great houses there for a newlywed couple just starting out. Great party to use the excuse to look around."

"I hear it's going to be big," Geoff commented with a wide smile.

"Really big. You all take care now," he said as he swept out the door.

Cheris slumped.

Yeah. He could relate.

"Come on. Let's go hang out in Lauren Cooper's sitting room."

In a few moments they sat on the couch, Geoff's arm still around her. The silence nearly deafened him as he waited on her to speak, scream, anything.

Finally she drew a shuddering breath, shifted under his arm, and tucked her feet underneath her.

"Cheris, do you want to tell me what's going on?"

She didn't speak for a while, only settled further into the couch and him.

"Where I grew up...how I grew up when the police appeared, it was never a good thing."

The words hovered in the air, their implications heavy on Geoff's heart for the little girl she had once been and the fear from days long gone haunting her tonight. He reached over and clasped her hand intertwining their fingers.

"I never went without food. Mama worked as a waitress in a truckstop restaurant, and we lived in a little apartment over it. But she...she had a lot of boyfriends and several husbands. Some of them weren't very nice."

"Did they...?"

"No. They never touched me. Most of the boyfriends never even saw me. After her shift, Mama would buy a twelve pack from the cooler and start drinking with whichever man was available. They'd stumble up the stairs after the beer was gone, and I'd shut my bedroom door and turn up the television. Late at night the only station without infomercials was the classic movie channel. So while my mom was falling in love or falling apart in the next room, I was watching Gloria Swanson and Doris Day."

"Where was your dad?"

"I don't think my mom even knows who my dad is. She should have been on Maury Povich pointing fingers at guys making them get paternity tests to find out who her baby daddy is."

"Her baby daddy is now Chip Arrowood, and he's quite pleased about it. As is his wife, his elder daughter, and especially his son."

Cheris scrambled from the couch. She glared at him as unshed tears glittered on her lashes. "I'm from the worst kind of Appalachian hill trash there is. I don't belong in your family."

Dammit. Not the reaction he wanted.

He stood as well. "Yes, you do."

"Geoff, this is stupid. Stupid! It was a one night stand."

"We're at a week now."

"No. Don't you see? I'm not fixable. I don't fit in with you or the Arrowoods. I'm not the kind of wife you want."

"Never deny that you are Dulcinea."

Her face crumpled, and he knew she had recognized the quote from *The Man of La Mancha*. It's what Don Quixote had said to the woman of his heart when she had tried to convince him she was a tramp and not worthy of his affection.

But she had been worthy of it, and his foolish heroic belief in her was what had redeemed her. In the end it was what had saved Don Quixote as well.

"Open your eyes and see me as the woman I really am."

"You have shown me the beauty of the sky."

Cheris shook her head as a tear trailed down her face. She sniffed and wiped it away. "Take me home, Geoff. I can't live this impossible dream."

Geoff sighed and resisted the urge to break out in song of dreaming the impossible dream.

Okay, so maybe the *La Mancha* allusion had been too much. He should have gone with *The Sound of Music*. Cheris was more nun than whore, he supposed. But the voluptuous image of her at the pool had put him more in the mindset of Sophia Loren than Julie Andrews.

Without a word, Geoff followed her to the front door. They piled into his SUV without a word, and he drove them to her apartment. His soul screamed foul, but what could he do? He'd pushed her to the verge with the movie quotes, and he knew he needed to give her a little space to process what they'd said through Cervantes' truths.

Patience.

That's what he needed.

To give her time and space to realize she was his Dulcinea to her Don Quixote, his Maria to her Captain Von Trapp, his Princess Leia to her Han Solo.

Could he do it?

Yeah.

From two states away he was about to give her plenty of space.

Chapter Ten

"Well, that is another hope gone. My life is a perfect
graveyard of buried
hopes. That's a sentence I read in a book once, and I say it
over to comfort
myself whenever I'm disappointed in anything."
"I don't see where the comforting comes in myself," said
Marilla.
—*Anne of Green Gables* by L.M. Montgomery

Why hasn't Geoff called me?

Two whole days had gone by, and not even a text.

Was he living by the out of sight out of mind rule?
Had he so many things to take care of back in Georgia that
he hadn't bothered to call?

She *could* call him.

His number on the front of her refrigerator was
branded on her brain. Every time she walked in the kitchen
the neat handwriting drew her attention.

Sitting at her computer desk, she stretched. It was
nearly midnight, way past her bedtime, but she knew if she
lay down, she'd toss and turn. She was too restless,
too…what?

Unsettled.

She Googled Newbie River Institute, the school where
Geoff had said he worked. Finding the correct one, she
clicked on the link and found the menu for faculty and
staff.

Scrolling down the list, she saw him.

Dr. Geoff Arrowood, Ph.D.

Professor of Science and Astronomy

His office location, telephone extension, and an eddress were listed.

Logging onto her account, she sent an email.

Insomniac seeks Pool Boy for companionship. Cullsbaier natives only need apply.

She bit her lip as she pressed send. So, what's the worse that would happen? He'd get the email tomorrow and ignore it. What's the best? He'd get it tonight and email her back. Getting up from the desk, she wandered around her apartment. She picked up the remote and aimed it at the TV and flipped through the channels.

Nothing good.

Back at her computer, she got on Hip Granny's site. A large animated box, brightly wrapped with a bow danced across her monitor.

What was that about?

When she attempted to click on the gift box, it skirted away from her cursor and a timer appeared counting backwards a little less than twelve hours.

What was happening on Hip Granny at noon tomorrow?

She began to log in to her IT account when a pop-up screen appeared on her computer. Cheris smiled.

Pool boy has challenged you to a game of Intergalactic Monkey Wars. Do you wish to play?

The game site was one she had played on before. Logging on, she opened a chat box.

Who R U

Don Quioxote. Y no sleep?

Too much time. Not enough windmills to fight.

Easier 2 defeat space monkeys.

UR on

She clicked on the start game button and waited for Geoff on his end to do the same. In a few seconds, they began fighting the outer space primates. The battle and its heightened skill levels continued until a quarter to two when Geoff called it quits. The chat box appeared.

8am class in a few hours. Enjoyed the game.

Sorry to keep u up.

Don't be. I usually crash about 2 anyway, but any later and I'll sleep through the alarm.

Night owl?

Hoot. Hoot.

Call me tomorrow?

As is your command.

Cheris' heart skipped a beat as she read the words from her favorite movie. Did he realize only Gensa's lover responded to her orders that way? Her fingers moved over her keyboard.

Do I detect a movie quote?

Gensa's Genesis. Sweet dreams, General.

She sighed in appreciation for the man who quoted poetry and science fiction.

****

Cheris had been summoned.

By Annie Hill.

The older woman sat in her straight backed chair gazing with her wise owl eyes at Cheris who fidgeted with Annie's computer. The excuse to have Cheris find out why her Internet was not working had been just that.

An excuse.

Cheris had spotted the disconnected cord when she'd walked in the room. But she'd faked calm and dumb. Truth be told, Cheris was glad for the company. Here it was Monday afternoon, and with a whole week of no work stretching ahead of her, she was glad for something to do.

"How do you like being married?"

"It has its moments." Cheris dropped to her knees and crawled to the telephone outlet.

"When Bill gave you two weeks off, the intention was for you and Geoff to spend it together."

Well, here it was. The purpose of the summons.

Cheris picked up the cord and plugged the end into the receptacle.

"Virginia Lassiter recognized you in the grocery, and she plays bridge with Monnie and me. Monnie told everyone that you and Geoff are spending this week down in Georgia since he couldn't get the week off from teaching. Now I love Monnie, and I wouldn't want to see her embarrassed because her son and his wife are not being truthful with her."

Cheris turned and sat on the Persian rug crossing her legs. "Annie, Geoff and I did something really dumb when we got married."

Annie arched an eyebrow, Cheris raised her hands in surrender.

"My dear, if you're telling me marrying Geoffrey Arrowood was a mistake, I have to disagree."

"I'd never met him before that night. I was drunk."

Annie pursed her lips. "I find that very difficult to believe."

Annie knew Cheris' mother was an alcoholic, and Cheris had sworn never to drink in case she turned into one, too.

"Janie was one of the artists at the Children's Classic Literature Gala at the art museum. At the Alice in Wonderland exhibit I ate the cake—"

"And drank the punch, oh my heavens, you didn't." Annie clutched her chest. "The museum already has one suit against it because of that stunt Gary Sheirer pulled. Are you okay? Is Geoff? Is that all you two did? Run off and get married?"

"Running off and getting married was plenty. Somehow Geoff's mother found out and made that announcement at the party." Cheris sighed.

"Oh, my." She touched her head to her temple. "Oh, my dear. That's just the beginning of it. Have you seen Hip Granny today?"

"No."

Annie stood and approaching her desk, she moved the mouse. Instantly, the screen came to life.

Trying to ignore the panic rising in her chest, Cheris joined Annie in front of the computer as she clicked on the icon to connect to the World Wide Web. Instead of the familiar logo of Hip Granny's website, bells materialized. Church bells.

Wedding bells.

A fuzzy video morphed of a staircase with people standing on it.

The Arrowood family and Cheris.

Oh, no. Oh, no. No. No. No.

The scene Cheris had lived last week replayed on the monitor.

Monnie talking. The toast. Monnie and Chip kissing. More of Monnie talking.

The crowd egged her and Geoff to kiss. Geoff called to the crowd before Cheris quoted a line from *It's a Wonderful Life* and pecked him on the lips. The crowd jeered. Then....

The scene zoomed in on them gazing at each other. Geoff spoke to her.

"Are you sure?" he had said.

She nodded. "Yes, I'm sure," she'd said back. "Be quick about it."

And the not-quick-enough kiss began.

Cheris stared in fascination at the scene before her.

Her jaw dropped when she watched herself wrap her arms around the man and pull him closer. And on the kiss went. The catcalls and applause began. Finally, Geoff lifted his head breaking the contact.

Geoff. Not her.

Her stomach churned when words popped up on the screen.

Congratulations, Geoff and Cheris.

Enter the Whirlwind Wedding Workshop

The what?

Cheris reached forward and clicked the wedding bell icon. The screen changed to an unfocused scene of a church wedding and a menu containing everything from The Perfect Bridal Registry to Honeymoon Havens.

Bill Connor, the money-grubbing opportunist at Hip Granny, had been busy.

Cheris collapsed on the chair and moved her fingers across the mouse as she entered the how-to guide for planning the perfect wedding.

"Bill has launched Hip Granny into the wedding and marriage market," Annie informed her. "And as soon as your honeymoon is over, he's making you the spokesperson of it."

Cheris blinked at the screen. She shook her head. "No."

"I know you're not much on being in the spotlight, but Bill's been wanting to update Hip Granny's image for a while."

"Geoff and I aren't staying married, Annie. I'll make a terrible spokesperson."

"Just because you married in haste doesn't mean you and Geoff won't stay together. I think you make a lovely couple."

She turned to the older woman. "I can't believe you're saying that. You know what I came from."

Annie's eyes narrowed. "What do you mean?"

Cheris gestured to herself. "Come on. I've told you

about my childhood. I'm a bastard child out of Athens County."

Annie sniffed. "You've become better than just that, my dear."

"Maybe so, but I'll never fit in with eating petit fours on real bone china." Cheris stood and pushed the chair away from her. "Not ever. Excuse me, Annie. I've got to go." Picking up her purse, she marched out of the room.

****

Cheris drove over to Web Enterprises and bounded into Bill's office. He sat behind his desk with his ear plastered to his telephone yapping to some stupid person about Windfire web speed. She folded her arms and glared at him until he hung up and rounded the desk with arms outstretched.

"How's the wedded woman today, huh?"

Cheris pointed at him. "Don't you pull that with me. How dare you launch a marketing campaign using my marriage."

Bill rocked back on his heels. "Cheris, it's perfect." He grinned.

"No, it isn't. This is my life you're prostituting, and I won't have it. I'll quit before I let you use me and Geoff to pad Milton's Stewart's pockets."

Bill shook his head. "You've got me all wrong here. We're on borrowed time with Hip Granny. We need to—"

"'Keep it current. No flash in the pan for us.' I've heard it all before, and you're not going to use my private life to do it. I want that video taken off the site."

"Babe…"

Cheris shot him a murderous look at his endearment.

"Sorry. Cheris, that video is not your property."

"It's got me in it."

"And as an employee you signed a contract giving Net Enterprises permission to broadcast you on our website."

"For tutorials," she defended.

"In what capacity is not specified, especially when it is Stewart making the video."

"No way."

"Way, Mrs. Arrowood. This was his idea." Bill placed his hand on her shoulder, but she shook it off. He waved his hand to the door. "Now, then. This is still your honeymoon. People don't work on their honeymoon. When you get back next week, we'll negotiate your promotion."

Cheris raised her face in disdain. "I quit."

Bill threw his head back and laughed. "You want to resign? Come back next week and do it on company time."

"I'm serious."

"You might be, too, as I'm sure you'd like nothing better than to shop all day and live out the Cullsbaeir version of *Desperate Housewives*."

"I don't like you very much."

"You and my three ex-wives. Why don't you all start a club? Get. Get. Get. Out of here and the premises. Don't make me call security." He shooed her out of his office and closed the door behind her.

Cheris meandered through the building just so Bill wouldn't think he could bully her about *everything*. As she passed her cubicle, she ducked in it and sat at her chair. Pulling herself up to her monitor, she pressed the power button drumming her fingers impatiently on the keyboard as she waited for it to start.

Fine. He wouldn't take off the video. She would.

She logged in to her computer and entered her password.

A pop-up appeared on her screen.

Access denied

What?

"Sorry." Rhoderman Crantz, her co-worker, peered at her from over his side of the cubicle. "Bill made me wall your input until he meets with you next week."

"Rhoderman!"

He hung his head and peered at her with his big puppy dog eyes.

"Take it off."

"Can't. Bill said he'd fire me if you got access to Hip Granny. Said it'd be my personal failure."

Cheris beat the desk with her fist. "He won't fire you. Other than me, you're the best IT guy they have."

"Sorry." His sad face disappeared as he sunk back in his cubed rat hole.

She wrenched her chair back, stood, and stalked out of the building fury causing her teeth to clinch. Deciding to swim out some of her anger and frustration, she stopped by her apartment to get her suit and towel and headed to the Y.

After half an hour of laps in the pool, the edge of Cheris' anger had dissipated. In the locker room, she stripped off her swimsuit and pressed the towel to her damp skin.

Bill was smart. She'd give him that. He knew if she realized Rhoderman's job was on the line, she'd be less likely to hack the site.

Still.

Having her private life for all the world to view, especially when that private life was in shambles, was a nightmare.

Her cell phone dinged signaling reception of a text.

Cheris slid on her panties and bra before picking the phone up to read the message.

How R U?

Geoff.

Hmm. Did he know their kiss was all over the World Wide Web? Would he care?

She typed a message:

Grrrrr. Hate my boss.

Working?

Not allowed. Swimming @ Y now

Right now?

No. Changing n locker room right now.

Cheris grinned mischievously. Let him wonder what she was or was not wearing. She placed the phone down and finished getting dressed.

In seconds her phone dinged again.

Too bad, big boy. You'll have to wait, she thought as she reached for her pants.

Fully clothed, she read Geoff's text as she exited the locker room.

Unfair

Cheris chuckled. Since their pool disaster Friday night, she hadn't spoken to him though they'd played online battle ship and punch monkey several times.

On my way home. Wanna play a game in @ 10 mins?

Class in 3 mins. L8R @6?

K

She had just settled in her car when her phone rang. Was Geoff calling her now? She peered at the screen. No. It was a local cell number. She hit the answer button and greeted the caller.

"Mrs. Arrowood?" a man's voice asked.

"No...oh. Umm. Who are you looking for?"

"Is this Geoff's wife Cheris? I'm Larry Preston. We met the other night when you and Geoff had the police called on you at Lauren Cooper's house."

"Right. Yes. I remember you, Mr. Preston."

"Call me Larry. I got a hold of Geoff, but he tells me he's in Georgia. He gave me your number and said you might be willing to meet with me at Lauren's house."

Cheris stared through the windshield at the cars surrounding her and the YMCA building beyond. *What had Geoff done?*

"Mrs. Arrowood?"

Cheris huffed. Why did he have to call her that? "Cheris, please."

"Certainly, Cheris. When are you available?"

Cheris shook her head. "What is this about? If there was any damage—"

"No, no, no. Of course not. Nothing like that at all. Just a friendly visit at a beautiful home."

Yeah right.

"I can't speak for Geoff. If you have some business with him, perhaps you should wait until he comes back to town."

"I agree with you completely. Completely agree. But I'd like to meet with you today, and if Geoff and I have business at a later date, I sure as heck am going to meet with him when he gets back."

"I didn't do anything in that house other than swim, eat, and sit on the couch. We did walk through it, but I didn't mess with anything."

"Dear, Lauren's tickled pink that you enjoyed her house up until the police came, that is. I'd like to make that up to you."

"There's no need, Mr. P—"

"Larry. Come on. Don't make me beg here."

Cheris sighed. "I suppose I could meet you."

"Great. Wonderful. Are you free right now? I've got forty minutes that are yours if you want them."

Fine. Get it over with. Whatever *it* was.

"Very well. I can be there in about fifteen minutes."

"Fantastic, Cheris. You won't regret it."

"It's an offer I cannot refuse, Don."

"Huh? What was that?"

"Forget about it," she said in her best mobster voice, then, "I'll see you there, Larry."

When Cheris arrived at her dream house, Larry Preston was already there standing in front of the wrought iron gate leading to the front porch. He waved to her as she climbed out of her car.

With a jovial grin and an outstretched hand, he greeted her. "Well, Cheris, thanks for meeting me here." He grabbed her hand and squeezed instead of shaking it as she expected. "Come on in, and let's talk."

Ushering her inside, Larry's contented sigh echoed in the large room. "What a gorgeous set-up. A crying shame it's empty."

Standing with her hands clasped tightly in front of her, Cheris cast a quick longing glance around before settling on Larry.

He watched her, waiting. "What do you think?"

Never tell anyone other than the family what you're thinking.

But she wasn't *in* this family. The Arrowood family. Ugh.

"What can I do for you, Larry?"

The older man announced, "I'd like to see you and Geoff in this house."

Cheris' mouth dropped open. She shook her head.

"Now don't think this isn't doable because it is."

"It's not doable on levels you're not even aware of."

He crossed the tiled expanse of the pool room, and Cheris reluctantly followed. At the base of the wrought iron stairs he paused and gestured for her to precede him. The spiral staircase had been one she and Geoff hadn't taken the evening they spent here. She ascended the steps noting the sound of their shoes against the metal. On the landing she admired the water below them, remembering when she and Geoff had been there.

"You're renting an apartment now, isn't that right?" Larry said from behind her.

"Yes." Cheris glanced behind her at the man, but the

view in the plate glass windows snagged her attention. The house was on a hill overlooking the east side of Cullsbaeir and the bridge spanning the river beyond it.

Oh, wow.

"How'd you like to wake up to that view every morning?"

A sigh of appreciation escaped her lips.

"What if you lived here for what you and Geoff are paying there?"

Cheris turned away from the windows and gave Larry her best Annie Hill no-nonsense stare. "It's impractical. Sure, I could live here for what I'm paying in rent, but the cost of electricity and gas in a place like this is exorbitant, I bet."

"There's a gas well on the lot so the cost of heating the house and water is non-existent. The air conditioner is state of the art. All of the bulbs are LED. You belong in this house."

"This house is too big for one person."

Larry's eyebrow's rose in surprise.

"Even two people," Cheris added hastily. "This house needs a big family in it. Or several. Maybe one of those families on that reality show with three wives and twenty kids."

Larry didn't take the hint. He led her on a tour of the house spouting its attributes. Once he'd shown her the rooms inside, he took her outside to the back of the house with its smooth bricked patio and built in barbecue grill. Rounding the house they entered the front yard, and Cheris' tree swing came into view.

Larry walked right up to the swing and grasped the chain hanging from the branch above. "This house deserves someone to live in it. To love it," he declared.

"That someone's not me."

"You live in the apartments over in Cullsbaeir Terrace, right? In three months their rent is going to increase by seventy dollars."

Cheris had recently received a letter about it. "How do

you know that?"

"I'm a realtor. It's my business to know. I'll put you in this house for what you'll be paying at Cullsbaeir Hills in three months with a three hundred dollar cap on electricity per month."

"Look. Just because you know Geoff's family—"

Larry shook his head. "It's not personal. It's business. I start cutting deals for all my fraternity brothers, I won't be able to make my own mortgage which will make my wife very unhappy."

"You'll lose money on this deal."

He nudged the swing a bit, and it moved back and forth. "An empty house is a loss, and I think there's a lot of potential here, Cheris."

The motion of the swing drew her eye. She knew there was potential here. She yearned for the house, its space and beauty. The swing. The pool. The unique architecture of the open rooms. All of these things called to her like a siren song.

Cheris wasn't stupid. Larry was making this deal too sweet, an offer she really couldn't refuse.

It's not personal. It's business, he'd said.

No doubt. If Geoff wasn't behind this, his parents had to be. They had the means to pay whatever it took to set their son up with his new bride. And Cheris may be hillbilly trash, but she could *not* be bought.

She took a shuddering breath and stuck her arm forward. "Thank you, Larry," she said as they shook hands. Stepping back, she settled the strap of her purse on her shoulder. "I'll talk to Geoff about this."

Boy would she ever.

"Great. And don't forget my open block party this weekend. If you win that TV, you can mount it in the pool room. Watch TV while you swim."

Cheris marched to her car without looking back at Larry, the tree, or the house.

Pulling into the lot of her apartment complex, she parked and walked to the bank of boxes to check her mail.

Pulling a square linen envelope from the slot, she peered at the name on the front.

Cheris Arrowood

Gritting her teeth, she turned the envelope over and tore open its scalloped seal. For a moment Cheris stared at the pearl white card with its filigree border inviting her to a celebration of the marriage of Geoffrey Watkins Arrowood, III to Cheris Leigh McDowell.

What?

A small crisp paper with a monogrammed *A* on the top fluttered to the floor. Stooping to pick it up, Cheris read the loopy script:

Cheris,

I hated to bother you two on your honeymoon, so I went ahead with the after-the-fact wedding shower. Hope this date suits you and Geoff. I've sent out about eighty and can send out as many more as you need if you want to give me addresses ASAP as you notice the date is in two weeks!

Hugs and kisses,
Monnie

P.S. If you and Geoff haven't already, register for your patterns. Please do so today. Hip Granny has the links to the stores ☺

No, no, no!

Why was everything today about throwing her and Geoff together in this marriage?

Cheris stalked to her car, started it up, and drove to Janie's. Janie had twenty-nine years of dealing with Monnie Arrowood. Maybe she could help Cheris figure out how to rein in the woman.

At Janie's studio Cheris stood immobilized at the door's threshold and surveyed the disaster before her. Broken pieces of Janie's sculptures littered the floor. Black paint had been splashed and poured on her paintings and the walls.

Who would have done such a terrible thing?

Breaking into a run, she hurried to the office noting

the destruction in the back hall as well. Turning the knob to the smaller room, Cheris opened the door. She expected to find the computer and camera missing, but everything was in order except for Janie slumped on the desk.

"Janie, are you all right?"

The other woman raised her head revealing mascara smeared tear trails down her blotched cheeks.

Cheris knelt next to her friend. "What happened? Are you hurt?"

"Get out of here, and leave me alone." She put her head back down on her folded arms resting on the desk's top.

"No way. I'm calling the police." Cheris stood and reached for the cordless telephone on the desk.

"You're not calling anybody." Janie straightened and snatched the phone out of Cheris' hand. She slammed it down on the recharger. Wiping her cheeks and sniffing, she said, "Nothing happened. I'm fine."

"You're not fine. Look at you. Look at your studio. Your beautiful art, oh, Janie."

"Don't. Don't do that. Don't say anything about it."

"But we've got to call the police. Somebody destroyed—"

Janie stared at her paint-blackened hands. "No."

"Why?"

"Because I hate it. I hate it, and it's a lie."

Cheris shook her head in confusion. "What's a lie? What do you hate?"

"The painting. The sculpting. I've been lying about everything all this time, and I...I'm never painting again."

"You don't mean that. I know this is your work. I've watched you paint and sculpt."

"I've worked my whole life to be who I am, to play by my own rules."

"Yeah. What's changed?"

"Everything. Me. I can't do this." With shaking hands, she covered her face.

"Do what? What's changed? Did Bobby hurt you?"

"No. I ditched that loser."

"He did this."

"No. I did it! I've trashed everything here because none of it means anything to me anymore. I have to give it up."

Cheris pulled Janie's hands away from her face. Peering into her friend's eyes, she grasped her fingers tightly. "Tell me what happened."

"I think I'm in love with...with David Denton."

"Who?" The name clicked in her memory. David was Kelly's minister friend from Clarksdale who had caught Janie when she'd fallen off the chair. "Oh." Cheris hid her surprise. "Well. I think it's great."

"You would. But I'm not going to...I'm not doing that."

"Why not? He seems like a sweet guy."

Janie wrenched her hands out of Cheris' grasp. "He's a preacher, Cheris!"

"Right. Not a priest. He's allowed to date. Have you guys been out on a date?"

"You don't get it, do you? He's a minister. In a church."

"What? You're not good enough to date a minister?"

Janie moved her chair back and pushed past Cheris. She turned to face her friend. "No, I'm not. I don't fit into that lifestyle. I'm a rebel, a dissident, an artist."

Cheris straightened and sat in the chair Janie vacated. "I guess he likes his women a little wild, huh?"

"It's not funny."

"Come on, Janie. Enjoy a guy who is nice for once. It's not like you're going to marry him or anything."

Janie stared at her friend. She blinked, and a tear rolled down her cheek.

What?

"Did he ask you to marry him?"

"No, but I...I've...." She glanced at the ceiling and ran a hand through her disheveled hair. "I get what happened with you and Geoff now. I know why he drove you to

Serenity. I saw his face the night of the gala when he looked at you. I lived that look the day in the church nursery. I looked at David, and it was like my soul was ripped open. I knew he was the one."

Cheris shook her head in disbelief. "Marriage is more than a soulful feeling. If you're talking about a lifetime commitment, you need more than a...a look. You need common interests, goals, dreams."

"Now you're beginning to see my dilemma."

"So, you think your only choices are to give up your art, or give up David?"

"Can you honestly see me as a preacher's wife? The church will take one look at me and David will be out on his ear."

"You don't give the church people enough credit. You're a good person."

"I'm not good enough for that. I'll screw up, and he'll suffer for it. I care too much about him to do that." She picked up a wood and clay prototype piece from her Secret Garden exhibit and threw it through the open doorway where it hit the wall in the hallway and fell in pieces to the floor.

Cheris sighed. "Come on," she said rising from the chair. "Let's get out of here before you destroy everything." She grabbed her friend's hand and pulled her toward the front. "Don't touch anything else." She pulled the curtains across the plate glass windows, thankful Janie had installed them when she moved her studio to the storefront property. "I'll cover this mess so nobody calls the cops until you can get your head on straight."

Cheris took Janie to her apartment and pushed her into the bathroom to clean up. While there, she noticed all signs of Bobby had been removed. He'd obviously moved out, but when? After Janie had met David? Why hadn't she said anything before now?

When Janie emerged later after showering and putting on fresh clothes, she seemed calmer though reserved. Cheris ordered Chinese food, and they ate it on the floor while watching Animal Planet.

At nine that evening, she drove Janie back to the studio to get her car and made the woman promise she would call her if she needed her.

"I'm your friend. Let me be there for you, okay? Want to come home with me?"

Janie shook her head.

"Sure?"

"Yeah, I'm sure. Thanks."

"All right. Go home and get some rest. Things always look better in the morning."

Janie nodded and climbed into her car. Without any other words, she shut the door, started the engine and left.

Cheris rolled her shoulders then stepped to her own car.

What a day.

She drove home with thoughts of Janie in love with a minister and she and Geoff living in the dream house running through her mind.

At home she saw an invitation to play a game from Geoff on her computer.

Oh, yeah. They'd had a net date at six.

Not that she was in any mood to do anything with him other than bite his head off. They were in a hole so deep with this marriage, she wasn't sure they'd ever get out.

Picking up her phone, she saw a missed call from him around seven but no message. Why wouldn't he leave a message? She hated people who didn't leave messages.

If he wants me to call him back, then he needs to let me know.

Timmy strolled in the room and meowed a greeting. Cheris reached down, picked him up, and settled on the couch with him.

"That's right," she crooned as she stroked his snowy fur. "You're the kind of man I like. Uncomplicated."

Timmy purred in response.

Chapter Eleven

It made her think that it was curious how much nicer a
person
looked when he smiled. She had not thought of it before.
—*The Secret Garden* by Frances Hodgson Burnett

"Cheris."

Cheris awoke from a sound sleep.

What?

She blinked in the darkness of her bedroom and
looked at her digital clock.

12:15 am.

"Are you awake?" Janie asked.

"What?" She sat up to find her friend sitting at the
foot of her bed. "How'd you get in here?"

"I broke in. Hey, listen, I've been thinking about what
you said, and I know what we need to do."

"Huh?"

"Road trip." Jumping up, Janie switched on the
overhead light.

"Turn that off! I'm trying to sleep here."

Janie opened a dresser drawer, pulled out clothes, and
tossed them on the bed. Another drawer open, and more
clothes.

"What are you doing? Stop that."

"We'll just get in the car and drive. Won't that be fun?"

"I can't go anywhere, Janie. Would you stop?" Cheris
crawled across the bed and caught a shirt Janie had thrown.

"Why can't you go? I thought you had two weeks off."
She peered on the shelf in the closet. "Where's your

suitcase?"

"I can't leave Timmy." Cheris began refolding the clothes and putting them in piles.

"He's a cat. Put out extra food and water. He won't even know you're gone." Closing the door, she walked out of the bedroom. "Aha. Found it." She returned a moment later with the suitcase Cheris stored in the hall closet.

"Where do you want to go?" She slid off the bed with a stack of clothes in her arms intending to put them back where they belonged.

"What's it matter? We get in the car and drive. It's a road trip. The point is getting the hell out of here for a while. When we get tired, we'll stop."

"Look, Janie, you're welcome to stay here with me, but I'm not getting in the car in the middle of the night and driving across country because you have the hots for a preacher man. It's insane."

****

Their road trip ended in Cider Falls, Georgia, the city where Geoff lived and worked. Asleep in the passenger seat since about three in the morning, Cheris had awoken as the sun had risen over the north Georgia mountains.

Janie swore she hadn't planned this.

"I just sort of pointed the car, and here we are," she defended. "And, hey, even better. We can stay at Geoff's."

"I am *sick* and tired of everybody trying to throw us together," Cheris groused as they entered the city limits.

"You are so grumpy when you haven't had enough sleep. Want to see where he works, or go by his house?"

"Maybe we should call and warn him that we're here."

"No. Let's surprise him."

"Where is he now?"

"It's after eight. I bet he's at school. He's such a conformist."

"I certainly don't want to go to his house if he's not there."

"Why not? I can get in."

"I know, but it isn't nice to break into people's

homes."

"He's my brother. He doesn't care. Besides, I'm wiped out. I'm ready to crash."

Cheris grabbed her cell phone and opened a text box.

Janie and I are in Cider Falls. Where R U?

She waited for a response but didn't get one.

"Here's the campus," Janie declared as she turned left onto a long straight road lined with Bradford Pear trees fully in bloom.

"Oh, my gosh," Cheris breathed at the beauty of the white blossoms blanketing the trees.

"I know. Aren't they gorgeous?"

A majestic white building stood at the end of the row, and Janie guided the car into a parking space marked *visitor* in front of it. Exiting the car, the two women ascended the smooth stone stairs to the massive black double doors in front of them.

"This doesn't look much like an institute," Cheris commented alluding to the name of the school as they walked through the entrance to an open room four stories high lined with balconies on each level with doors beyond. Their tennis shoes squeaked on the polished marble floor as they walked across the room to a door beyond.

"We'll cut through here. The science building is on the back campus."

Soon they found their way to Geoff's closed office door. Janie grasped the knob and pushed the door open.

"Don't you ever knock?" Cheris asked. "What if he's in there with a student?"

"He's not." Janie stepped into the book-lined room and settled on the couch under a window on the far wall. She lay back and closed her eyes. "His schedule's posted on the door. Why don't you see if he lectures any better than he swims?"

Peering at the printed sheet, Cheris' eyes followed her finger across the page to Tuesday morning.

AST 191 Room 108 B

Wonder what AST 191 is? Or where I could find room 108B?

"You think he'd mind if I sat in his class?"

"No, he wouldn't care. Close the door, will you?" Janie curled on her side with her back to Cheris who went to find Geoff's class.

In a few moments she stepped inside the door of the large amphitheater and stood waiting for her sight to adjust to the darkness. Cheris walked the few steps to a theater seat in the back row and watched the stop motion movie playing on a large screen in the front of the room. A rap song belted out the lyrics of *Bang You Hard* while oddly shaped objects hurtled toward a brightly striped ball in front of a black background. With each impact a cloud shot out from the ball.

Oh, I get it. That's something hitting a planet in outer space.

The scene morphed to clay people hunched around a toy computer screen. They jumped up and down in delight, and a ripple of laughter spread throughout the room.

Credits began rolling across the screen, and the lights came up.

Geoff, dressed in khakis and a buttoned down navy blue shirt walked away from the wall, grinning widely.

Cheris' heart flip-flopped at the sight of him so handsome and...there.

"Well, great job, Group One, also known as the Organic Rock Stars. Come stand here with me, and we'll see how well your film taught the class." Three women and three men—all looking to be fresh out of high school— came to stand in the front of the room. Geoff walked across the low stage as the screen rose behind him. He picked up a large bag of candy from the edge of a desk next to the wall. "Okay, your reward for correct answers will be Jolly Ranchers in a variety of flavors."

He held the bag in one arm and reached into it with his other hand. "First question, what's the name of the planet in the movie?"

"Jupiter," came an enthusiastic voice in the front row.

"You got it." Jeff threw a piece of candy to the student.

"Who were the astronomers looking through the telescope at the beginning?"

"Shoemaker and Levy."

Geoff gazed at the woman who had answered. "There were three clay figures. You've only given me two names."

"Shoemaker, Shoemaker, and Levy."

Geoff threw three pieces of candy to her. "I'll give you three more pieces if you can tell me first names."

She groaned.

"Who can?"

"Eugene, Carolyn, and David. Can I have three green ones?" hollered a man sitting on the aisle stairs.

Geoff fished in the bag and tossed them.

"Next question. What did they discover?"

"A comet!"

"Called?"

"Shoemaker-Levy Nine."

"Two candies for two correct answers."

"Can I have watermelon?"

"You guys are getting too picky." Geoff sorted through the bag and withdrew the requested flavor. "I'm going to switch back to Tootsie-rolls if you keep it up. What year did Shoemaker-Levy Nine slam into Jupiter?"

There was a pause.

"Come on. It was subtle, but it was in there. Anybody catch the clip of the top grossing movie of that year Organic Rock Stars included in their clay masterpiece?"

"Nineteen ninety-four."

"Got it, Erin." Geoff dispensed the prize.

"Okay, ready for the bonus question. If you get it right, our Organic Rock Stars will have earned an A for their group project. What's the difference between a comet and an—" Geoff's gaze fell on Cheris and held. The relaxed expression and easy smile disappeared as he stared at the woman in the last row. A Jolly Rancher fell from the bag followed by another until a steady stream poured to the floor unnoticed by Geoff.

One by one every student turned in their chairs to find

out what had captured the attention of their teacher. Cheris glanced at the curious faces of forty students before returning her gaze to the man with the empty candy bag.

The Organic Rock Stars gathered up the spilled treats.

Finally, Geoff looked down as one of the students tugged the bag from his grasp. "Oh. Thanks. Thanks." He strode over to the blackboard and began erasing it as several students leaned into each other and whispered. The murmurs increased with frequent head turns in her direction.

Cheris bit her lip as she watched him stretch his arm in wide sweeps. This was a mistake. What had she been thinking coming in here and interrupting his class?

With the board clean, he sat on top of the desk next to the wall on the low stage. Taking off his glasses, he placed them next to him and rubbed his eye. "Let's get quiet." He rapped on the wooden top. "Where were we? Oh, yes. Charles? You're group leader of the Organic Rock Stars. If we get a right answer to the difference between a comet and an asteroid, you dispense the candy. All right?"

"Yes, sir."

"Great. How about it? What's the difference?"

"The comet is mainly ice, and the meteor is rock."

"Great job, Josh. Okay, Charles, throw Josh a Jolly Rancher. Let's give the Organic Rock Stars a hand for their Grade A movie."

Cheris joined in the class in applauding the students who grinned and preened at the praise.

Geoff gripped the edge of the desk as he waited for the applause to die down. "Thursday we'll see presentations from Interplanet Janets and Zeus' Realm. Class dismissed."

The students rose from their chairs and filed to the stairs lining the stadium seats. As they passed Cheris, each studied her with curious or amused expressions on their faces. She touched her fingers to her burning forehead and ignored them. She turned to Geoff who still sat on the desk, his glasses lying beside him.

As the last of the students left the room, excited voices

reached her from outside the door. Cheris listened as Geoff placed his glasses on his nose and sprinted up the stairs.

"Who was that?"

"Dr. Arrowood's girlfriend!"

"Didn't you notice? He's wearing a wedding ring. She's not his girlfriend. She's his wife."

"He got married over Spring break? Killer."

Geoff shot past her and closed the door sighing audibly when the barrier shut out the noise. Grinning as he reached the stair next to her, he entered the row below her and stepped over the chair to occupy the one next to her. His smile and the welcoming twinkle in his eyes made her heart flop once again.

"Hi."

Another flop.

"Hey."

"So, is this business or pleasure?"

Cheris shrugged. "Why did you remove your glasses?"

"So I wouldn't be tempted to watch you while I finished the class."

"I'm sorry… I shouldn't have come."

"What? Because you distracted me? Don't be. This is a great day to be here. They're presenting their mid-term projects. It's a fun class to sit in on. And I don't have another class until seven o'clock tonight. I'm yours until then."

"Mine and Janie's. She's asleep in your office."

"Uh-oh. What happened?"

"What do you mean?"

"She usually shows up when she's upset about something."

"She's…umm… She has a new boyfriend, and she doesn't think she's good enough for him."

"Hmmm."

"I found her at her studio. She completely trashed it."

Geoff shook his head. "I hope the new boyfriend is a step up from Bobby."

"The new boyfriend is about forty stories up from

Bobby."

"Good. Have you seen much of the campus? I'd love to show you around."

Two hours later Cheris stood in the middle of a massive field staring at a series of white iron bars which formed a large dome high above her head. It was supported by a perfectly circular base with numbers stenciled on it.

Geoff lifted his arm and pointed. "These trace the path of the sun. This one is the line across the sky of the Summer solstice, that one the Winter solstice, and the middle one is the equinox path."

"Hmm," Cheris said pursing her lips. "I always thought the sun just moved from east to west."

"Generally, that's true, but depending on the season of the year, the sun's path is a few degrees north or south of due east to west."

"Did you build this?"

"Mostly." He stood with hands resting on one of the bars above his head. "I did have some help from an Astronomy for Educators class and several shop students. What do you think?"

"I think it's pretty cool. Will you be sorry to leave it when you move?"

Geoff shook his head as his gaze rested on her face. "It'll give me a chance to build a new one in Cullsbaeir."

"Speaking of Cullsbaeir. I don't really appreciate being bullied into living in the pool house."

Geoff dropped his arms. "What are you talking about? Who's bullying you?"

"You or your parents. Larry Preston was pulling a Godfather act with me trying to get me to move in."

"An offer you couldn't refuse, huh? He did call me yesterday wanting to meet with us. I told him I was here. He said, 'My business is really with your wife anyway. Can I have her number?' I gave it to him. I'm sorry about that. I should have asked you first. As far as Mom and Dad are concerned, I don't think they've spoken with him since the party. Mom's not a big fan of his."

"Really?"

"Yeah. He divorced one of her friends and married a much younger woman."

Cheris ducked beneath the rim supporting the iron beams and strolled toward a large circle paved with white rocks. As she neared the display, she studied the neatly painted numbers on the stones.

"This looks like a clock."

"It is."

"What happened to the hands?"

"We're the hands." Geoff who had joined her caught her fingers and tugged her toward the middle of the circle. "It's a sun dial actually, and luckily it's a sunny day." Sliding his hands to her shoulders, he nudged her to the left and pointed to the ground.

Cheris's skin tingled where he touched her. She watched their melded shadow where he pointed. Behind her his breath stirred her hair as he spoke.

"We're nearing eleven now. See?"

Eleven o'clock on the rock.

"This is really neat. Did you do this too?"

"Not exactly." His shadow broke away from hers. "I give most of my classes a group project assignment to benefit the community."

Cheris turned to watch him stride over to rock seven. He knelt down and repositioned it.

"Who will take care of this after you leave?"

Straightening, he stepped back as he studied the rock then approached it again to move it. He nodded briefly. "All of this belongs to the Institute so they'll mow the grass, and there's a pretty active astronomy club here so they'll keep it up at least for a while."

Cheris covered her mouth as she yawned.

"Tired or bored?"

"Tired. Sorry. Janie drove the whole way, but it's hard to get good sleep in the car."

"Come on then." Geoff stood with hands in pockets. The sun glinted on his glasses making it hard to see his expression. "We'll go by the office and get Janie, then you two can go on to the house and take a nap if you want."

"I'm sorry," Cheris said as they walked toward the science building.

"Don't be. I'm glad you're here. Both of you."

****

Geoff treated Janie and Cheris to a quick lunch before they headed to his house. The modern one story gray shuttered house barely registered as Cheris climbed the five stairs to the front porch. She followed Janie into what the woman had deemed 'my room', a neat space with a double bed, a cabinet, and an easel propped in the corner. Wild, colorful pictures of people on a main street setting dominated one wall of the room with another wall depicting a graphic scene of corpses in various states of decay.

Cheris didn't think she could sleep in here with the grotesque figures, but Janie pointed her to the other side of the bed which faced a blank wall with the cabinet and a window. They lay down, and to her surprise, Cheris fell asleep almost immediately.

When she awoke later that afternoon, Janie was gone. Cheris sat on the edge of the bed orienting herself to where she was.

Oh, right. Georgia. Geoff's house. Janie's room.

Cheris glanced back at the skeleton wall.

Ick.

She stood and walked out of the room closing the door softly behind her. Hearing jazzy music, she followed the sound to Geoff's living room where Janie sprawled across a leather recliner and Geoff sat at an oak desk in the corner typing at a computer.

She was about to speak when a framed painting on the wall caught her eye. Drawn to the yellow and golden hues she approached the picture.

Her jaw dropped as she recognized the woman lying in a suggestive pose on the wheat-painted field.

She turned accusing eyes to Janie who had risen from

174

her chair and shifted from one foot to the other refusing to meet her stare. Beyond her Geoff had joined them as well. With crossed arms he gazed at the framed print with a satisfied smile on his face.

"What is this, Janie?" Cheris demanded.

"It's just a picture I did last year."

"Of me asleep?"

"It's not exactly you. The face is—"

"Geoff, do you think this looks like me?"

"Yes."

Janie glared at her brother. "How about helping me out here, Bro?"

Geoff shrugged. "I'm not going to lie. It looks exactly like her."

"I've never been asleep in a field. When did you do it?"

"It...it..." Janie sighed. "You were at the apartment one night, and you fell asleep on the couch. You were so cute all curled up that I took a few pictures then converted them in this painting program I was fooling around with. Geoff saw it at the studio and really liked it so I gave it to him for Christmas."

"How could you?"

"Well, I didn't mean for anybody to really have it. I just needed a subject, and it's your fault for falling asleep with that yellow shirt on and your red hair. The colors were too good, and the curves of your boobs against the—"

"Janie!"

"Well, not like that. The curves and lines worked really well. It's not like a painted you naked or anything. If I'd done that, it really wouldn't have been you since I've never seen—"

Cheris smacked her friend on the arm. "Don't you even think about painting me without clothes on. I will kill you."

"Oww."

"It is beautiful."

Cheris' face burned at Geoff's comment. "Didn't you think you should have told me, asked me for permission?"

"It's not you. Not really." Janie placed her hand over the eyes and nose of the picture. "See? Your face is not this narrow. And that mouth? So not yours. I had to redo it because you were drooling in your sleep."

"It's my mouth only closed."

"You think?" Janie squinted at the painting then shook her head. Turning to Cheris, she grasped the woman's face between her fingers. "Relax your mouth and let me see."

Cheris shook off her friends hands. "Stop it. I am so mad at you right now."

"And you." She turned to Geoff. "Why didn't you tell me Janie... Wait a minute. Last Christmas? You've had this since last Christmas?"

Geoff nodded.

"But you...you didn't even know me then."

"It's one of Janie's best, I think. I didn't really know it was a real person until I recognized you on *Hip Granny*."

Cheris shook her head in astonishment. "But it just seems too much of a coincidence."

"It is too much of one. She was always talking about *Cheris this* and *Cheris that*. One day Janie was bragging about you being a computer guru, that Hip Granny had just posted a podcast of you. I got on there, watched it, and there was Woman in Gold."

"Woman in Gold?"

"The name of the painting," Janie supplied.

"Oh." Cheris sighed. "When you saw me at the gala, you knew exactly who I was."

"Yes."

She waved her arm at the wall before turning her back on it and glared at Janie. "You set me up."

"I didn't make you eat that Alice in Wonderland crap then twist your arm to go all wedding bell crazy with my brother. That was your doing."

"Promise me you'll never use my likeness again without asking me."

"Okay."

"Really promise. Pinky swear."

"What are we in fourth grade?"

Cheris held out her hand. "Do it."

Janie huffed but hooked her finger through her friend's. "Okay. Pinky swear."

****

The light clicked on waking Cheris up with its brightness.

"What are you doing?" Cheris groused as she squinted at her wrist watch. "It's the middle of the night."

"Sorry. I needed the light," Janie said without a smidgeon of repentance as she stood in the room and stared at the door.

"What's wrong?"

"Nothing's wrong. I'm going to paint." She opened the cabinet revealing shelves of tubes of paint, brushes, and jars.

"Right now?"

"Yeah." Taking a charcoal pencil, she sketched a long flowing line across the white wall.

"How am I supposed to sleep?"

"Get in Geoff's bed." Sitting on the floor, Janie quickly drew a clawed foot resting on the baseboard.

"I'm not sleeping with him."

"He's not here. He left about an hour ago."

Cheris sat up. "Why?"

"He's a geek. He spends most nights with his eye stuck to a telescope. He'll never know you're using his bed." Another claw and a reptilian leg.

"What if he comes back?"

"Then keep it down when you jump him. I don't want any distractions." A second leg with a disturbingly large dewclaw.

Cheris threw back the covers. Why couldn't Geoff have a couch? Who owns a house and not a couch? It was absurd. She could stretch out on his recliner, she supposed.

"Do you know where he keeps his blankets?"

Janie exhaled in exasperation. She stomped over to the bed, grabbed the comforter and a pillow and shoved it in

Cheris' hands. "Here, though I don't know why you need it. Geoff's bed is plenty warm, I bet." She returned to the wall scraping the charcoal up in a graceful mark against the white paint.

"Why am I friends with you?"

"Because you've got very bad taste in friends. Now quit bugging me before I lose this picture."

Cheris trudged to the living room to settle herself in one of the two recliners. Though it was dark, she could still make out most of her picture. She sighed as she stared at it. Janie had done a beautiful job.

Still.

It bothered Cheris to think about Janie painting it on the sly and it hanging on Geoff's wall all this time.

Minutes or hours later she awoke when the sound of the garage door opened then shut. Shortly thereafter Geoff walked into the dark room from the kitchen paused, then continued on into the hallway. Low voices and silence. Cheris shifted and slept until the aroma of coffee beckoned her.

When she entered the kitchen, Geoff leaned against the counter sipping from a mug. He set it down when she approached.

"Good morning. I see Janie's midnight inspiration drove you out of the bedroom. Want some coffee?"

"Sure. What time did you get in?"

"Just before two. Want to come to work with me? Janie's not going to be much company today." Geoff poured her a cup of coffee and added some creamer from the refrigerator. He set it on the counter and gestured for her to take it.

So when had he learned how she drank her coffee?

"What do you mean?"

"She's in OCA mode." At Cheris' questioning look, he continued. "Obsessive Compulsive Artist. She'll paint and sleep until she's done with the wall. I've been through this several times with her. After she painted a scene of Auschwitz in the living room, I made her paint over it and relegated her to the guest bedroom for any future tormented artist inspirations."

Cheris grimaced. "I thought sleeping in there would give me nightmares."

"Yeah. The skeleton pile was after Dad had his heart attack. The people on the street is nice enough. She painted it when she came down for our twenty-fifth birthday."

"What about Auschwitz?"

Geoff took a sip of his coffee before he answered. "She had some difficult things to happen around the time of her college graduation."

Oh.

Once Cheris had commented on a dark scene Janie had painted in black, red, and gray which hung in Janie's apartment. Janie had told her she'd named the picture Kaylis, in memory of a classmate that had been murdered a week before they graduated. Deciding Geoff's vague answer was a cue not to pry, Cheris changed the subject.

"I can hang out in the library at the Institute so I wouldn't be in your way."

Geoff set his coffee cup on the counter and crossed his arms as he regarded her. "You're welcome to stay in my office or sit in on any of my classes. We have an impressive media center and computer work-up station on campus."

Cheris brushed a strand of hair out of her face. "Do I have time to take a shower and get ready?"

Geoff checked his watch. "I leave in forty-five minutes. If you need more time, I can meet you over there."

"That's enough time."

****

Geoff exhaled the breath he hadn't realized he'd been holding when he heard the bathroom door close down the hall.

When Cheris had walked in the kitchen looking all rumpled and sexy, it had taken all Geoff had not to take her in his arms and kiss her. Instead, he'd played it cool and poured her coffee. He'd taken deep breaths and thought

179

about chemical compositions instead of oogling the length of legs exposed past the cotton shorts she wore.

Knowing she was in the bedroom down the hall had been enough to keep him awake until he'd thrown on some clothes and gone out to the observatory until he could barely keep his eyes open. Now that Janie was in full artist mode, she was going to be little help as a chaperone. And if she kept to her M.O. she'd up and disappear as soon as the wall was done without a word leaving Cheris here with him.

On their honeymoon.

How was he supposed to give her space to fall in love with him when she was sleeping in his front room and wandering around the house in shorts showing her killer legs?

Driving with Cheris to Newbie River had Geoff so distracted he ran a red light. She'd worn a skirt which came mid-thigh when she sat next to him in the car.

Plowing into another car because he couldn't keep his attention on the road was not an option.

He decided to mentally plot star courses until they got to the college.

Once there he parked and they walked across campus to the math and science building. His basic physics class met first, and Cheris found a chair in the back row amid whispers, Geoff had no doubt, concerning her presence.

To his surprise he made no mistakes during the lecture and went through a third of a bag of dum-dum suckers as he quizzed the students over the content of their reading and notes.

All with his glasses on.

And only a few glances to her legs.

When all the students had gone, Cheris strolled to the front of the room. "How come you use a chalkboard?"

"Because I like a chalkboard."

"But there's a Smartboard in this room." She sat down at the computer on the desk and began typing. The light on the smart projector illuminated the smooth surface on the screen.

Yeah. He'd had the same gripe from the department chair, not to mention unearthing the portable chalkboard from the furnace room at the beginning of each semester.

"A chalkboard is more efficient, and I'm not limited by the Smartboard programmers."

She clicked her tongue in disapproval. "You're missing some great opportunities by refusing to use the technology readily available to you." Coming around the desk, she picked up the marker from its holder.

Janie was right. Cheris looked beautiful in yellow. Her shirt skimmed her curves and rested at her hip. She reached up and touched the pen icon then turned to him.

"Whatever you write will be more attractive in color."

Geoff smiled. Exactly what he had been thinking though he'd have a little more color with her hair not pinned up.

"And you can easily pull up a picture to illustrate your point."

She touched another icon, and a keyboard appeared. She pecked out the word molecule, then chose a model from a list.

"See?"

"I can draw that in less time than it takes you to find it. And besides." Geoff picked up another marker. "This is wrong. The proportions are off." He drew a similar model. "This is more accurate."

Cheris studied the two models then touched another icon at the top of the board. She moved her marker over the first picture and changed the size of the nucleus. "There. They're the same now."

"Why would I want to go to all of that trouble when I can draw my own accurate model in the first place?"

"Because it's more interesting in color. And you can't draw a photograph of Jupiter on a chalkboard."

"True enough. But unless you need to show a photograph or a complex picture, a chalkboard is the better choice. It's simple and unpretentious. If the electricity or the wireless goes out, that Smartboard is useless."

"If the electricity goes out, your students won't be able to see the chalkboard to take notes."

Geoff walked over to the window and opened the blinds. "Sure they can."

Cheris blinked at him. "You'd continue with class even with the electricity out?"

"Why wouldn't I? Unless it's a night class, there's no reason not to."

"There won't be any air conditioning or heat."

Geoff shrugged. "It'll take a good half-hour for there to be a noticeable temperature change in most of the classrooms. And anyway, if the students are a little uncomfortable, they're more likely to stay awake and listen."

"They're not going to listen to you. They're going to be thinking how cold or hot they are."

Geoff tapped his chin thoughtfully. "Hmm. That might be a good experiment to have one of the study groups to undertake. If they learn better all warm and cozy with their blankies or in a straight chair with their feet in ice buckets."

Cheris giggled. "I hope you're kidding."

"Sort of. The Institutional Review Board frowns on the professors performing experiments on their students. However I have found my classes learn better when food is involved as a reward."

"So that's what the candy is about?"

"Yeah. It also encourages participation and makes me seem less like an ogre who would continue lecturing even if the lights go out."

Cheris flashed him a smile that made his knees wobble. He pulled a sucker out of the bag on the desk and held it out to her.

"What's this for?" she asked as she took it from him. "I didn't answer any questions."

"For a lively debate." *And looking like springtime in front of the Smartboard.* "I've got a committee meeting in ten minutes. Want to meet up for lunch in the cafeteria?"

"Sure."

Chapter Twelve

"Oh my ears and whiskers how late it's getting!"
—*Alice in Wonderland* by Lewis Carroll

Obviously people had taken notice of Cheris and her connection with Geoff. He'd fielded several questions at the faculty meeting earlier in the day hoping to put off the inevitable discussion of moving to Cullsbair or the reasons for doing so. No matter what happened with him and Cheris, Geoff had committed himself to teaching in his hometown. It was a gamble he hoped would pay off, but if it didn't, he would still be closer to family and have a great teaching and research position.

When he walked into his Che 212 class the Smartboard displayed an Internet feed of the Hip Granny website. He watched fascinated as a video played from his parents' anniversary party.

Of him and Cheris kissing on the stairs.

Hmmm. Good thing she wasn't sitting in on this class.

Congratulations, Geoff and Cheris, noted the script across the picture.

Oh, boy. Had Cheris seen this?

Another reason to despise the Smartboard, he supposed. He'd be willing to bet Cheris would be with him on this one.

He picked up the remote and hit the power button. Turning to the men and women sitting silently before him, he picked up a piece of chalk and wrote the day's lecture topic on the blackboard.

"Dr. Arrowood?"

"Yes, Haley?"

"Did you get married over spring break?"

"Yes."

"Is it true you're leaving Newbie River and moving to Kentucky?"

Obviously nothing was wrong with the rumor mill on campus. He'd tendered his resignation only yesterday.

"Yes. But not until the summer. Let's get back to—"

"I didn't know you were getting married," Patrick Restull commented.

"I may have neglected to mention it since it has nothing to do with *college chemistry*."

"You know Cheris is the technology chick on that website. Does she know you don't let us use calculators on our tests?" Carter Stein added.

"You ought to be able to work simple equations without a calculator, Carter."

"It must have been a small wedding if none of us got invited."

"You all want a pop test? I'll be glad to write up a few problems on the board for you to solve." Several groans emanated from his audience. "That's what I thought. Now, let's get back on topic. Who can tell me what characteristics are unique to metals?"

****

When Geoff drove Cheris back to his house, they found the scent of paint heavy in the air.

"She's still at it, I guess," Cheris commented as they walked into the kitchen from the garage.

Geoff hung his key ring on a hook next to the light switch. "If she's consistent with her past behavior, she'll paint until she's done."

"I think I'll check on her." Setting her purse down on the floor next to the dining table, Cheris continued to the bedroom door and knocked.

No answer.

Pushing it open, she saw Janie standing on a step ladder stroking the wall with a brush. She still wore the clothes she'd gone to bed in the night before, and her hair was in a tight ponytail.

"Janie? You okay?"

"Yeah."

"Want to go get something to eat?"

"No." Her hand never paused. "You guys go on."

Cheris stepped into the room to see what she'd painted.

"Get out, Cheris. I'm not done yet."

It was an outdoor scene in lush greens and plants of every color, but a large white hole remained in the center where she hadn't painted yet. "I need to get my suitcase."

"I put it in the hall."

Cheris backed out and shut the door behind her. Geoff leaned against the wall where her suitcase had been placed.

"I've been kicked out."

Geoff picked up the bag and carried it to his room. "You can sleep in here."

Setting the case on the floor, he turned to face Cheris where she stood on the threshold. With maroon walls and gold curtains lining the windows, his bedroom was unlike what she expected.

"I can't take your bed."

A nice bed it was, too. The antique mahogany four poster topped with a brown and gold comforter dominated the room. A matching bureau with mirror was the only other piece of furniture.

"Sure you can. I'll be at the observatory most of the night anyway."

"Do you go out every night?"

"When it's a new moon, yes, and especially with no cloud cover. Tonight it's supposed to be clear. A good night for viewing."

Cheris walked over to the bed and ran her hand over one of the posts, admiring the carved wood. "This is beautiful."

"It was my grandparent's bed. When I bought the house, Grandma gave me her bedroom suit."

Cheris' bed at home had been a mattress on the floor. When she'd moved to Cullsbaeir she'd bought a second hand bed from a consignment store. She'd never owned anything as exquisite as this.

Glancing up, she caught Geoff's reflection in the mirror. Behind his glasses his gaze caressed hers, made her heart beat hard in her chest. Gripping the post, she turned to face him wanting....

What?

Before she could name the emotion, Geoff left the room without a word.

Don't go.

Why not?

I want him to stay. Here. I want to....

You want to...?

Cheris closed her eyes in frustration. The voices were back. She shushed both of them and followed the sounds of the faucet running where Geoff filled a pasta pot full of water in the kitchen sink.

"Spaghetti okay with you for supper?" he asked without looking up.

"Sure."

"Great. There are fixings for salad in the fridge. Want to put one together?"

Cheris dutifully opened the refrigerator door and pulled the crisper to retrieve the ingredients. By the time they sat down together at the table, the tension she'd felt in the bedroom was gone. Cheris quizzed Geoff about the other projects his class had presented and what he expected for tomorrow's small groups. Janie was a no-show for the meal as Geoff had predicted though Cheris did fix her a plate and took it to her. Sitting it inside the room, she noted the other woman asleep in the bed, the light still on.

Closing the door softly behind her, Cheris returned to the kitchen as Geoff began to wash dishes.

"You're good to her," he commented. "She appreciates it though I'm sure she's never told you."

"How do you know?" Cheris wet a sponge and wiped

the table.

"For close to a year she'd been telling me about you. 'Cheris brought me something to eat today.' 'Cheris gave me balloons for my birthday.' 'Cheris came to pick me up when I got drunk at Crazy Eddie's.'"

"She was really drunk that night. I took her home with me and woke her up every two hours to give her water to drink." Cheris wiped down the counters and the stove. "That's a trick my mom told me about. If you drink plenty of water after getting drunk, your hangover isn't so bad the next day. I guess it helps to have a lush for a mom."

"That kind of knowledge is more useful than what my mom taught me."

"What was that? Which fork to eat your salad with?" She paused in her task to look at Geoff.

He quirked an eyebrow. "How many forks did you see me eat with tonight?"

"One."

"Then obviously it wasn't that. It was the Foxtrot." He wiped his hands on a towel and pulled her into his arms.

"What're you doing?" Cheris gasped.

"Showing you how much smarter your mom is than mine." Geoff adjusted her arm by nudging it with his. "This is a proper dance so no grabbing butts. Rest your arm on mine."

Cheris rested her hand on his shoulder as he held her other hand in his.

"Good. Now, I'm going to step forward with my left foot so you have to step back with your right." With his thigh, he pressed into hers. "Then my right foot, your left and we move to the side."

Cheris stepped on his foot as they moved out of the kitchen. "Sorry."

"No problem. Try it again. Back right, then left, now to the side. Let's do a corner step to get out of the way of the table. Back right. You always go back right first. Then left."

Cheris stepped on his foot again. "Sorry." She looked

down to watch their moves. "Maybe I should take off my shoes."

"If you take off your shoes, it will really hurt when *I* step on *your* feet. Now slide." He moved them to the right. "And we turn a bit. You see how lame this is? What good did it do me in college?"

"Like I'm sure you partied there," Cheris commented as she tried to follow Geoff's lead.

"I tried. The first time I drank, I was so sick, I couldn't eat for three days. Your little tip could have saved me a lot of trouble. As far as what my mom considered *necessary knowledge*, I never danced with a woman. Never."

"Until when?"

"Until now. Pathetic, right?" Geoff dropped his hands and stepped away from her.

"Probably when your mom was dating, it was necessary knowledge. You know, with cotillions and the country club and such. But with our generation, it's different."

"Different how?"

"How we socialize. Date." Cheris folded her arms. "Think about what we've done since the gala. Movies. Watching television. Swimming. Eating. The Park. Playing games on the Internet. Texting. Even though..." Cheris dropped her gaze in embarrassment. "The dancing was nice." Doing her best Groucho Marx, she quipped. "I could dance with you until the cows came home. On second thought I'd rather dance with the cows until you came home."

Geoff laughed, and Cheris smiled in response. For a moment they studied each other.

"Do you...want to dance? There's more to the Foxtrot I could show you if you're interested."

"Okay."

Geoff moved the recliner from the middle of the room next to where the other one sat against the wall.

"There. That'll give us some space." He grasped her fingers and placed his other hand on her shoulder blade.

Remembering her stance, she settled her arm on his and tilted her head back to watch him.

"One thing to remember is if you slide your feet as we're going forward and back, you're less likely to step on your partner. Not that I mind, but this part of the dance is more of a shuffle than a step. And it's slower, too. When we move side to side, then we'll step and pick up the pace. Ready?"

Cheris nodded wondering if the butterflies in her stomach were from learning to dance or being so close to Geoff. As they danced to bluesy music from the Bose and Cheris became more comfortable with the steps, she relaxed into him.

"You're a good teacher," she said as she slid her hand further up his shoulder.

"Maybe there's some use in knowing the Foxtrot after all."

"What? Something to do because you don't own a TV?"

"Yeah."

Leaning in a bit more she rested her head against his chest. This was nice. "It is weird that you don't own one."

"What?"

"A TV." His heart beat against her ear.

"Oh." His fingers flexed against hers.

"How come you don't?" Cheris stopped moving her feet and leaned back to see his face.

Still embraced, Geoff stared down at her. He shrugged. "It's a distraction I don't need although…" His caramel eyes sparkled warming her.

Tingles began in her stomach and radiated outward.

His face lowered a fraction.

He's going to kiss me.

Okay?

Yes.

"Although?" Cheris whispered and lifted her face.

"Although there are probably a few things worth watching." Geoff's lips punctuated hers at the last word.

His mouth opened, and she tasted his warmth, the tingle of pepper and oregano which lingered on both of their tongues. Dropping her hand, Geoff wrapped his arm around her body and brought her flush against him.

Cheris felt the corded muscle of his shoulders and back beneath his Oxford shirt examining the curves and planes of this man. The well-defined body she'd seen the night they'd swum in the pool attested to the fact that he frequently worked out on the exercise machines in the third bedroom of his house. Geoff also sought contact for his fingers kneaded the skin of the small of her back as his mouth left hers to rain kisses down to her neck.

Cheris arched her shoulder to accommodate the attention to her skin he'd pushed her shirt aside to reveal. Fire licked at her wherever he touched. She even heard....

Beep. Beep. Beep.

Beep? Beep? Beep?

"Geoff, I hear something," she whispered.

"Ignore it," he said against her collarbone. He must have undone a few of the buttons. *Yes, he had.* One hand was cupping her bare shoulder now.

"What is it?"

Geoff lifted his head. "It's my watch. It'll stop in about thirty seconds" He kissed her again.

Cheris' fingers moved to his shirt buttons and had three undone by the time the watch was silent again.

He was wearing an undershirt.

What a shame.

She wanted to see his chest, this time close enough to touch. Maybe she'd even get to the BVDs. Oh, he'd looked gorgeous at the edge of the pool trying to entice her out with the blanket. If she hadn't freaked out because of the cops, she could have appreciated the view a little more.

Another button, and she was nearly to his waistband. Pulling the material from his pants, she had the shirt completely open all without breaking contact with his lips. She grinned against his mouth in triumph.

Progress.

Sliding her hands up, she peeled the Oxford away from his shoulders and tugged it off his arms.

The watch beeped again, and she glanced at the clock on the wall. Twenty after nine. Why was his watch beeping now?

He pulled off the shirt and pressed the side of his watch until the sound ceased.

"Why is your watch beeping?"

Cheris loved the undershirt. James Dean with glasses.

Geoff shook his head. "Don't ask."

Skimming under the material, she splayed her fingers on his stomach gazing at him to gage his reaction. "Is it bad?"

"Really bad." Geoff worked on her shirt now, his hands fumbling over her breasts as he slid the buttons through their holes until he pulled her blouse aside to kiss her shoulder.

"You have to take your medicine?"

"No," reverberated against her skin.

"Appointment?"

He growled and pushed down her bra strap. Cheris closed her eyes and sighed in pleasure when he nibbled at the tender skin at the inside curve of her arm. His mouth sought hers again, and she realized his glasses were gone now.

What had Annie said about taking the glasses off?

That simple gesture demonstrates a deliberate willingness to show your deep affection.

Deep affection.

Lovely.

Cheris reaching behind her to unhook her bra, but Geoff's hand grasped hers.

Hugging her to him, his mouth whispered in her ear, "Don't."

"But—"

"If you take any more of your clothes off, I'm going to stay here and love you for the rest of the night. And I can't do that because people are depending on me to be somewhere else right now." His fingers traced a pattern on her back and ran under the elastic cloth.

From his pants pocket, his cell phone rang.

His sigh rustled her hair and tickled her ear.

"Is that call from the people depending on you?"

"Most assuredly."

Cheris stepped back and out of his embrace. "A new moon and no cloud cover."

"Yes, dammit." He picked up his glasses from the bookshelf behind him. Adjusting them on his face, he grimaced. "I've had this set up for months. Way before…"

"Way before me." She nodded as she smiled at him enjoying his reluctance to leave.

"If it were only me, there would be no question about staying." His gaze traveled over her. "I don't want to go."

"I know. I'll be here when you get back." Cheris walked toward him and placed her hands on his cheeks. She brushed her lips against his. "Maybe a big ol' thunderstorm will come up and you can get back sooner."

"Yeah. That'd be good. We'll hope for that."

She gently pushed him away, picked up his shirt, and handed it to him. She retreated to the other side of the room so she wouldn't be tempted to wrap herself around him and ask him to forget about the people depending on him. "Go on then. See you after while."

He shrugged into it. "In my bed, right? You're not sleeping in the recliner again, are you?"

Cheris smiled and shook her head.

"Good." Striding to her, Geoff cupped her waist with both hands and kissed her. Drawing back he sighed then brushed her lips again. "Last one," he muttered against her mouth and withdrew. Heading to the kitchen he began buttoning up his shirt. "Call me if you need anything, okay?"

"Sure."

He disappeared into the other room. Cheris heard the clink of his keys and the squeak of the kitchen door. Immediately the mechanical sound of the garage opening reached her.

Ohmygosh.Ohmygosh.Ohmygosh.

What had happened?

She pulled her shirt together and took several calming breaths.

First they were dancing, and it had been fun. Then she'd asked why he didn't have a television, and he'd kissed her, and, oh, boy had she kissed him back.

He'd unbuttoned her shirt, and she'd undone his. He'd stopped her at the bra, saying he had to leave, but he'd be back later.

And they'd have sex.

Her stomach flipped, and she gripped her middle.

That's a good thing, right?

It didn't mean they'd have to stay together forever. She could still get the divorce after the two weeks if she wanted to. This was just a natural progression to their relationship. They'd already done it anyway in the hotel. She just couldn't remember. It'd be good to know if she liked it, if he was sweet and tender like she thought he'd be.

A voice surfaced from her subconscious: *It'll be good, baby. You'll see.*

A brief flash came to her of being pinned with her back against cold stone, a hard male body at her front, and fighting fear, trying to stay calm.

Get off of me!

Cheris gasped. Had she remembered something else from the night at the Gala? Had Geoff forced himself on her?

Nausea rose up inside her, and she swallowed a few times trying not to throw up.

No.

Geoff wasn't like that. Not once. Not once had he *ever* given her reason to be afraid.

Right?

What, then, was she remembering?

Chapter Thirteen

One of the strange things about living in the world is that it is only now and then one is quite sure one is going to live forever and ever and ever.... Then sometimes the immense quiet of the dark blue at night with millions of stars waiting and watching makes one sure; and sometimes a sound of far-off music makes it true; and sometimes a look in some one's eyes.
—*The Secret Garden* by Francis Hodgson Burnett

The tail lights of three school buses shone as they rumbled toward the main road taking the high school students away from the field night onsite expedition Geoff and the high school science teachers organized each year in March.

Geoff walked back across the field to the top of the gently sloped hill where Joel was already setting up his telescope.

Joel and Tony were the most committed of his stargazing colleagues. Joel, chair of the music department at Newbie River Institute, had founded the astronomy club before Geoff had arrived five years ago. He and Geoff had done most of the work to set up the observatory on the four back acres of his land. Tony's passion for astronomy had him out here most nights. Geoff knew his dream was to discover and name a comet.

"Man, I'm glad that's over. I don't know why we have to go through this every year," Tony complained. "Half those kids use it as an excuse to hide behind the observation buildings and make out."

"We do it because some of the kids are actually

interested and might want to get into amateur astronomy," Geoff returned.

"Geoff, you had me scared when you were late. If Tony and I had had to play star guides to those hoodlums there would have been a disaster of cosmic proportions. Now that they're gone, I can get my scope out without worrying about some teenager knocking it over."

"Guys, I think I'm going to call it a night," Geoff said eliciting groans from his friends.

"I knew it. You go and get married and now you're too busy screwing your wife to star gaze."

"Watch your mouth, Tony. I'm out here now, aren't I?"

Joel opened the back of his SUV, and began unloading equipment. "I don't blame you, Geoff. If she drove all the way down here, she's probably pissed that you're not at home."

Geoff pulled Joel's folding chair out of the vehicle and carried it to where the man was laying a tarp on the ground. "She didn't come here voluntarily. My sister Janie suckered her into a road trip and didn't tell her she was bringing her here. Want your trunk out here too?"

"Yeah."

The two men retrieved a large wood trunk housing Joel's telescope equipment.

"Seems like she'd be glad to be here if you two just got married last week."

"She's not sure she wants to be married to me." Kneeling with care, they set the heavy box on the ground.

"Puzzling."

They straightened and walked back to get Joel's telescope.

"We got married on the spur of the moment. She's got all these hang-ups because her mother serviced half the state of West Virginia if you know what I mean."

Joel shook his head sorrowfully while Tony's laugh rang across the hill. "How much does she charge, and is she hot?" He called, "I'd drive across the state line for a little servicing."

Crap. He hadn't meant for Tony to hear what he'd said. "She's not a hooker, you ass. She just had a lot of boyfriends."

"Even better. I won't have to pay to play."

"I've never met the woman, but I doubt she'd get close enough to touch you."

"I'm with Geoff on this one," Joel said as he adjusted the legs of a metal stand. "Tony, you smell like you haven't had a bath in a month. Didn't you notice how none of the kids would stand within three feet of you?"

"I'm allergic to antiperspirant, and being around all those obnoxious teenagers makes me sweat. I hate field night."

"The grant I get us for field night pays for six months of electricity and water for out here," Geoff commented. "So unless you want to start running an extension cord a half a mile to power your laptop or driving home every time your irritable bowel syndrome acts up, you need to get over it."

"Yeah, Tony. No one's used that bathroom more than you. Go make a pot of coffee for us."

"Why do I have to do it?"

"Because I'm the president of the amateur astronomy club, and I'm telling you to."

"You're the president, but you act like a dictator." Dutifully Tony headed to the headquarters, a low cinderblock building at the edge of the field sporting an office, meeting room, storage space, and a lavatory.

"Geoff, would you give me a hand with this?"

Geoff held the stand while Joel set his telescope on it, then tightened the nut over a screw at the scope's base to hold it in place.

Joel glanced up and asked in a lowered voice. "So if she doesn't want to be married, are you two fighting all the time?"

"No. We get along really well actually though she doesn't quite trust me. I'm trying to take it slow. Let her get to know me, see that unlike her mother, some relationships can work out."

"Want my advice?" the older man asked. He'd been married for thirty years so Geoff thought the offer was a sincere one.

"Of course."

"Don't have sex with her. Instead just hold her, cuddle her at night. Women need that touch without the bang bang. They crave it."

Geoff flinched. "Joel, that's a tall order. I think I finally have her where she's willing to do something."

"Don't. If you love her, I mean. You wait and show her affection first. Convince her being married to you is a good thing. Don't you know you demonstrate more love with your arms around her than your genitalia inside of her?"

"Can't I do both?"

"Impossible if she's having doubts. Sex is one of the most self-centered physical acts we commit because it's about getting the climax by benefit of another person's body." He looked through the eyepiece of the telescope and adjusted the grips.

"But if she orgasms, too, then it's mutually beneficial."

"You're trying to justify getting off with her."

"I had her stripping for me three hours ago."

"You think any of her mama's boyfriends ever offered to cuddle the woman when she took her clothes off? I guarantee you every one of them got their rocks off and to hell with what she really needed."

Dammit. Joel was making too much sense.

"Trust me, Geoff. I know. Patty was raped before I met and married her. Hey." He stepped aside and gestured for Geoff to look into the telescope. "Take a look at this. What is that?"

"I'm sorry about Patty. I didn't know."

"Why would you? My point in telling you is she and I had to create a galaxy of good will and love before we brought sex into it because sex meant something ugly to her even if the sex felt good with me. Do you understand?"

"Unfortunately, I do." Geoff peered into the eyepiece.

"Good man."

"Did you clean the lens? You either have lint on the glass or you've discovered a celestial object."

Opening a small plastic case, Joel retrieved some window cleaner and a cloth. "Why don't you stay out here a while and let the chilly night air cool down your mojo before you go home to your wife? What'd you say her name was?"

"Cheris."

****

Some time in the night Cheris awoke when the bed dipped with Geoff's weight. She turned her head toward him holding her breath and waiting. Dreading yet anticipating. He sat on the bed's edge, his back to her. Stretching he pushed back the covers and swung his legs onto the mattress then folded the pillow under his head.

He yawned as he lay on his side away from her.

Seriously? He was going to sleep?

"I'm awake," she whispered.

Geoff flipped on his back. "Sorry. Didn't mean to wake you."

"It's okay." Cheris' skin tingled in anticipation.

Nothing.

"Do you," Cheris expelled a breath, "want to kiss me?"

"Very much."

Her muscles tensed, but she willed herself to relax.

He closed the distance between them, and leaning over her he paused. "I like you here." He kissed her cheek and lay back down throwing his arm over her body and pulling her to his side.

She gave him two minutes to make his move, and he didn't.

What was he waiting for? She was ready to do this. She'd shaved her legs all the way up to her thighs.

"I thought you were going to love me all night."

His mouth curved upward. "It's nearly four. That's not

199

nearly enough time to love you."

"So what? All I get is like?"

"No. You get it all."

What's that mean? She blinked at him. She'd resolved that they could have sex. Now she was throwing herself at him, and he was talking in riddles. "You're a pedophile, aren't you? You wanted the teaching job all along, and I'm a cover so they don't suspect."

Geoff gripped her body, and turning his, he spooned her. She gasped when she felt his erection against the back of her thighs.

"I want you. I want to make love to you. Do you believe me?" he murmured in her ear.

Not trusting herself to speak, she nodded her head.

"But I need you to know I can sleep with you and not make love to you. That's loving you, too, for what's left of tonight."

"You need more than three hours to love me?"

His hand found hers, and he interlaced their fingers. "Absolutely."

"How long does it take you?" Cheris was torn between fascination and fear. What kind of technique did he have?

"Oh, I don't know. Four or five."

"Four or five hours?"

"Lifetimes. Can we go to sleep now?"

"You're crazy."

"Yeah. So, I've been told."

Cheris squeezed his hand in response. How could he expect her to sleep when he'd just uttered the most romantic thing she'd ever heard in her life? No movie she'd seen could even come close.

****

The next morning when Cheris awoke, Geoff was still beside her.

She'd heard his alarm clock buzz at six-thirty. She'd watched him rise up, hit the top of it, and lie back down before pulling her against him. And she'd drifted off to sleep with a smile on her face as he'd snuggled against her.

She'd slept with him, and they'd actually slept.

Now the clock read a quarter to eight in the morning. On his stomach, he had an arm thrown across her body, his hand curved around her hip. She was safe with him. His body next to her in bed was comfortable. Excitement prickled her skin when she realized the intimacy of being in bed even if he had chosen to forego the sex.

Cheris reached over and smoothed his hair across his scalp.

He took a deep breath and rolled on his side. Opening his eyes, he blinked a few times at her.

"What do you see?" she asked wondering without his glasses what he could see.

"A vision."

"What time's your first class?"

"Eight o'clock."

"Geoff," she exclaimed. "You only have fifteen minutes to get there."

Geoff jumped up and dashed to his closet grabbing his glasses off the dresser on the way. From her vantage point, Cheris enjoyed watching the nearly naked man pull slacks from the closet and step into them then grab an undershirt from one of the drawers. He strode to the bathroom and shut the door.

When he came out, he had the undershirt on and reached into the closet again, this time retrieving an Oxford and a sport coat. "I can come back at eleven, and we'll go out to lunch. Okay?"

Without waiting for a response, he left the bedroom, and the house.

Lunch sounded good.

Being here with Geoff was good.

"Hey." Janie stood at the door in the same clothes she'd worn for three days.

"Hi." Cheris sat up and leaned against the bedframe. "How's your wall coming along?"

"Pretty well. Geoff installed canvas covers over the

actual walls in there so if I ever want to take the pieces, I could." Janie entered the room and sat on the bed's edge. "You and he are doing okay, it seems."

Cheris nodded. "I think so, but you and I need to get back soon. I worry about leaving Timmy alone this long."

"I'll be done tomorrow at the very latest."

****

Because Geoff had no afternoon classes, he and Cheris came back to the house after lunch. When they pulled into the driveway, Janie's car was missing.

"We should have taken her to lunch with us," Cheris commented. "She said she was getting close to finishing."

"I doubt she would have agreed to go." Geoff guided the vehicle into the garage. They left the SUV and walked into the kitchen.

"Wonder where she is."

"Maybe she'd done, and she went to grab a bite to eat."

Cheris excused herself to use the restroom.

"She's gone!" Cheris exclaimed, a piece of paper clutched in her hand. She marched out of the bathroom and held up the note up to Geoff.

Gone back to Cullsbaeir. I'll take care of Timmy 'til you get back. Janie.

"She left me here on purpose." Cheris snatched her phone out of her purse and punched Janie's number on her keypad. Of course, the jerk didn't pick up. Pushing the end button, she huffed. "I talked to her this morning. She didn't say a thing about going."

"Yeah. When she gets in that artist mode, she has little regard for anyone else." Geoff opened the guest bedroom door and walked inside.

Cheris followed him.

Before them a colorful depiction of the Garden of Eden covered the wall with a beautiful crouching dragon dominating the scene. His wings stretched up behind him and his face seemed more playful than sinister. Eve stood naked before him, gazing longingly at the beast as her arm stretched up for an apple hanging from a shimmering tree. Behind her, Adam glowered at Eve, his dirty claw-like hand reaching for her.

"I can't believe she did this in two days. It's incredible." Cheris pointed to the woman. "She's painted herself as Eve."

"Yes, and this," Geoff indicated Adam, "is Bobby. See his tattoo? The dragon, though. That's an interesting addition to the Garden of Eden story."

Realization dawned on Cheris. "Oh, my gosh. David Denton said something to her about what the serpent would look like before God's curse."

"Who?"

"Her new boyfriend. He's a minister."

Geoff burst into laughter.

"He is. That's why she's so upset."

"Hmm. Look." Geoff stepped to the wall. Without touching the painting, he traced the lines on the animal's scales. A capitalized D hung from the corner of another one in a monogram near the dragon's breast. "He's the dragon."

"Wow. That's different."

"That's my sister."

****

Things were moving fast.

But it was okay.

Cheris and Geoff had met with Larry Preston when they'd come back to Cullsbaeir over the weekend, and Larry had disclosed he and her boss had negotiated using the dream house as a backdrop for the wedding line on Hip Granny's website.

When Cheris had called Bill Connors to verify the story, he'd confirmed it.

With an offer of a six month lease, Cheris waited until she met with Bill before deciding. Geoff had gone back to Georgia, and Cheris had gone back to work on Monday to discuss her career options.

On Monday she sat before Bill in his office wearing

her best business woman suit and her hair in a neat chignon. "What are your terms?"

He opened a drawer, pulled out a stapled document and pushed it across his desk toward her. "Double your salary. You come public as Cheris the newlywed. Daily blogs and ad ops. Weekly webcasts on wedding planning and domestic topics, including spots at businesses."

"Weekly?"

"It doesn't have to focus on you. And none of Geoff. Weddings are women's realm. I'd like to have him as completely absent. It lends to the mystery and the everyman aspect of the groom."

"And also you wouldn't have to pay him if he doesn't have an active role on the site."

Bill chewed on his cigar. "There is that."

Like he hadn't already thought of it.

Bill's chair squeaked as he straightened and spoke. "I want your matter-of-fact approach here like you've done for the computer tech stuff. You're smart and practical. The market will respect your opinion. And you're pretty, so that makes you attractive to the wanna-be brides on the net. It's a brilliant move for us. We'll progressively transition from Hip Granny to a more general advice and market online shop with a host team approach. That way if in two years you decide you don't want to do it anymore, we're not in a lurch."

"Two years?"

"For you on the wedding site."

"What about the house? If you want it for Net Enterprises, why not lease it yourself? Why try to manipulate me and Geoff into it?"

"Babe..."

Cheris stood up to leave.

"Sorry. Sorry." Bill stood and hurried around the desk raising his arms in a placating gesture. "Cheris, Larry and I are old friends. We happened to be on the golf course the other day, and you and the house came up. But I'm not into real estate. If Net Enterprises gets into property rental and purchase, it'll create all kinds of headaches I don't want to fool with. But Larry sees it as an opportunity. That's why he's willing to rent it to you so cheap. We'll contract with him through you for on location webcasts to do with setting up housekeeping. It's ingenious."

"Why weren't you and he just upfront with me about it?"

"Because you were on your honeymoon. Milt said leave you alone, but Larry?" Bill shook his head and laughed. "He's on a scent. He's overzealous, but that's why he's the best realtor in the state." Going over to the chair she had vacated, he patted the back of it. "Come. Sit back down." He crossed the office and settled back in his chair as Cheris sat down. "Don't move in the house if you don't want to. Don't sign the contract, but I'm telling you, I think the setting is perfect. You can live in one part of the house, and we can do the spots in the other. It's convenient without being intrusive. And with your name on the lease, you have more control. Do you see that?"

"Yes, I do."

"Okay. Well, those are the terms." Bill eyed her for a few moments. "I'll give you a couple of days to read it over and think about it. Milton is coming back into town Thursday. We'll meet with him if you decide you want to do this."

It didn't take long.

Bill had wisely created a position for her so that she could host the wedding site without infringing on her private life. No matter what she and Geoff decided personally, she'd have a raise and control over much of the content.

By Thursday she'd moved into the role of the online newlywed and brought two advertising contracts along with a timeline for the upcoming month to her meeting with Bill and Milton.

With Monnie's after-the-fact wedding shower coming up, Cheris had already made three webcasts at area stores as she picked out china patterns and registered for gifts while

Rhoderman worked the camera. His awkward countenance and her accompanying banter had Milton over the moon and Bill scrambling to negotiate a new contract with Rhoderman as the geeky sidekick cameraman on Cheris' wedding adventures.

Chapter Fourteen

"Don't have a mother", he said. Not only had he no
mother, but he had not the slightest
desire to have one. He thought them very over-rated
persons.
—*Peter Pan* by J.M. Barrie

Cheris smiled as she unwrapped a silver rimmed glass
salad bowl. The name on the card was unfamiliar. She
handed it to Geoff who sat next to her. He read the script
and nodded. "They are Mom and Dad's next door
neighbors." Glancing around the room, he searched for
them. "Very nice. Thank you."

"Yes, Thank you," Cheris added.

"Such nice manners," a raspy voiced declared. "Hard
to believe you're my kid." Sarah McDowell stood in the
doorway, her flinty gaze piercing her daughter's.

Cheris heart stopped.

Mama.

How had she gotten here, and why?

"Guess you wasn't going to tell me about your party or
gettin' married."

Oh, no. Please.

The last thing Cheris wanted was her mother making a
scene in front of Geoff's family and their friends.

She glanced at Rhoderman who held a small camera in
front of his face.

Or the world wide web.

Rhoderman lowered the camera.

The room was completely silent, and Gerald, Mom's
boss, appeared and stood behind her. He waved to Cheris,

his mouth crooked in a half grin.

Monnie stood and approached Sarah and Gerald, a welcoming smile on her face. "Bless your hearts for coming all this way. How wonderful to have you." She reached over and hugged Sarah, startling her though the woman accepted the embrace. "I'm Monnie, the groom's mother. It's so nice to finally meet you. I'm glad you got the invitation."

Sarah studied Monnie. "Did you know about me? 'Cause I sure as hell didn't know about you."

Monnie chuckled. "Young people." She shook her head. "Too busy living their lives to stop and tell us about it." She offered her hand to Gerald. "Hello. You must be..."

"Gerald Smithson." He shook the hand she offered before pulling her to him in a bear hug. "I'm Sarah's boss, and today I'm her driver since she lost her license for that DUI back in aught eight."

The affectionate pose elicited a surprised yelp from Monnie, but she recovered quickly.

"It was oh-seven, Gerald, and I'll thank you not to air my dirty laundry in front of Cheris' new family."

"Mama—"

"You finally got you a family you don't have to be ashamed of."

"Oh, Sarah. I'm thrilled to pieces you're here," Monnie said, "May I get you and Gerald something to drink? We've got punch and just about anything else you'd like."

Sarah turned back to Monnie, and Cheris held her breath hoping Sarah wouldn't cuss her out. For ten seconds they stared at each other.

"I'll take some punch. I'm a recovering alcoholic," she stated in her no nonsense way. "So if it's got liquor in it, you better just give me water."

"I'll take whatever's handy," Gerald added.

"Please have a seat if you like." Monnie called for her husband. "Chip? Would you get Sarah and Gerald settled?"

At her bidding, Chip moved to help the newcomers find a place to sit. Geoff wrapped his arm around Cheris' waist and leaned in to her.

"Want me to open the next one?" he murmured to her.

She nodded blinking quickly so that the tears in her eyes wouldn't fall.

Monnie had invited her mom? Why? Why was her mom even here? Cheris hadn't even talked to the woman since Mother's Day last year when she'd called her an ungrateful daughter and hung up on her.

Geoff pulled a gaily wrapped box from the mound of gifts on the table next to them. He opened it, made the appropriate responses, and opened the next several before calling for a break. Monnie stepped in and invited everyone to refresh their plates. Grasping Cheris' hand, Geoff led her out of the room, and down the hall to the den under the stairs where they had kissed when she'd had Sunday lunch here several weeks ago.

Geoff shut the door and locked it before pulling her into his arms and holding her tightly to him. The gesture was to offer comfort and strength. For a moment they stayed in that position until Geoff kissed the top of her head and stepped back.

"I'm so sorry, Geoff. If I had any idea your mom was planning on inviting her, I would have—"

"No, I'm sorry. Mom should have okayed it with you."

"I can't go back out there. Not with her here," Cheris said brokenly.

"Okay." He nodded.

"What do you mean 'okay'? I have to go back out there."

"No, you don't. Not if you don't want to."

"What about the party?"

Geoff shrugged. "What about it?"

"We have to finish opening the presents."

"I can do that. You can stay in here, or go up to my room. I'll send Janie up to stay with you."

"I have to go out there," Cheris said tearfully.

Geoff pressed his hands on either side of her face.

"No, you don't."

"But my mom. She'll...she's—"

"My mom can handle her. She's had lots of practice with Janie. It will be fine. I promise."

"You don't know my mom."

"I know her daughter, and that's good enough."

"I'm nothing like her."

"I know." He grinned down at her. "You were insistent I drive the night you knew you were intoxicated. You lectured me about safety on the road, and made me walk a straight line and touch my fingers to my nose with my eyes closed to make sure I was sober before you'd hand your keys over to me."

"Really?"

He nodded.

Cheris became aware of how close they stood, their bodies touching from knees to chests. Her gaze dropped to his lips. "Kiss me," she whispered. "Kiss me like you mean it."

Geoff lowered his head, his lips just touching hers. "We're in this together. Remember that." He molded his mouth to hers then, touching and tasting her, gentle, unhurried, deepening their connection, emotionally, physically until the tension drained away from her.

Pressing her head to his shoulder, he stroked her hair. "Feel better?"

"Yes."

"Okay. I'll send Janie in here."

"No. I can do this. With you."

"Sure?"

Cheris nodded.

"Okay."

With hands held, they walked to the door. "Man, I hope we get the robotic vacuum cleaner. We're halfway through the presents, and we still haven't gotten one."

Cheris grinned and determined if they didn't have one by the end of the party, she'd go out and buy one for Geoff.

Sarah McDowell said nothing more during the rest of the shower. Cheris noticed her absence as people congregated in groups preparing to leave.

Had she and Gerald left too?

Thump. Thump. Thump.

Annie Hill's cane hit the floor with her progress toward Cheris. The older woman's knowing gaze settled on her, making Cheris' stomach churn.

"My dear." Annie stood in front of her. "You made me very proud how you handled yourself today. The potential for a scene was rather high, but you practiced graceful restraint."

Cheris' throat stung with emotion.

"Did you know she was no longer drinking?"

No. She'd had no idea. Cheris shook her head.

"She's probably in AA. This trip is an opportunity for her to make amends. Be gracious, but cautious. Do you understand?"

Cheris nodded. Annie reached forward and kissed her forehead as Good Witch Glenda had done to Dorothy in protection against the Wicked Witch of the West.

Oh, please. I need those ruby slippers.

"You call me if you need to."

"Thank you, Annie."

Annie smiled in response and walked to the door as Geoff appeared beside Cheris and settled his arm around her shoulders. "Still doing okay?"

Cheris took a shuddering breath. The uneasiness in her stomach continued. "I think so."

Monnie approached, all smiles. "Wasn't it a nice party? The weather couldn't have been better for it, and how exciting to know you might use it on the wedding site."

"Monnie, did my mom leave?"

"No, dear. I think I saw her headed to the kitchen."

Cheris glanced at Geoff. "I think I need to check on her." If there was going to be a fight, it'd be better to do it privately while Monnie was seeing the rest of the guests off.

Cheris found her mother washing dishes in the sink.

"Hi."

Sarah didn't look up.

"You shouldn't do that."

"Why? Afraid I'll break your mother's pretty dishes?"

Cheris came to stand next to her, attempting to ignore the tension of the years of bad feelings and resentment. "*You're* my mother."

Sarah snorted. "Nice of you to remember."

Cheris swallowed hard when a wave of nausea rose up in her throat. "Mom, I don't want to fight."

"That why I have to find out from the U.S. Mail that my only daughter got married? Inviting me along with all of Margaret Arrowood's uppity friends?" She rinsed a serving platter and set it on the counter.

"I probably should have told you, but—"

"But, I know. You've always considered yourself better than your raisings. And now all of you get to rub it in my face. Why don't you go out there with them, and I'll stay in here and clean up. It's where I belong in this house. Tell Mrs. Margaret Arrowood she won't have to dirty her manicured hands with the dishes, and she can count the silver after I leave."

"She's been perfectly gracious to you ever since you walked in the door. It's not fair to insult her." Cheris held her stomach trying to quell its uneasy rumbling.

"Fair." Sarah shook her head. "Is it fair to live in a house like this without lifting a finger while I'm on my feet forty hours a week at the diner?"

"Stop it, Mama." Cheris' voice rose in anger. "Why do you have to make everything seem like it's a personal insult to you? These are *nice* people."

A sound from behind her caught her attention. Geoff and Monnie stood in the doorway.

Stomach acid burned her throat. *Oh, no.*

I'm going to....

I can't....

Cheris clapped her fingers over her mouth and ran to the garbage can before throwing up.

Hands—but not her mother's hands, Geoff's hands—pulled her hair away from her face while she lost everything she'd eaten. She dropped to her knees and closed her eyes in misery and humiliation, tears streaming down her face.

When she'd finished, she sat down and tried to catch her breath. Geoff knelt beside her his hand still holding her hair.

Sarah stood with arms crossed as she studied her daughter. "Well, I guess this explains a lot. You went and got yourself knocked up. I guess the apple really don't fall too far from the tree, do it? Except for *your* daddy never stuck around long enough to do the right thing by me."

Geoff glanced at Monnie. "Mom, help." He lifted Cheris in his arms.

"Now, Sarah, aren't you sweet to wash up," Monnie commented as Geoff and Cheris left the kitchen. "Here, I'll dry. We'll have this done in no time."

Geoff carried Cheris upstairs and set her on a bed in one of the rooms. He walked out as fear and realization paralyzed Cheris. Could she be...?

She counted up days in her head.

Late. Three days.

No! She didn't want to be pregnant.

Geoff came back in with a warm wet bathcloth and wiped her face and neck.

She couldn't have a baby. The wicked witch downstairs in the kitchen attested to the fact that Cheris had no business bringing up a child and screwing it up like her mother had screwed her up.

She pushed Geoff away and covered her face with her hands. "She's right. She's right. Oh, Geoff, didn't you have enough sense to use a condom that night? How could you do this to me?"

"You're not pregnant. You can't be."

"It only takes one time, you jerk. I haven't been with anybody else, and I should have started menstruating three days ago. I don't care if we were married, what kind of man has sex with a woman who's too drunk to say no?"

Geoff sat back as if he'd punched her. For a moment he studied her face then he set the bath cloth on the bedside table and left the room.

****

"Mom?" Geoff called as he flew down the steps. "Mom!"

Monnie hurried into the hallway, her excited face greeting him.

Typical.

The world was falling apart, and Tsunami Monnie was happy about grandchildren.

"Where's Janie?"

"She left a little while ago. Said she was going to the studio."

"Please. Don't let Cheris leave, and keep her mother away from her. I've got to go out for a little while."

"Is she feeling better? Is she really pregnant?" Monnie clinched her hands excitedly. "When's she due?"

"I'll talk to you about it later, Mom. Thanks for handling this." Geoff charged through the door on his way to find Janie.

When he arrived at her studio, he noted Bobby's beat up truck out front.

Just the prick he wanted to see.

When he walked in, Janie's angry voice carried across building.

"...done, Bobby. You might as well leave because you're wasting my time."

Geoff stalked through the front room and found Janie with hands on hips in her office and Bobby lounged against the doorframe.

"I don't get why you've got this attitude all of the... Hey, look. It's the college boy. What's—"

"Did you touch my wife the night of Janie's gala?"

Bobby's gaze narrowed, then his mouth split in a lecherous grin. "Yeah, Cheris. Janie told me you got married. I warmed her up real good for you, didn't I? Took her right there next to that stone horse. Man, she was hot."

Geoff grabbed him by the neck and shoved him into the wall pinning him there. "You stay away from my wife *and* my sister."

Bobby clutched at Geoff's hand struggling to breathe. "Geoff, don't. He's not worth it."

Geoff pressed his thumb and finger a centimeter inward feeling the pulse and the swoosh of blood beneath the skin. *It wouldn't take much to—*

"Geoff!" Janie shook his arm. "Let him go."

Glaring at the man, Geoff broke contact and stepped back.

Bobby grabbed his throat coughing.

Geoff flexed his fingers and waited. "If you don't leave in five seconds, I'm calling the police."

Bobby straightened. "I'm the one who should call the police. You coulda killed me. It was just a damn joke."

"Go ahead and call the police," Janie remarked. "They all know you on a first name basis. They'll think you started it."

He glared at her and spit on the floor. When Geoff took a step toward him, Bobby stumbled toward the front. The door opened and slammed shut.

"Shit, Geoff. What the hell was that about?"

"Who's that friend of yours? The nurse practitioner?"

"Traci Chew?"

"Yeah. You have her number? Do you think she'd see Cheris today?"

"I don't know. I can call her. What's wrong?"

"Cheris thinks she's pregnant. She and her mom got into it. She's so upset. I think she needs to see somebody. Now."

"But..." Janie shook her head. "You don't seriously think she and Bobby—"

"Of course not. Please will you call?"

＊＊＊＊

Cheris didn't move when Geoff came back in the room. Though her back was to the door, she knew it was him. She recognized the sound of his shoes as he walked in the room, the movement of his body when he sat on his bed.

"Are you awake?"

"Yes."

"Janie's got a friend who's a nurse practitioner. She's agreed to see you this afternoon. Give you an exam. Make sure everything's okay."

"I don't want to be...to be." She took a shuddering breath. "I can't be somebody's mother."

"If you're pregnant, you're already somebody's mother. You'll be a good mother."

Cheris turned on her back to look at Geoff. "How can you say that? You've met my mother. Is that the kind of person you want raising your child?"

"What makes you think you'd do one thing like your mother? Everything you've done until now has been exactly the opposite."

"Yeah. Like getting knocked up." Tears trailed down her skin.

"I don't think it's knocked up if it's on your wedding night."

She didn't answer.

"Think how much fun we'll have. Buying toys. Going to Disney World. Building model space ships."

Idiot. He had no idea. "Toxic paint from Chinese toys. Temper tantrums at Space Mountain. Going broke paying for college."

"Bill Connors is going to be thrilled. He'll triple your salary and make you the maternity and child Internet advice specialist."

"I'm not ready for this."

"Let's go see the nurse practitioner and go from there. Okay?"

Cheris sighed and sat up.

****

Cheris sat on a Queen Ann chair in a warmly decorated room and waited for Traci Chew. As a nurse practitioner, Traci specialized as a midwife and ran her medical office out of her house.

"Well, Cheris," Traci, a dark haired young woman with blue eyes walked in the room with a folder in her hand. "The pregnancy test is negative. The other tests will take longer to get the results back. But if something shows up, I'll let you know."

"What other tests?"

"For STDs. They're standard, but your husband mentioned he thought you should have them. Since you said he's been your only partner, I don't anticipate anything."

"I know I'm pregnant. I haven't started my period. I've never been late in my life, and I've been sick to my stomach off and on for three weeks now."

"I ran several tests to be sure. You're not pregnant. Your lab work shows nothing abnormal. Not even a fever."

"What's wrong with me then?"

Traci peered at her over her glasses. "What's going on in your life right now? Any changes in habits, diet? Stress factors?"

Cheris rolled her eyes. "Where do I start? I ate cake and woke up married to six feet of stress sitting in your waiting room. My boss made me a marriage consultant, and I have to do webcasts every week. I'm going to move into my dream home, and my horrible mother showed up at my wedding shower and made a disgusting scene in front of everybody."

"Well." Traci opened the folder and wrote on a paper inside. "That sounds indicative of stress to me. It can really play havoc with your menstrual cycle. Are you ready to start a family right away?"

"No."

"You'll probably want to get on some birth control pills then." She tore a sheet from a pad of paper and handed it to Cheris. It was a prescription. "I'll see if I have any samples to get you started. You'll want to use another form of birth control for the first month, okay?" Traci walked to the door. "Go ahead and start the pill today. If nothing else, it'll regulate your period."

Cheris made sure she stuffed the pills down in the lowest part of her purse before she walked into the sitting area Traci used as a waiting room in the front part of her house.

When he saw her, Geoff stood up and searched her face. She shook her head slightly, and relief flickered across his face.

Just as she thought.

All of his big talk of Disney World and her being a good mom had been a put-on.

He didn't want a baby any more than she did.

And he'd used to opportunity to have her tested to make sure she wasn't a slut like her mom.

Silently they walked to his SUV and settled inside.

"I don't sleep around," she declared.

"Okay."

"So I can only assume you wanted me tested for STDs because you do."

"I don't. I've never—"

"So this just shows how stupid all of this is, that you would have sex with me without knowing anything about me, Geoff. I had an excuse that night, but you didn't. And I thought the reason you hadn't had sex with me since then is because you cared about me, but it was really because I wasn't born into a nice family like you were."

Geoff started the car.

"Do you want to go back to my parents' house and your mom, or do you want me to take you home?"

Cheris rubbed her eyes and ran her hands through her hair. "I don't want to deal with her right now, but I don't see that I have a choice."

Without a word, Geoff drove her to the house. When he pulled into the circular driveway, he left the engine idling. Cheris sat and waited.

"I'm going back to Georgia," Geoff announced.

"Right now?"

"Yes. Janie said she'd be here in a little while. She can

take you home."

"You're mad at me."

"You know, Cheris." Geoff stared through the windshield. "It doesn't matter how much I love you if you're always ready to think the very worst of me because you don't think you're worth loving."

"You don't love someone after only three weeks."

"I'll be back in Cullsbaeir May thirtieth. That's a little over two months from now. Want to continue this conversation then?"

"What about the divorce?"

"You waited two weeks as I asked. If you still want to file, I'll sign."

But I don't want to get a divorce.

Tears filled her eyes, but she blinked them away. Opening the door, she slid out of the vehicle and walked toward the house while Geoff pulled around the driveway and onto the street.

****

"So, it was a nice party. I would thank you for inviting me, but since *you* didn't I thanked Margaret Arrowood instead," Sarah commented as she and Gerald stood in the yard preparing to drive back to West Virginia.

"You all could stay with me tonight."

"Gerald's already lost a day's worth of business over this."

"I didn't mind," the man interjected. "You only get married once, unless you're your mama."

"Shut up, Gerald. If I could have found somebody who didn't drive me ape shit, I might've stayed married." Her gaze traveled across Cheris, examining her from head to toe. "Geoff seems okay. His mother's a little too happy, but it's because she's on Zoloft. I saw it in her medicine cabinet."

"Mama!"

"Chip's on blood pressure medicine. I'd have to take it too, if I had to listen to her yack, yack, yack all the time."

"You was doing plenty of yacking yourself," Gerald

quipped. "Telling her all your stories of people who come into the diner."

"She does like a good story. How's your stomach? You always was a nervous child."

"I wonder why?" Gerald winked at Cheris and hugged her before climbing into his ancient El Camino.

"You need to get over that. Remember that time I took you to the mall and you threw up all over Santa Claus?"

"No."

"All that drama, and for what? It goes and upsets everybody. But at least you ain't pregnant."

"Geoff said he thinks I'd be a good mother."

"Well, I guess he'd know since his mama's all cuckoo taking drugs and acting like we're best friends. She asked for my peanut butter pie recipe, but I'll be cold in my grave before I let her have it."

"Get in the car, Sarah. I don't want to be driving half the night."

Sarah didn't move. She continued to stare at Cheris. "She invited me and Gerald for Thanksgiving. You believe that? Seven months away and she's already planning it. I told her flat out no, that we're too busy cooking for people like her who won't lift a finger in the kitchen."

"Geez, Mom. Would it kill you to be nice to her?"

"It don't bother her. She said all of you would just come over to the diner for Thanksgiving. I'll believe it when I see it though. People like her like to use their good china and linen cloths too much."

"Maybe she'll bring her dishes with her. Come on, Sarah."

Sarah laughed. "Oh, yeah. I like that idea. Cheris, you tell her to bring her plates for Thanksgiving. That'll be her contribution."

"I will not."

"Sarah, I'm leaving, and you can just stay here with your new best friend." Gerald put the car in gear, and it rolled forward a few feet.

"All right. All right." Sarah marched to the car. "Pick up the phone and call me every once in a while, why don't you?" she called over her shoulder before getting in the car.

Cheris breathed a sigh of relief when it turned the corner at the end of the street.

Chapter Fifteen

I am never afraid of what I know.
—*Black Beauty* by Anna Sewell

Where was Rhoderman?

Cheris stood in the office of the *Loving You* Chapel and tapped her foot impatiently.

She couldn't very well interview the Chapel host if Rhoderman wasn't here to run the camera.

It was hard enough soliciting wedding stores for marketing options when her own marriage was on shaky ground. All of the happily ever after and gushy framed images of couples hand in hand hanging on the wall churned her stomach.

Not pregnant.

She hadn't heard from Geoff in two weeks. Of course, she hadn't contacted him either. What could she say?

I'm sorry you wanted me tested for venereal diseases? I'm sorry I'm not pregnant? I'm sorry you'll sign the divorce papers if I send them?

She was sorry.

For all of it, and that they had moved so fast the first night she'd met him. If they'd waited on everything, they'd probably be dating right now. She'd remembered the strong pull of attraction as they'd talked in the Wonderland exhibit—his beautiful eyes and clever conversation, not to mention how he'd looked in the tux.

Her stomach flopped, this time from the memory of his hand on her when she'd stumbled over the looking glass frame.

She really wasn't pregnant. Another two weeks' worth

of pills, and she wouldn't have to worry about getting pregnant. Not that it looked like the possibility was ever going to happen.

Geoff had sat with her as she wept that day, terrified, thinking she was.

If you're pregnant, you're already somebody's mother. You'll be a good mother.

He'd been so sweet, so confident that they'd be a family going to Disney World and playing with toys.

He'd talked in terms of presence, being together. Him, Her, and a baby.

What would their baby look like?

Curly dark hair like his, or auburn like hers? Blue eyes or warm gold? Boy or girl?

Charles Mason, owner of *Loving You*, entered the office dressed in a charcoal suit complete with tie. "Has your cameraman shown up yet?"

"Not yet. I texted him to see why he's late."

Charles checked his watch. "There's a couple coming in at eleven. Maybe we should reschedule?"

"I really wanted to post something today since there's a gap for a wedding chapel on the site. I have a friend who lives close by. I could run and borrow her Flip and be back in ten minutes."

"Her what?"

"It's a video camera. We could do a quick piece to fill my space, and it would serve as a teaser for the real interview. Okay?"

"All right."

****

Later that afternoon Cheris sat in her cubicle with Janie's flip ready to upload the recording she'd made to the Whirlwind Wedding Workshop. Pushing the menu button which displayed the thumbnails on the small screen, Cheris was about to choose the video she'd shot that morning, when a picture of Geoff on the video thumbnail next to it caught her attention.

When was a video of Geoff taken?

Cheris clicked on it.

In his tuxedo, Geoff stared into the camera as he stood inside a hotel room.

Hotel room!

"I'm not sure you're going to want to remember any of this, Cheris."

From off camera, her voice responded. "Yes, I will. Everything. Now go ahead."

Geoff took off his glasses briefly and wiped his eyes. "You're a handful."

"I was a frightful girl before you married me, and I made no secret of it. I didn't deceive you, Sir."

He grinned. "Where did you hear that?"

The picture shook. "Elizabeth Taylor said it to Rock Hudson in *Giant*. James Dean died during the filming. Did you know that?"

"I did not." He strode over to the bed and pulled back the covers. "Come on. Get in the bed."

The camera moved toward Geoff. "Eager, aren't you?"

"We're going to sleep. That's it. You've had too much champagne."

"I haven't had any champagne. I don't drink. At. All."

"So you keep telling me. Come on. I'm tired." He reached forward and their clasped hands appeared at the edge of the screen. With his other hand he took the camera and set it down face up so that the lamp stand filled the picture.

"You think midnight putt-putt was too much? I beat you fair and square all three times."

"I let you win because you're so cute when you do that little victory dance."

"Want me to do it now?" Cheris suggested silkily.

Rustling and a zipper.

"Stop it," he admonished. "Keep your clothes on."

"I can't sleep in this. The skirt is too tight, and my bra is digging into my skin."

"Sleeping naked is not an option… Would you quit?"

"What kind of wedding night is this? You promised to

worship my body."

"I also promised to love and honor you. Worship connotes reverence. Let's sleep on it tonight, and work on reverent lovemaking another night."

"I've never known a guy who didn't want to have sex if given the opportunity."

"Well, the opportunity hasn't exactly presented itself before."

"You're a virgin? I don't believe it. Why wouldn't anybody sleep with you?"

"Because I spend most of my nights on a field looking at stars. It's not conducive to an active social life."

"Come on, Geoff. All those nineteen and twenty year olds gazing at you longingly from their desks?"

"First of all being involved with a student is an ethics violation. Second of all, most of them have nose and tongue piercings. Unless it's the ears, I think it rather disturbing."

"Are you sure you're Janie's brother? Not only does she have a naval ring, but she was afraid Bobby gave her herpes because—"

"Shhh. There are so many reasons I don't want you to finish that sentence, I can't even list them all. Here. I'm going to shower. Take my shirt. You can sleep in it."

"Mmm. It smells nice. Like you."

"In bed. I double dog dare you to be asleep by the time I get out of the shower."

"You're so cute when you dare me. I'll try." She yawned noisily.

"Good."

A sound of a brief kiss against skin. Footsteps fading, and a door shutting.

The Flip picked up a loud feminine sigh. Clothing rustled, and something landed on the lampshade knocking it askew.

Cheris flinched.

She'd bet it was her skirt and panties hitting the light covering.

She picked up her cell phone and dialed Janie's number.

"I've got to talk to you," she said when her sister-in-law picked up.

****

"Just for the record. I don't have Herpes." Janie sat on Cheris' desk chair in her apartment as the video feed on the computer monitor cut off. She swiveled the seat toward Cheris who sat next to her on a kitchen chair. "And there's no chance you have it either."

Cheris shook her head and shrugged in confusion. "I know I don't have it. Traci tested me."

"Yeah, because Geoff asked her to. He was afraid you and Bobby had had sex."

Cheris' mouth flew open in shock. "What?"

"Bobby was being an asshole and told Geoff you and him got it on in the *Black Beauty* exhibit. Remember I told you I walked in on them about to fight? Apparently it was because Geoff caught you two together after he got back from picking up Aunt Nancy."

Cheris swallowed the bile which rose in her throat.

"Now don't get all sick to your stomach. I didn't believe it so I took my Taser and threatened Bobby's balls if he didn't tell me the truth. He said he propositioned you, and you said something about his mom not having any kids.

It was hard on your mother, I'm sure, not having any children

The scene flashed in her head. The remembered fear sped up her heart.

Yes.

It had been at the Black Beauty exhibit.

Her bad vibe radar had gone on alert the second she realized Bobby had cornered her in the room absent of anyone else. When he'd pinned her against Black Beauty's statue and unzipped his pants, she'd fought to stay calm.

"Get off of me before I knee you, scream my head off, and sic the police on you." Cheris dug her nails into his hand when he'd pulled at

her shirt.

Bobby held her fast, his breath hot against her face. "You give me three minutes, Babe, I can have you begging me take you right here."

Cheris braced her foot. "It was hard on your mother, I'm sure, not having any children."

A sound from across the room caught Bobby's attention. Cheris pushed him away as hard as she could as Geoff approached them, his eyes glittering angrily.

"Everything okay here?" Geoff asked Cheris.

"Yes." Cheris smoothed her sweaty palms down her shirt and tried to stop her knees from wobbling. "Bobby was just telling me a funny joke so I threw him a Ginger Rogers' line which of course he didn't get."

Geoff glared at Bobby who glared back.

"You got a problem, bro?" Bobby tugged at his too low pants and zipped up.

Geoff held Cheris' gaze. She took the hand he offered to her. His eyes ran over her, but not as Bobby's had. Geoff's gaze was assessing, checking to be sure she was okay. He nudged her away from him and toward the door before dropping her hand.

Finally he turned to Bobby. "Does my sister know you sleep with other women?"

"Why don't you mind your own damn business?"

Geoff stepped closer to Bobby murmuring something to him Cheris couldn't hear.

Oh, no.

Were they going to fight? She wrung her hands wondering if she should get the security guard she had seen near the entrance.

"Gentlemen," she called. "There will be no fighting here. This is the war room."

Janie entered the room and walked past where Cheris stood. "What's going on?" she asked as she watched the two men, their postures stiff with tension. "Geoff?"

"I'm getting the hell out of here," Bobby grated and stalked out.

"Man, I wish I could have one—" Janie's phone chimed signaling she had a text. She looked at the screen and grimaced. "It's Judith, the director. She needs me." Janie appealed to Cheris. "You're

getting lots of video, right?"
"Yes."
"Great." She sprinted away. "See you in a few. Geoff? I'll take Aunt Nancy home, all right?"
"Sure, Sis."
Janie's brother turned to her searching her face, his own expression troubled. "Cheris, did Bobby...was he——"
She linked her arm through his and began to walk to the door. "I have spent many a day around men who like to push and shove and shout thinking they make things happen by being aggressive. And I'm not terribly anxious to have another man like that around the place." She winked at Geoff. "I'm starving. Won't you take me somewhere and feed me?"

"Oh, Janie." Cheris turned to the other woman. "What have I done?"

"Nothing yet. But you need to fix that. I swear I cannot believe that man is still a virgin and almost thirty years old."

"I've been so awful to him—accusing him of taking advantage of me and thinking I wasn't good enough for him. He told me he loved me and I threw it up in his face."

Janie stuck out her tongue in disgust. "You threw up in his face?"

"No." Cheris smacked her on the arm. "He said it didn't matter how much he loved me if I was always so ready to believe the worst of him. Then I brought up getting a divorce." Cheris gasped. "He knew the baby wasn't his, and he wanted to take it to Disney World."

"What baby?"

"Our potential baby. The one I thought I was pregnant with."

"Oh man." Janie chuckled. "You were a few days late and he was planning to take a baby that didn't exist to Disney World?"

"He knew it couldn't have been his, and he never said anything."

"Well, see, that's his problem. He needs to put his

cards on the table. Tell you what happened." Janie shook her head. "I would tell you to go to the Whirlwind Wedding Website for advice, but you are the Whirlwind Wedding Website."

Cheris clapped her hands with inspiration. "Here's to plain speaking and clear understanding."

Janie griped, "Are you quoting old geezer movies again? I hate it when you do that."

All starry-eyed, Cheris hugged herself. "Geoff loves it. In fact, I think he loves me, and I'm going to love him right back via the World Wide Web."

"This isn't going to be pornographic, is it?"

****

Geoff and Joel walked down the hall in the Music and Arts building. Joel had asked Geoff to accompany him for a demonstration the older man had made for the observatory.

"So, when's the last time you talked to Cheris?"

"Almost three weeks. Maybe I shouldn't have followed your advice. She accused me holding back because I think something's wrong with her."

"Did you tell her otherwise?" Joel asked.

"She didn't give me the chance."

Joel motioned Geoff to enter the classroom as he spoke. "Didn't give you the chance? How long's it take to say 'I love you. I want to make sure you're ready before we do this.'"

"It isn't that easy."

"Sure it is. What's she say when you tell her you love her?"

"Well." Geoff leaned on the table and stared at the floor. "I didn't outright say I loved her."

"What'd you say?"

"I said it didn't matter how much I loved her if she didn't think she was worth loving."

Joel shook his head. "To be so smart you sure are dumb. Just say 'I love you' and let that be it. Then hug her and wait until she returns the sentiment."

"I am waiting," Geoff returned. "She's got until I

move back there. If she hasn't filed for divorce, I'm going to sweep her off her feet."

"And if she does file for divorce? What are you going to do then?"

"So far I've managed to avoid thinking about it." Geoff rolled his shoulders. "Why don't you show me what you got?"

"One more piece of fatherly advice?" Joel clapped his hand on Geoff's back.

Geoff nodded.

"Loving is a process. When she responds, keep being patient. You've got the rest of your life to love her."

"I hope so."

"Good man." Joel walked over to the computer sitting on the desk but when Geoff followed him, Joel held up his hand to stave him off. "No. You go over there and sit down in one of the desks. I want you to get the full effect."

"Not the Smartboard. You know how I hate it."

The projector light clicked on illuminating the white screen with its icons across the top.

"Isn't Cheris some kind of computer tech person?"

Geoff chose a chair in the front row and waited. "Ironically, she's in charge of a wedding and marriage advice website."

"Interesting."

The Hip Granny Website appeared on the screen, and the mouse moved to Cheris' wedding site.

"Joel, haven't we beaten this dead horse enough today?"

"Oh, a few more whacks might just be what we need to resurrect it."

The mouse moved to a video feed Geoff hadn't noticed the last time he'd checked the site. Cheris' face filled the screen.

Her hair was down around her shoulders, and she wore the same outfit she'd had on the night of the gala.

Complete with the turquoise spiked heels.

He loved those shoes.

She stood on a high columned porch with marbled stairs. It almost looked like...

Geoff sat up straight.

"Hi, this is Cheris, and today I wanted to talk about wedding vows. Some people choose to write their own, and some use more traditional versions. You'll find both kinds on the links labeled 'Your Vows' and some informative tips to help you make your decision. When my husband and I said our vows, we chose the ancient words from the early Christian tradition.

With this ring I thee wed.
With this body, I thee worship.
With my earthly goods I thee endow.

What do I like about it? It incorporates the symbol of the ring, takes into account our reverence for each other through our affection, and declares our intention to blend all of our assets as we begin our life together."

Geoff stood at her word *reverence.*

Was it possible?

Had she remembered their wedding night?

Cheris held up her hand in which her wedding band glistened in the outdoor light. "I wear this ring as a reminder to myself, my husband, and the world of those vows that I intend to keep until death do us part."

With graceful steps, Cheris approached the front door of Newbie River Institute's Main hall and opened it.

She was here.

She was here, and she had on her wedding ring.

Inside the foyer of the main hall, she crouched on the area rug next to a...

A grin split Geoff's face.

Oh, I love that woman.

"Here's a fun domestic gadget: the robotic vacuum cleaner. My husband was so excited about these little cuties that he asked for one for our wedding shower."

The camera followed the metallic disk as it moved

across the Persian rug.

"The beauty of it is it cleans the floor at night while you're sleeping. It's reasonably priced and comes with an AC powered charger station. Since no one gave my dear husband one for the shower, I bought it myself to give him."

The picture moved from the floor to Cheris.

"To my husband, I'd like to say, yes, I love you." She smiled prettily. "And you can clean my floors any time."

The picture morphed into the Whirlwind Wedding logo.

Geoff looked at Joel who still sat behind the computer monitor. The older man nodded sagely.

"Did you know about this?" Geoff asked.

"Who do you think worked the camera?"

"How—"

The robotic vacuum whirred into the room.

Cheris.

Geoff charged to the door reaching it as Cheris stepped onto the threshold. Her fingers clasped in front of her and one foot poised in front of the other, she looked beautiful. Geoff cupped her shoulders and skimmed down her arms until he held her hands.

Opening his mouth, he managed one syllable. "Hi."

She stared in the vicinity of his throat. A glance upward and she lowered her gaze again. "I'm wearing white for you, to help me say how humbly I need your forgiveness."

A movie quote. He'd bet his life on it.

Geoff slid his arms around her, and did his best Bogie.

"Of all the joints in all the towns of all world you walk into mine."

Cheris face tilted, her mouth breaking into a smile. Geoff placed his lips on that smile, sealing all of the unspoken words and healing all of the misunderstandings in the kiss.

He raised his head and held her against him, breathing in her sweet scent, reveling in her soft frame pressed against his.

"I'm sorry, Geoff."

"You don't need to apologize. You're here now. That's what matters."

"I don't want to get a divorce. Not ever."

"Okay."

Joel moved into his line of vision. He waved his hands in a hurry up gesture.

What?

Joel rolled his eyes and mouthed *I love you* then pointed at Cheris.

Oh, right.

"I love you, Cheris. I haven't said it before because I didn't want to—"

Joel shook his head, his eyebrows furrowed. He ran his finger across his neck in a cut throat gesture to desist.

Oh, yeah.

I love you, and that's it.

Cheris arched her back away from Geoff, a crestfallen expression on her face. "You didn't want to?"

"No. I mean, yes, I wanted to love you, but I didn't want to scare you off. Joel says I should just tell you I love you, hug you, and wait. So, I love you." He tightened his embrace.

Joel made a disgusted sound and moved past them. Nudging them from the doorframe, he shut them inside the room.

"What are we waiting for?"

"Ummm. For you to return the sentiment."

"Oh….Okay." She stepped away from him and retrieved the robotic cleaner. Tucking it under her arm, she opened the door and clasped his hand. "When's your next class?"

They walked into the hallway. "I'm done for the day."

"Good." Cheris pulled him down the corridor. "Let's go to your house so I can return the sentiment."

THE END

A NOTE AND A POEM FROM THE AUTHOR

I love classic movies and wanted to incorporate some of the more colorful quotations from my favorite movies into a book, hence Cheris' habit of reverting to movie quotes when she gets nervous. But I wanted to respect copyright so each quote has been tweaked a bit to stay within the law but keep the flavor of the quotation. Except for Gensa's Genesis, which exists only in my imagination, the rest of the quotations are close approximations from actual movies.

I also have a great love for books, especially some of the wonderful works of children's literature. Each quotation at the beginning of every chapter is in its original form as all of these works are now in public domain.

I had a lot of fun with all of the quotations as well as writing the original poem Cheris and Geoff quote to each other in the planetarium. I had another poem in mind, but, again, wanted to respect copyright and was unable to get permission to use it. I call my poem *Fair Use* because of my frustration at the time with copyrighted works and wanting to use them for the book, but also wanting to respect the work of the author. This pushed me to be more creative, and I see now that copyright not only protects the artist and their work, but also challenges the rest of us to give birth to something new and fresh. Following is *Fair Use* in its poetic form:

Fair Use

In the black expanse Orion, that great hunter, waits with
arm raised,
Arrow poised and twinkling belt—silent, searching.
While below I pull my sweater to me thinking soon I'll see
my breath.
The hunter pays me no mind, so focused is he on his aim.
Trembling, the crisp leaves beside me hang on for dear life.
They know the eminent fall and crunch underfoot.
And I'll strike a match to them, breezy cinders, and bitter
smoke
Will rise, rise, rise to that great one who may, at last, stop
and look at me
And have his turn to gaze and wonder.

ABOUT JENNIFER JOHNSON

I have aspirations to be Wonder Woman but find high-heeled boots uncomfortable. However, I appreciate that she values truth and she's never had a bad hair day.

I have the heart of a writer and am blessed to be able to write both professionally and recreationally. I reside in the southern United States with my awesome family. They're okay with me not being Wonder Woman, as long as I take a break from the fictitious worlds I create and join them for supper.

You can read more about me and my books by visiting my web site: www.**booksbyjenniferjohnson.com**.